The Pursuer

The Pursuer

James Clayton Welch

THE PURSUER

iUniverse books may be ordered through booksellers or by contacting:

iUniverse LLC
1663 Liberty Drive
Bloomington, IN 47403
www.iuniverse.com
1-800-Authors (1-800-288-4677)

Because of the dynamic nature of the Internet, any web addresses or links contained in this book may have changed since publication and may no longer be valid. The views expressed in this work are solely those of the author and do not necessarily reflect the views of the publisher, and the publisher hereby disclaims any responsibility for them.

Any people depicted in stock imagery provided by Thinkstock are models, and such images are being used for illustrative purposes only. Certain stock imagery © Thinkstock.

ISBN: 978-1-4917-3808-5 (sc)
ISBN: 978-1-4917-3807-8 (e)

Library of Congress Control Number: 2014910953

Printed in the United States of America.

iUniverse rev. date: 07/09/2014

Prologue

The deserts of the earth are filled with ghosts. They are the great calm pools toward which flow the vanished civilizations, the corrupted wisdom, the lost dreams, and the abandoned gods. The spiritual vestiges of a thousand centuries of forgotten religions and unanswered prayers lurk in the sunbaked canyons, the dusty arroyos, and the momentary whirlwinds.

The great San Juan Basin stretches out mile upon mile across the Colorado Plateau northwest of Albuquerque, New Mexico. It is a desert of intricate rock structures and enormous, flat stretches of gray, alkaline sand, cut through by innumerable dry washes and red-orange arroyos. The dominant floras are the gray-green sages and tumbleweeds and cacti of every variety—pear, stick, Palos Verde, even saguaro—the stately, druid-like forms standing silent sentry over the homeland of the Navajo. In ancient days, this land was verdant and fertile, the land of choice for a people who believed that they had found the center of the world. In it flourished a religious center, a place where the Old Ones came to their contemplative work in dark structures called kivas, in the hope that the prayers of many would have greater efficacy than those of a few. In time, the intricate knowledge of astronomical events and processes was accumulated from thousands of careful observations, and records were left of this knowledge in petroglyphs and in the architecture of their buildings. This knowledge was incorporated into their religion, in the reverent hope that a way could be found to control the natural processes of the earth and sky. When the land dried up from drought, the people died or fled; some say they were driven out by the gods who were offended by the arrogance of the supplicants.

Chapter 1

He opened his eyes in the dark little room and could not remember where he was or how he came to be there. He lay still, waiting for some vestige of awareness to come to him so he would know what to do. The predawn light filtered in from the small window above where he lay. He sat up and looked about him. Desert debris was strewn about on the dirt floor, and there were small tracks, patches of dried hair and skin, and tiny bones where the predators had left them. A door hung from one remaining rawhide hinge in the wall in front of him, and pieces of the roof lay scattered about where they had fallen long ago. He looked through the other open doorway and saw another room identical to this one but missing its far wall. He rose slowly from his pallet and stood waiting for his head to clear. He rubbed his hand across his eyes and forehead and saw little fragments of skin drop. The radiation sickness was getting worse.

A misty blue was seeping into the black sky at the eastern horizon in advance of the sun and the suffocating heat and odor of oven-baked rock and sand. There was no movement or sound. The desert was its own reason for being, and it killed and nurtured whom and what it willed with eternal indifference. It was pure and stark, and there could be no comfort or compassion there, only the struggle to survive, suffering, and death. What sanctuary there was consisted only of penance for the anguished soul who yearned for silence, solitude, and simplicity. It was where the mystics came, those who sought nothing more than to see into their own hearts and consign to oblivion all else with which the world had corrupted them.

* * *

As his memory of the signal horror of his life edged back into his consciousness, he remembered the last whispered words of Thomas, the first pope of that name, as he lay helpless on the floor of the now shattered Sistine Chapel: "Da mihi veniam. Da mihi veniam, Domini. Forgive me." So Father Michael Francis Kintner, S. J., Knight Commander of the Sacred Order of the Keys of St. Peter, traced the sign of the cross with his thumb in blood on the forehead and, in extremis, absolved his pontiff. "Ego te absolvo, ego te absolvo, ego te absolvo. In Gloria patris, et filio, et spiritui sancto, sicut erat in principio, et nunc, et semper, et in saecula saeculorum. In pace requiescat. Rest in peace, little priest."

"Little priest of the poor," his countrymen had called him.

And Father Michael Kintner laid the head of the bishop of Rome back down on the broken stones and rose to his feet, filled with a terrible resolve.

* * *

He couldn't remember what day it was. He hadn't for a long time and did not care. He didn't know who or how many, but he knew they had been after him for some time. It felt as if they were all around him now that he'd stopped for a while. He could almost hear them gibbering in the darkness when he lay down on his pallet last night, trying to trick his mind into falling asleep.

They thought they knew him, took him for someone they could isolate and finish off when they were damned good and ready. Let them think that. Let them think anything they wanted. He was already dead, but he was still dangerous. They'd learn that before all this was through. He also had the advantage of their hatred for him, a rage and an insane desire for revenge, which would distort their judgment and make them underestimate him. He would send them all to hell, the same everlasting hell into which he had sent so many of their kind.

The room was starting to brighten, and he opened the flap of his rucksack and brought out some matches. The ruined little adobe house was rife with tinder material, and this he gathered into a small pile and surrounded it with dry sticks and slabs of wood from the fallen roof. He lit it, walked outside to his truck, retrieved a thermos and some food in plastic bags, along with a small stew pot and cup, and brought them inside.

He poured the last of the coffee into the stew pot and set it on three small rocks, which he had placed around the fire. He stood up and stared down at the pot as if he expected a djinn to appear. As it heated, the coffee started to smell like old socks. He took the cold cornbread he had made two days before out of the sack and sat down. It was the only bread he knew how to make, and it lasted about as long as tortillas and was easier to eat.

In a little while, the coffee was hot. He poured his cup full and took a sip. Then he bit into the cornbread, which tasted almost as good as cardboard, with the coffee that tasted like he thought dirty socks would. He sat looking down into the cup for a moment and then reached over to his rucksack and took out a bottle of brandy. He sweetened the coffee and tasted it again—like socks with brandy poured over them.

In ten minutes, he was pulling away from the ruin. He stopped the pickup short of the dirt road and looked back east. The sand had blown across the little road in several places so that it might just as well have been a cow path across a sparse prairie of sage grass and mesquite. He turned west, as he had for the last week, and headed off toward the dark sky. Ahead was a deep arroyo with a precarious wooden bridge. He didn't know if it had running water in it, but if it had, then it might as well be called *El Rio de las Animas Perdidas*, the River of Lost Souls.

He crossed the bridge slowly, and it popped and cracked, making sounds like distant rifle fire as his tires rolled across it . . . the mournful mutter of the battlefield. As he started the climb out of the little canyon, the nose of the truck pointed upward, and he caught sight of the full moon against the dark western sky. A good omen, perhaps. If it were, then it would be the first in a very long time. It had helped him a great deal to stop again at the Benedictine monastery—Christ in the Desert, it was called—and have his old mentor, Father Abbot Toriano, hear his confession. After the absolution, the abbot had spoken further:

"Michael, you remember that I once told you that the most profound values of a society, of a culture, can be transformed and reconstituted by spiritual renewal but only at great cost. The blood of martyrs has not always nourished a transformation and regrowth. But such profound changes never occur without it. Most of the martyrs are unwilling ones, of course. I don't think anyone can know how far one ought to go in the preservation of one's culture or one's religion. I don't know if anyone has yet gone as far as you have. The sacrifice of one person for many is considered holy, yet the sacrifice of thousands for the sake of many other thousands is considered monstrous. An appalling contradiction. I think the answer must lie in individual accountability. If not, where does it lie?"

* * *

Commissaire Divisionnaire Joffre set his coffee down hard, rattling the spoons on the polished walnut desk.

"What in god's name makes you think he's still alive? It's been— what?—six weeks since that thing was set off down there. Is anyone else still alive who was in the building?"

Agent Renseignement Henri Breuger sighed, having tired long ago of the exaggerated anger of middle-aged, overweight bureaucrats. Joffre was typical of such officials, who never got close enough to the actual intelligence agency activities to understand how they really worked in today's environment.

"No, Commissaire, not that we can find."

"What sort of bomb was it? The explosion was too small to have been nuclear. So where did all the radiation come from?"

"It was very similar to the one they used on the Cathedral de Notre Dame de Paris. The intelligence reports I read said that the bomb consisted of three to five pounds of plastic explosive wrapped inside at least twenty pounds of cesium 137 and covered by a frangible radiation shield. That means, among other things, that the chapel might not be habitable for several decades. A bomb that size would be difficult to conceal, but not impossible, obviously."

"So, out of three hundred thirty-three people, most of whom were farther away than he was, he's the only survivor?"

"He's been the only name mentioned in the communiqués we've been able to intercept. But if he's dead, why would they still be trying to find him?"

Joffre looked intently at Henri Breuger for any trace of emotion, but as he expected, he saw nothing other than his hard and implacable stare. The agent stood about six feet and looked and moved as an athlete would. His face was sturdy with regular features but was usually devoid of an expression of any kind. There was no question that Breuger was one of the best operatives in the whole of the French counterintelligence and counterterrorism organization. He had more experience with the Islamic terrorists than any other agent, dating back to his tenure as an officer in Le Legion d'Etrangere. A master of Aristotelian logic, as any French Renseignements Interieur officer should be, he was an excellent judge of these people, but they did not act according to logic. Their motivations sprang from centuries-old resentments and frustration toward the older Western cultures for reasons both real and imagined, colonial domination and later postcolonial dependence on American oil money and Soviet military technology. To Joffre, whatever intellectual and cultural refinements they might have had stopped developing in the seventh century. But Breuger had dealt with them in Algiers and fifty other third-world toilets around the globe, and he knew what they were like. Joffre had spent most of his early career as an intelligence agent in the so-called Cold War, fought out in little surrogate wars in Korea, Indo-China, Afghanistan, and lesser dustups in Africa and the Levant. The Americans and Soviets had eventually learned from these unwinnable little wars that engagements and counterengagements exhausted morale, as well as military, economic, and political capital, at an unacceptable level and finally abandoned them altogether. These latter-day terrorists had not yet learned that lesson, detached as they were from state sponsorship and geopolitical structure.

"Why, indeed?" replied Joffre. "Why do they do any of the things they do?" He swiveled his maroon leather desk chair around and looked out his window. The carefully kept lawn swept down and away from the main building to the river below, the stately French oak enfilading down the slope like a grand army awaiting orders from their emperor. The early spring buds were pushing the thick brown leaves off faster than the grounds crew was able to keep up with them. Any disorder offended Joffre, as it did any Gallic soul, but disorder was the key to mystery, and any evidence of it in an investigation rang alarms in his mind as reliably as sidereal movement.

"Have you talked to Bohemund about this, Henri? Have our people kept up with him?" Joffre turned his chair back toward his desk and looked across at Breuger, who was still frowning at what he believed to be his superior's deliberate obstinacy. Breuger shook his head and shrugged, as if Joffre ought to have known better.

"Sources and methods, Commissaire. Reveal nothing of sources and methods—isn't that rule one?"

"*Bon Dieu*, Henri! Bohemund was in French military intelligence for ten years after graduating St. Cyr. Don't you think he already knows what our methods are? He has helped us before, when our interests have coincided with his. And a source in Rome is always useful. Especially a man whom one can actually believe. Go and speak to him. Find out if he can confirm what happened to Kintner. If he can't, ask him to name someone who can."

Breuger stood up and walked across the broad expanse of carpet toward the door. Trust the Direction Centrale du Renseignement Interieur (DCRI) to acquire a chateau to house their headquarters. They saw no contradiction between the need for secrecy and ostentation. What had one thing to do with the other?

* * *

The sky was now a light pastel of blues and pinks, and Michael could easily see anyone behind him. The road would join the blacktop in a few miles, and then there would be the turnoff through the Navajo reservation. If he remembered rightly, the turn was very hard to see, commencing just beyond a blind cliff, and you could drive past it and not know that you had missed anything. Maybe they would miss it and he would get a better margin ahead of them. Not that it would matter. Somehow, they always guessed correctly which way he had gone. He had kept off main roads, gone down badly kept county highways and even across private ranch roads, but eventually, he would see them again, always in that red pickup with the massive black custom grill, until he began to think that they must have fifty of the same kind of truck, all deployed for the purpose of keeping his trail.

He wondered for the hundredth time if he were delusional and if that meant psychosis had finally taken his consciousness irretrievably beyond reality. Of course, it could be argued that that had occurred a long time before this chase had started. The recent war against terrorism was in many respects like all wars. The instincts and proclivities one must have, not just to survive, but to bring the war to an acceptable conclusion, were clinically psychotic. But this war—the press had dubbed it the Ninth Crusade—was exceptionally close to utter insanity. When ancient Christian and Jewish edifices began to be destroyed by the Muslim terrorists, Israel, France, and the Vatican formed an alliance to prevent anymore of these obscenities from occurring. The loss of the West End London Synagogue and Notre Dame Cathedral, among others, appalled the entire Western world. Almost as appalling—to many—was the formation of a military order by the Vatican, the first in centuries.

His mentor, Father Toriano, had been able to put some of these contradictions into a context of faith:

"Michael, the truth is always more than the sum of its parts. All the faiths of the world since time began do not, in their individual essence, add up to the sum of what faith means or of what the truth is. Yet, each of us can glimpse his piece of it. And therein lies individual accountability.

"The 'holy war' of Muhammad and the 'just war' of St. Augustine surely were contradictions to religions that taught spiritual peace and love. But, Michael, you know from your own experience that the path to truth is narrow and torturous, and few there are who travel it to the end. Wise men have known this for thousands of years."

It was growing lighter, and the road entered a wide curvature to the left. He could see the towering red butte on the horizon to the left of the road. All else was flat and brown and devoid of vegetation except for the scrub pine and juniper and the gray-green sage in little pockets across the plain. Far up ahead, he could just make out the high jagged karst climbing vertically out of the desert, looking for all the world like a massive black clipper ship under full sail. That was the sign, wasn't it, the sign that the turnoff to the reservation was a few miles—ten, fifty, what?—past the massive black ship rock? In his subconscious, the rock reminded him of the converted bomber he had flown on that last day, just after the suspension of hostilities.

It was painted black, the flying ship, the airplane with the stubby nose, the high shark fin for a tail, and the engines that didn't sound like engines at all but like the hiss of a cobra whose bite was a nightmarish fire that looked as if it could burn up half the world.

His mind was beginning to cloud, and he wished that he had drunk more of that awful-tasting coffee. But it would pass, and he was pointed away from the rising sun so that he could see clearly. Just keep going, that was the key. If he didn't stop for very long, they wouldn't get him. There were a thousand miles between him and the sea, and a lot could happen. Maybe a hiding place would appear, one even they wouldn't think of as a hiding place, maybe one so obvious that they would just pass it by. And maybe the archangel Gabriel would appear and take him to paradise. Both were about equal in likelihood.

He topped a small rise. He felt a familiar feeling without really knowing why and guessed he was close. He slowed and looked for it. There it was. Just beyond an abrupt drop in the terrain was a narrow blacktop stretching off to the north into what looked like nothing at all for as far as he could see. He slowed further and eased off onto the little road, glancing once into the mirror and seeing only the golden glow in the sky behind him. He knew there was a long, empty road ahead with little commercial traffic and not much local, either. More than a century and a half ago, the government had picked out the least valuable land it could find and put the Navajo on it. They went because they had no choices other than slow starvation or slaughter. They had been given a lot of land, though, so that when anyone asked an embarrassing question about what had happened to the people, the government could say what an enormous territory it had given to them.

An hour passed, or maybe more, he couldn't tell, and the only artifacts he had seen were a few small government-issue modules of what looked like two or three rooms. Twice, he had seen, far out on the prairie, an isolated wickiup, if that was what it was, no doubt built to prove a point if nothing else. One had to admire that kind of attitude. The sun was full up now, and he couldn't see the road behind him for it, but he didn't care. Crowding out all the other thoughts just now were the final words of Father Toriano:

"We both are near to the end of our lives, Michael. You, perhaps, nearer than I. But we must carry to our graves the simple truth that any claim to spirituality that is not solidly based on morality or on the essence of love is false. Love is nothing else but love and is its own reward. It merits no other reward nor fears any punishment.

"But how fleeting are the most closely held values and principles when driven out by the human thirst for revenge, for justice, for retribution. What are those compulsions, really, but an indulgence of one's most primitive and destructive instincts, no matter how we justify or excuse them? Yet they have formed the basis for human sociology for tens of thousands of years. They will never disappear. And some questions will forever remain unanswered."

* * *

Monsignor Robert Bohemund was a tall, urbane Frenchman from an ancient and noble family, which traced its lineage to Norman provinces in France, on the Italian peninsula, and in Sicily before and during the time of the First Crusade to drive the invading Seljuk Turks from the eastern Christian empire. His background in French military and intelligence departments before becoming a Jesuit had served him well during the most recent, and probably bloodiest, crusade.

Robert Bohemund looked at the neatly dressed but rough-looking Frenchman and remembered that all intelligence agents were thoroughly paranoid. It was a useful and absolutely predictable characteristic of their vocation. But he still found it annoying.

"Your pardon, Monsieur, but are you seriously suggesting that Michael Kintner is still alive? Do you not realize that the radiation alone would have finished him off by now, if I may put it crudely, and it is still the official position of the Holy See that he died in the blast? I do not see what the Renseignements Interieur hopes to gain by this charade."

He remembered the first time he had laid eyes on Michael Kintner at the Vatican—when was it?—five, six years ago now, before the Ninth Crusade. He was a youngish, athletic-looking man; his appearance belied the brief he had read about him only a day or two before. It had described his scholarly attributes, his doctorate in astrophysics, his original research in complexity theory, his book *The Just War: A Critique*. There had been nothing in it that addressed his military background—first in his class at the US Air Force Academy, outstanding graduate at the Air War College, and his combat experience as a fighter pilot in Indo-China, Bosnia, and the Gulf War. And it had been these that had secularized his profile, even among the Jesuits, arguably the most worldly of the clerical orders. Pope Thomas had chosen him to lead the Crusade with Bohemund as his deputy commander. In retrospect, Bohemund wished he had not accepted any part of it—not that he could have foreseen the horror, but even if he had, how could he have refused the pope?

Henri Breuger wiped his hand slowly across his face, his hopes that they might have been able to dispense with the tiresome bureaucratic dance the Vatican seemed always to insist upon before actually giving up any helpful information fading.

"Monsignor Bohemund, please do not misunderstand me. I am not empowered to take issue with the diplomatic position of the Holy See. I am only a minor functionary of my government whose sole duty at the moment is to resolve some . . . inconsistencies . . . in our information regarding what we know of some current terrorist activities."

If the monsignor wanted bureaucratic double-talk, he would be happy to oblige. As anyone in government service knew, a diplomatic position was a lie everyone pretended to believe so that the lies of their own governments would also be accepted as truths. It sometimes avoided, if only temporarily, an inconvenient confrontation until everyone had exhausted all other alternatives. But it still was a monumental waste of time and effort for people such as himself who tried to keep their governments from lying to themselves or, more precisely, from believing their own lies.

Bohemund knew the only chance he had of eliciting any information from the Renseignement Interieur was to offer them something they needed. There was always a quid pro quo, and if the French had information about another possible terrorist catastrophe, it was very much in the church's interests to get it. They could not afford to lose another irreplaceable edifice, such as the Sistine Chapel; nor could they lose another pope. The pope was, at least, replaceable. But the destruction of the Grand Mosque in Mecca, allegedly by an agent of the church in retaliation, after the official cessation of all other hostilities, had not yet met with a response. There had been an eerie silence from the terrorists, at least according to the church's own sources of information, since the day an aircraft with no markings had exploded a massive hyperbaric bomb over the Grand Mosque in the middle of Ramadan. The world and the church held their collective breaths, waiting for what surely must come.

"In that case, I am prepared to be as helpful as I may. What exactly are these inconsistencies on which you seek my help?"

* * *

It was only a small cantina in the middle of nowhere, but it suited Michael's purposes. It had plate-glass windows in front so that he could see whoever might show up while he was inside. It was close to noon, but there was only one beat-up car in the parking spaces in front, the kind they called an Indian car.

He pulled cautiously into the lot, turned the truck around, and pointed it back toward the road. *Still paranoid,* he thought. But even paranoids had enemies. He got out of the cab, walked over to the front door, and tried it. It opened, and he walked into an unlit and empty room. Four tables with Formica tops each sat attended by three or four unmatched folding chairs. There was a bar across the back of the room with a number of handwritten menus high on the wall behind it. Mostly Mexican food. Was that what Indians ate these days? The rest of the wall was covered with shelves loaded down with brands of whiskey, vodka, and wine he had never heard of. He walked to the bar and looked down it. He saw a little domed bell meant to call the help, he supposed. He tapped it, and the sound bounced forlornly around the room. He was just about ready to leave when a woman came through the door behind the counter. She was stocky and not very tall and looked as if she had been asleep. Her shiny dark hair had come halfway out of the beaded cord that had been holding it behind her head. She had a bad bruise on her left cheek, and her lower lip was split and scabbed over. She came up to the counter and stood silently waiting for him to say something. She stared hard but expressionlessly at his face, and he remembered what he must look like, the sloughed skin and white hair with the patches where it had not yet grown back—two people battered by things beyond their control or comprehension and each pretending not to notice.

"Can I have some scrambled eggs with toast and coffee?"

"Anything up there," she said, pointing over her shoulder at the menu, "you can have, except you get tortillas 'cause we ain't got no light bread."

"All right."

He turned, walked over to the nearest table, and sat down facing back toward the front. He heard her start getting things together in the back, and because there was nothing else to think about, he tried to imagine her exact movements in the kitchen from the small sounds he could hear. He quickly grew bored of it and thought about who might have given her the beating and why, but he knew it was pointless to speculate on what surely must be the most common of pastimes for people with too much time and too little hope on their hands. Like himself in a way, he guessed.

In a few minutes, she had the eggs, warm tortillas, and coffee in front of him. He asked for butter but got a few pats of artificial something that tasted vaguely like lard. He ate it down in about five minutes and sat sipping the coffee so he wouldn't get any of the dregs. She came back out and stood at the table without saying anything. He took out five dollars and handed them to her. As she started away, on impulse, he spoke to her.

"Would you happen to know of a place to stay around here that was quiet? I wouldn't need any maid service and could pay in cash?"

It sounded stupid to him as he said it, but it pretty well summed what he wanted if there was such a place.

She looked at him for what seemed like a long time, as if she were trying to decide something, and finally answered him.

"I got a spare room out back next to where I live if you just want someplace to sleep where nobody would bother you. What would you be willing to pay?"

"Whatever you had to have for it. In cash. Would you take twenty dollars? A day? In advance?"

She was silent again for a long time.

"I guess it'd be all right. But you got to put your truck back there. People know I'm here by myself, and I don't want nobody askin' who it belongs to ever' time they come in."

"All right. I'll drive it back there now if you want."

She nodded and walked back to the kitchen with his dishes stacked on her left arm and the five-dollar bill in her right hand. He got up, went out to the truck, started it, and pulled out slowly in a wide arc to his right, going around the cantina and looking for the room she said was out back. The ground dipped down and away from the building and leveled out again where there was an adobe cabin. He drove up to it and stopped by the front door. The lay of the ground concealed the cabin and his truck from the view of anyone parking in front of the cantina. It looked to be just what he wanted. Farther back was a dry creek bed lined along its banks with creek willow and Palos Verde. It wound out of sight in both directions between the shallow slopes of the hard, dry terrain.

It was early to be stopping, and he had thought when he started out that morning that he might make it to the Nevada line by dark, but this place was better for his purposes than anything he might find later on. Besides, he was trying not to be too predictable in how far he drove and where he stopped.

He got out of the truck, pulled his rucksack from behind the seat, and went into the little cabin. It smelled musty but was swept clean, and there was a bathroom attached. The little narrow bed was covered by a blanket with Navajo glyphs, and there was a decrepit chest of drawers against the opposite wall. There was a slender table with one drawer set in the corner, and on it was a cluster of burned-down candles surrounding a propped-up cardboard cutout of Our Lady of Guadalupe. He felt a sudden and unexpected stab of grief from somewhere inside him, an emotion that he had thought extinguished long ago. He walked over to stand in front of it and without thinking knelt down and crossed himself. He knelt there for a moment and then stood up hurriedly, feeling embarrassed without knowing why. He shook his head, trying to clear whatever unbidden feelings had intruded there in the last few minutes. He heard a sound and turned to see the woman standing in the doorway. She stood there without speaking for a long time.

"Is it going to do?"

He took a step backward and glanced around the sparse little room one more time.

"It will do."

She walked into the room and looked around. She went into the bathroom where she left the roll of paper towels she had been holding and then came back into the room. She looked down at his cloth case and then back up at him.

"There ain't no lock in case you got anything worth stealing. You got the twenty dollars?"

He took a plastic wallet from the front pocket of his jeans, peeled off a twenty that was wrapped around the outside of it, and handed it to her. She took it and wadded it up in her hand as if she intended to throw it away but held it tightly without putting it away in a pocket or somewhere. Then she stood looking at him as if she might be going to say something else. He stared at her, but the person he saw was someone from his past—a woman who had been both unforgettable and unattainable:

"Michael, is there something you need? What can I do to help you? Will I see you ever again? I have loved you too deeply for too long for you to leave me like this just when I might be able to help you the most. I cannot even think of the rest of my life without you. It doesn't matter what has happened. I can protect you for however much time you have left. Won't you even let me try?"

The young Navajo woman turned and walked out without looking back. He went over and sat on the bed, staring out the door for a long time, not thinking anything at all but just trying to keep from standing up and screaming.

* * *

"What I can say, Monsieur Breuger," began Bohemund, "is that if he had survived the blast, even for a few days or weeks, I am sure he would have returned to the United States. And if he had done that, there is only one person I know who might have seen him or talked to him. But I'm not sure how you would get in touch with her."

"Tell me what you can, Monsignor. I will do the rest."

Bohemund moved a small desk pad closer to himself. He picked up a pen and began to write on the pad. In a moment, he stopped, ripped off the top page, and handed it to the agent.

"Her name is Dr. Judy Weiss. She used to have a residence in Georgetown, near Washington. She was an advisor of some kind, I forget what, to the former American president."

Bohemund stood up, effectively terminating the meeting.

"I would be grateful if you could share with me any pertinent information you acquire that might help to avoid any further tragedies. I wish you *bonne chance* in your trip to the United States, if that's what you are planning. Needless to say, you have received no official information from me or from the Holy See."

Breuger took his proffered hand and gripped it briefly.

"Merci, Monsignor." He walked quickly out of the ornate office, stuffing the piece of paper into his jacket pocket. *Something*, he thought. Not much. But more than he had expected.

* * *

Michael sat on the edge of the bed listening to the staccato sound of a Stellar's jay somewhere off in the creek bed. There was no traffic noise or any other sound from the cantina, and he wondered how he would spend the next few hours until he could sleep. He had brought no books from his truck into the room, and he didn't feel like going back out to get one. His energy level was still very low, and he spent a good deal of time these days just sitting and wondering about things in general, trying not to recall specifics of any kind except those that had happened a long time ago.

He remembered the boring classroom at Georgetown University where he had taught physics and astronomy to groups of mostly undermotivated students. There was always one or two who made the drudgery worth it. His private research in the relatively new science of complexity theory was where his real interests lay, and the classroom duties made it possible. He had never really succeeded in developing a consistent and comprehensive system of mathematics for his theories, but he had gotten very close. If it weren't for the intrusion of affairs that were none of his doing, he might have had something worthwhile by now. But it didn't really matter. The stodgy community of physicists, which continued to resist any serious challenge to the prevailing scientific method, would certainly have rendered his work moot. To hell with them too.

Then there were the cool autumn days on Chesapeake Bay when the wind was good again and all he had to concentrate on was the point of sail, and the cool wind and spray coming over the bow transported him to a place where even the most troubled spirit could be at ease with the world and forget the man-made ugliness. Michael knew there would never again be such moments in his life.

It seemed only a moment later the darkness had descended outside, and he began to hear cars pull into the parking lot at the cantina. Music of some kind started up inside, and the raised voices drifted back to his little cabin. At first, they were cheerful sounding, and then as the evening wore on, there was more and more of an angry tone accompanied by the sounds of glass breaking and car doors slamming. He got up and pulled his door closed. He took off his boots and lay down on the cot. He drifted in and out of consciousness for a long time before the sounds from the cantina ceased altogether. He hoped he would not dream as he felt himself slip once more into the stupor that served as sleep for him now.

He came wide awake suddenly and held very still until he could figure out what it was that had waked him. A woman's voice begging in half-whine, half-scream came down from the direction of the cantina, and he lay still, waiting to see what was happening and whether it had anything to do with him or not. A man's voice, hoarse and angry and filled with hatred and violence, repeated one expletive used for every part of speech there was. Another scream from a different woman, it sounded like, and then all three were screaming and yelling at once. One of the screaming voices stopped, followed by the other two. Then there was only silence. The silence lasted for a long moment, and then the screaming started again.

He swung his legs off the bunk, found his boots, and put them on. He reached into the top of his rucksack on the way out the door and jammed his Sig Sauer nine-millimeter into his belt in the small of his back. As he came up over the rise, he saw a door standing open to a room in the back of the cantina, and he headed for it.

He saw a huge man standing with his back to the door, and he was holding the stocky woman by the neck against the wall where she hung as if nailed to it. In the far corner, another woman crouched on the floor naked, her eyes wide and her mouth open in one continuous scream. He walked up behind the man, drew out the automatic, and clubbed him hard with the barrel of the gun across the back of his head. The man stood still as if nothing at all had happened and then slowly turned to look behind him, letting the other naked woman slide limply down to the dirt floor.

The man's eyes were wide and staring, but no other expression at all was on his face. He thrust the hand forward that had been holding the woman and grabbed the throat of the man he saw standing there. He took three hollow-point rounds in the stomach before he slowly loosened his grip and then just stood there as if uncertain what to do next. As he slumped down to one knee, another round went through his left eye, splattering the back of his head and half its contents against the wall where he had been holding the woman. The woman crouched in the corner had stopped screaming and could only stare down at the great lump of meat on the floor, which a moment before had been a piece of the human race.

He let his hand with the gun in it fall slowly to his side. It had all happened so quickly that his hands hadn't even had time to begin to sweat. He walked over to the still woman on the floor and felt at her throat for a pulse, but he couldn't feel anything. Then he stood up, turned his head, and looked at the other woman, who was still staring at the dead man on the floor. They waited for a very long time just like that, and then he turned and went back to the little cabin where he repacked the few things from his rucksack that he had removed. In a few minutes, he was back on the highway headed west in the dark.

* * *

Henri Breuger was also packing a suitcase in his apartment just outside the wall of the Vatican. He had plenty of time to catch the Air Italia flight to Reagan National in Washington. He zipped up the bag and sat down at the little table where he took out a small notebook from his jacket pocket. He transcribed the contents of the piece of paper the Jesuit had given him and then burned the paper in the ashtray and pulverized the ashes with the top of his pen. He stared at the ashes blankly, wondering for the thousandth time what kind of world it was he had chosen to live in so many years ago. He doubted if any men ever really thought through the consequences of the decisions they made before they were really ready to commit the rest of their lives to them and without even knowing that was what they had done.

He had lost count of the seedy hotels, the stinking bars, the putrescent scum he had had to deal with, and those he had left with their blood oozing out from smoking holes in their flesh. Worst of all were those who did things just as bad as any waterfront thug but who lived lives they pretended were decent and honorable. He knew people could rationalize any repugnant act and excuse it by some overarching moral reason or by even the most half-assed or insane religious or patriotic fervor. Most of the time, it all boiled down to what you thought you had to do and whether you could get away with it. But then there were people in the world who did precisely what someone else could convince them was right in spite of and sometimes because it was suicidal to do it. He used to excuse what he had to do by telling himself it was to keep some semblance of sanity and security for what was left of the civilized world. But that was obviously ridiculous.

It was the twenty-first century, and there were a billion people in the world who still believed in a genocidal god invented by an illiterate desert nomad who convinced himself and his followers that his nightmarish deity desired the mutilation and murder of everyone who refused obeisance. And some of them were still so imbued with this self-induced psychosis that they could destroy magnificent edifices, such as the great Buddhist statues in Bamiyan, the Sistine Chapel, or the Cathedral of Notre Dame de Paris, and kill thousands of innocent people in the process. The religious leader of another billion people on the planet had convinced himself it served the interests of his god to form a holy military order to wreak vengeance on the first billion—a ninth crusade patterned after the first eight, which had ended in failure six centuries ago. So much for what was left of the civilized world.

Breuger recognized his reverie for what it was—a rationalization for an unaccountable worldwide insanity, which, if left unchecked, might destroy everything humankind had achieved in the last thousand years. Didn't that justify what he was trying to do? He fervently hoped so.

Chapter 2

Michael drove on through the desert, letting unbidden thoughts crowd into his consciousness. *Deus meus, ex toto corde me poenitet quia offendi Te . . .* How did it go again? He couldn't remember anything anymore. Things he had known all his life were as elusive as a mist. *Oh my God, I am heartily sorry for having offended Thee . . .* If the death of that man back there was anywhere nearly as offensive to God as his life no doubt was, then he guessed he owed him an apology. But he didn't. Not everyone had a soul. How could they? Maybe some were born without one, and certainly some killed it within themselves by the time they had lived for very many years. He had seen too much of this race of predatory bipeds to think that they were intrinsically and irreducibly holy. Not many of them, anyway. There would be no way to explain what they did otherwise.

He rubbed his hand across his face again, trying to stay awake. There was something else he had forgotten, something that plagued him every morning when he first got up or when he woke up in the middle of the night. Something important. But he couldn't remember. There was a good deal of pain, and it felt as if he were still swimming back from going out much too far, but maybe it would pass. If he had survived this long, maybe there was still hope. Life without hope wasn't life at all. But somewhere deep in his subconscious, he was trying to believe there was hope. Just to stay alive.

* * *

Breuger drove slowly down the quiet street searching the door facings of the trendy town houses for the number he had gotten from the French embassy. There were no empty parking spaces, he guessed because it was still early and not many had gone to wherever they worked. But he wouldn't mind walking. It was one of those rare spring days in Washington, redolent with the smell of dogwood, emergent daffodils, and star magnolia.

There was the number—1211 O Street. He slowed the car still further. It was a brick nineteenth-century structure covered in several coats of white paint and trimmed in black with open black shutters on the door and windows. To one side was a small gate leading between the houses to a presumptive garden in the rear. He drove on down to the end of the block and turned down the hill toward the business section until he found a parallel spot on the curb. He parked and started walking back toward O Street.

He glanced at his watch. Eight thirty. Still too early. He spotted a small park with some benches on the opposite corner, walked over, and sat down. Long ago, he had learned a mental technique of letting his mind go blank while maintaining an awareness of any small thing that might constitute a threat. The technique was very old, mentioned even in the writings of Tsunetomo on the "Way of the Samurai." A disciplined instinct was the most powerful weapon a warrior could possess. It seemed only a moment had passed when he became aware of something. He glanced up to see a large black man in baggy clothes standing a few meters away, watching him speculatively, trying to decide if the man on the bench was worth taking from. Breuger stood up slowly, looking straight into the stranger's face, waiting for any small indication of hostile intent.

A startled expression appeared on the man's face, and he turned and started walking swiftly away down the path that led back to the inner city. Breuger watched the receding form for a few moments and then looked at his watch again. Time to go see the woman.

He found the number again, walked up to the door, and pushed the bell button. No one came for several minutes. He had started to turn away when the door opened. The woman was nearly as tall as he was, but her posture made her look shorter. She had short dark-red hair, which needed a brush, and her face, which could have been striking, was swollen with the marks of her pillow still on it. She wore a white terry-cloth robe and was barefoot. She stared blankly at him, waiting for him to say something.

"Excusez moi, madame, I was under the impression that my embassy had contacted you about—"

"Yes, yes, they did. My apologies, monsieur. Please, come in. I will be just a moment. Please make yourself comfortable." She gestured vaguely in the direction of the sitting room just beyond the foyer where she stood. "Would you care for some coffee?"

"No, thank you, madame. I will be happy to come at a more convenient time if you—"

"No. I'll just be a moment. Please sit down."

She walked away unhurriedly without a backward look and disappeared beyond a door at the end of the hallway that led from the foyer. Breuger went into the sitting room and looked around. It looked as if no one had been in there for some time. A fine layer of dust covered the small tables by the chairs, and the only smell was that of the carpet, which looked newer than the other furnishings. The walls were mostly lined with books, some relatively new with expensive bindings and some that looked very old. The books were misaligned and seemed not to be in any predictable groupings, also indicating to him that the room had had no attention for some time. He walked along the shelves, reading the titles to try to get some insight into the woman's interests. There were many books on history, especially of warfare and politics; a few on the surprising subject of Jewish kabbalism, most of them by Gershon Scholem; and some on Catholic mysticism by Merton, Graham, and de Chardin. *A woman with depth,* he thought. He remembered that the people at the embassy had told him that Dr. Judy Weiss had been the national security advisor to the former president. Most of her books seemed consistent with that, but some were wildly inconsistent. He wondered what her exact relationship with Michael Kintner had been.

Several minutes later, Judy Weiss entered the room with a tray of coffee and sweet rolls, which she set on a low table to the right of where Breuger had been sitting. She was wearing faded jeans and a bulky sweater with leather shooting patches on the shoulders and elbows. She started pouring into the cups she had brought. She filled them and, as an afterthought, stood up straight and proffered her hand to him.

"Sorry, I forgot my manners. I am Judy Weiss, but I'm afraid I've forgotten what the person who called from the embassy told me your name was . . ."

"I am Henri Breuger, Doctor Weiss. Monsignor Bohemund in Rome recommended that I speak with you. It concerns Michael Kintner."

"Please sit down." She picked up her cup, walked over, and sat down in one of the Morris chairs by the bookshelves. "How is the monsignor?"

Breuger sat down and picked up the other cup. He looked across at Judy, who was staring vacantly out of the window toward the street. The way she had just inquired told him that she had no idea who Bohemund was. He knew her question was merely a diplomatic instinct, which was required and expected of all government employees. He wondered if she even remembered Kintner. It seemed to him as if she might be recovering from some illness or perhaps was still in its grip.

"Doctor Weiss, please forgive my presumption, but I perceive that you may not be feeling well. Perhaps at a more convenient time we may—"

Judy looked at him with some surprise. Her abrupt loss of composure indicated to Breuger that she was not accustomed to any lack of courtesy in her conversations.

"I am perfectly all right, thank you, monsieur. What exactly is it you wish to know?" she retorted sharply, with just a touch of temper.

Good, thought Breuger. *Now maybe we can have a conversation.*

"Madame, my government is very much concerned, as yours no doubt is, about the possibility of more terrorist attacks. We keep a close watch on their communications and actions. We have no wish to lose anymore of our citizens or our national treasures. Recently, we have noted in the terrorist communiqués the mention of the name of Michael Kintner and his possible connection with the destruction of the Grand Mosque in Mecca. My first question is: do you know any reason why they might have made such a connection?"

Judy looked at him with an incredulous expression. It looked as if her recent flash of anger was starting to deepen.

"Monsieur, you are very much mistaken. Dr. Kintner—Michael—was mortally injured in the Sistine Chapel where Pope Thomas and hundreds of others were killed. The bombing of Mecca occurred after that. What possible connection could he have had with it?"

Breuger sat back in his chair and put his cup back on the tray. He looked closely at her. It was possible that she had no useful information about Kintner, but it was also possible that she was unconsciously blocking out the things that she did know. At her previous level in the American government, she would have had access to the complete dossiers on everyone who had been involved in every major international incident—and to a great deal more besides.

"Doctor Weiss, may I ask . . . what exactly was your relationship with Michael Kintner? Did you have any contact with him outside of official channels? By that, I mean—"

"I know what you mean, Monsieur Breuger." She set down her own cup, stood up, and walked over to the window she had been looking out of earlier. She was quiet for a long time and then turned and looked at him again.

"I am not deliberately trying to mislead you. I knew Michael Kintner well. I met him about the time the Vatican was putting together its response to the all-out war the terrorists declared on the church." She walked over and sat back down.

"Michael was chosen initially as an emissary for the Vatican to the president for reasons that are not terribly relevant now. That was before he was given control of the Vatican military order. And over the course of the next few years, he and I grew very close . . . in spite of the fact that neither of us really sought such a relationship."

Appearing to grow embarrassed, she got up again and began to pace slowly around the room.

"When the Sistine Chapel was destroyed, he was the only one to survive. Well, I think there may have been a few others, but they all shortly died from the radiation. Michael came back home a couple of weeks ago to live out what he was told were the last few weeks of his life. And he stopped here for a while to say good-bye. He said nothing to me about any involvement with the bombing of Mecca. Then he left to go back and spend the rest of his time with an old friend, Father Toriano, the abbot of Christ in the Desert Monastery in New Mexico."

"But why would he go to such a place? If you and he were as close as you said, surely he—"

"Didn't you know, monsieur? Michael Kintner is a Jesuit priest."

* * *

27

Officer Billy Antelope from the Navajo police stepped carefully around the two bodies sprawled out on the dirt floor looking for something else, but he could see nothing. He had found four nine-millimeter cartridges, two empty whiskey bottles, and a condom with a small amount of cocaine in it and nothing else. Standard stuff for the back room of a cantina on the reservation, he thought.

Eddie Chavez had been trying to get himself killed for a long time, and he had finally made it. How little Betty Whitejack had put up with him for so long, he didn't know. She had come to him once or twice when he had beaten her very badly but could never bring herself to press charges the next day. Lots of women like that on the reservation. In the Anglo counties, too, he guessed. But she hadn't killed him. She wouldn't hurt a sidewinder if it bit her. Dolores, though, now she might get mad enough to. But she had said it was somebody else, someone she had never seen before. Maybe she had calmed down enough to talk some more. He ducked under the yellow tape and walked through the kitchen and back into the bar. Dolores was still sitting at the table where he had left her. He pulled out a chair and sat down.

"You thought of anything else? You sure you never seen him before?"

"No, Billy, I told you. He come out of nowhere. He was there just long enough to blow Eddie's head off, and then he left." She pulled her jacket tighter around her and moved her legs to one side so she sat looking out the window. It was still hard for her to believe Betty was dead. She never got mad, never hurt anybody, and you could borrow her last dime and never have to worry about paying it back. *Goddamn Eddie*, she thought. *Goddamn him to hell.*

"All right, then. Was he an Anglo or Indian? Was he in the bar before?"

"I never saw him before, I told you. I don't know if he was an Anglo or what. Looked funny, like he had been in a fire or something, face scarred up and hair all burnt off, or most of it."

She sat, trying again to remember something else about him, but she couldn't remember much. One thing she did remember was how calm and quiet he was. She and Betty had been crying and screaming, and Eddie had been yelling and cussing, but the other man might have been a deliveryman. He had just blown Eddie's head off and left.

"What about that condom with the dope in it? I know that's the way they bring the stuff across the border now. And women have twice the body cavities men do to carry it in. So . . . I'm asking you, were you Eddie's carrier?"

Dolores didn't answer and didn't look at him. She was still thinking about poor little Betty and what had happened to her. Finally, it dawned on her what she had been asked. She turned her head and looked at him again.

"Billy, is it just that you know you ain't got a icicle's chance in hell of catching whoever killed Eddie and so you want me to confess to carrying drugs to make it come out even? Or are you just looking for a fresh source for the police department?"

Billy's face grew dark, and his jaw muscles started to clench. *Just let it go,* he thought. *Dolores has got a right to bitch at me.* But she was right about one thing—he didn't have a chance in hell of catching Eddie's killer.

* * *

Michael had been driving a few hours now, and the sun was well up. Last night was already just a vague memory. He doubted anybody from the reservation would be coming after him. Wouldn't matter if they did. He would kill anyone who tried to stop him. Wasn't as if he had a lot to lose. He would just keep going.

The terrain hadn't changed much. Less vegetation, maybe. Up ahead, he could see a couple of lines of those huge power transmission towers converging toward the horizon. Was there a hydroelectric plant up there? Then he remembered—Lake Powell, built back during the Depression or during the war or sometime, on the Utah-Arizona border. There would be a town there, but he wouldn't stop. Lots of desert left to cross before nightfall. He needed some coffee or a drink or something. There was a five-gallon container with water in it in the truck bed, some cooking equipment, and a helmet bag full of cans and boxes of something to eat. He would keep watch for someplace to pull off where he wouldn't be bothered with tourists or other traffic. Get off this highway, in any case. Too much traffic.

He topped a gentle rise, and down below was the large lake stretching for miles from north to south. On the near bank was a small town, around which grew the only trees in evidence—juniper and cottonwood, some pine and mesquite. He drove right through the town and on the far side decided to stop at a little coffee shop adjacent to a truck fueling station. He walked in and looked around—clean and almost austere, with a bank of self-serve coffeepots and mounds of rolls with sweet toppings. A neat, middle-aged woman stood behind the counter looking at him while trying not to look at him as everyone seemed to do these days. People were almost always embarrassed by injury or deformity but were still fascinated by it.

He walked over, poured himself a coffee, put a roll on a paper napkin, and brought them to the counter. He paid the woman, and because she still looked embarrassed, he took the coffee and roll and left. Back in his truck, he set the coffee in the holder on the pull-down armrest, started the truck, and drove on. He came onto the high steel bridge over the lake and looked out the right window. The lake was surrounded by stark cliffs painted by enormous geologically horizontal stripes of orange, black, yellow, and red. He wondered at how much additional beauty had been covered up when they flooded the canyon. He drove on across the bridge into more beautiful desert, starting to fill up with dozens of tasteless houses on small lots, probably selling for a great deal of money because of their proximity to the lake. All over the country, people were in hock up to their collarbones with mortgages they couldn't afford because some realtor or developer had told them they were really saving money by doing so. The American dream, along with Prozac and abortion clinics and rehab farms and more penitentiaries than even the government could afford.

He thought he remembered from the last time he had looked at a road map that a small county road led from here northwest toward the Nevada desert. There it was, number 21, a narrow blacktop off to the left. He turned off, glad to be away from the RVs and trailers and other tourist traffic polluting the highways. He finished off the coffee and roll and sat back to absorb the emptiness of the land. He now understood completely why Central Asian mystics had regarded emptiness and oblivion as the highest attainment. Yet they regarded it as unattainable, only given. By what? By whom? No one could answer that. And it didn't matter, did it? An incomprehensible power, an unknowable source, all the names and anagrams and aphorisms and metaphors for what no one could adequately describe or even imagine. Yet, for as long as humans had been able to think at all, they had been aware of something beyond themselves, some greater pattern of which they were only one small part—or victims, servants, or supplicants, depending on which brand of spiritual mechanism one subscribed to. Right now, he would settle for emptiness.

He missed Father Toriano and their talks together, which continued long into the night, the only voices in that remote community of men sworn to silence. That gentle old man, who had incurred the wrath of the church because of his devotion to the poor in his native Ecuador, who had defended them against the landowners, the companies, and the government. He was a liberation theologian, a radical, a Marxist, and other equally degrading epithets to describe one devoted to the actual practice of Christianity as opposed to its theoretical application. So he had fetched up in that small monastery secluded in the canyon with the swift, deep river where his voice would never be heard again—except by him. He had heard it, that peaceful old man, telling him that he must go off to fight, to kill, to destroy those who would destroy the Christian world if they weren't stopped. And that was what he had done. When it was over, he had come back, when he was dying, when he had done everything in his power to make the church safe from the terror of the *jihadists*. Holy Warriors. Now there was an oxymoron for you. But Father Toriano had died first, just a few days after he had returned. And Michael had fled, with no destination, no intentions, and no hope for anything except a quick death.

That was when he became aware that they were following him. It seemed as if they weren't actually trying to catch him, but just keeping him aware that he was being pursued. He wondered if his confusion was one of the symptoms of radiation poisoning. Then he thought of another explanation. Maybe the pursuer was his own conscience.

* * *

Judy Weiss sat in her reading chair long after her visitor had gone. The last thing in the world she had expected was to have to talk about Michael. Now governments and terrorists were talking about him again, as if he had not been mortally injured, as if he were still around waiting to do their bidding, waiting to be killed again. She dropped her head forward into her hands, sobbing quietly, as she had done a thousand times, it seemed, over these last few weeks. How could they think about blaming Michael for the destruction of Mecca and its Grand Mosque? Was the church trying to lay the blame for it on him to deflect reprisal from the terrorists? It wouldn't surprise her, but what would the church realistically expect to gain by accusing Michael? If the terrorists were going to strike back, it would be against the church again. Killing Michael, if he were by some miracle still alive, wouldn't satisfy their bloodlust. Nothing about it made any sense. But neither did anything else.

She stood and walked down the hall into the kitchen in the back of the house. It was still morning, but she felt like she needed a drink. She opened the liquor cabinet and looked at the array of bottles. There was still a bottle of Kelt cognac, Michael's favorite. But neither of them had drunk very much in their last few days together. He hadn't seemed very much changed, not at all as if he had been through such an explosion as he had, but they knew that radiation poisoning would start taking its toll soon enough. She knew he wanted to be gone from her before he started to lose the skin and hair and turn into something he believed she would think was revolting. And now these people were inferring that he was still alive. Impossible, she knew, and yet Michael's religion provided for such impossibilities—she hoped it was true.

* * *

Henri Breuger sat in the window seat of the Southwest Airlines flight to Albuquerque going over in his mind what Judy Weiss had told him. She seemed to have no knowledge—or perhaps it was memory—of Michael Kintner's involvement with the bombing of Mecca. And she was certainly speaking sincerely of his death—his impending death—when she had seen him last. He did not know if anyone had ever survived exposure to radiation such as that which had occurred in the Sistine Chapel. He would check on that when he got back to Paris. But he should be able to establish his death one way or another at the monastery in New Mexico. There would be a body, or there wouldn't. And if there were, then the communiqués the Renseignements Interieur had been picking up about him were a ruse or a code of some type. If it were the latter, it would be only a trivial effort of the decryption experts to break it. Their computers were far more powerful than anything the terrorists might conceivably have. Not much compared to the Americans' NSA, but there were comparable machines in the DGSE. Why, out of the thousands who had responded to the pope's call to the holy military order— What was it? The *Ordo Sacer Clavium Sancti Petri*, the Sacred Order of the Keys of Saint Peter?—would they have chosen Michael Kintner's name as a code? He would need to do some more research when he got back as to exactly what role Kintner had played. Judy Weiss had said he was a Jesuit priest. So was Monsignor Bohemund. Perhaps they had both had military backgrounds before taking the cloth. Commissaire Joffre had said Bohemund was once in the Renseignement Interieur, or maybe it had been the Renseignement Electronique—perhaps Kintner had had a similar background in America. He would explore that possibility as well.

A pattern was starting to emerge in his mind. Suppose for a moment that Kintner's death had been a sham from the start. Suppose that the church had set up a circumstance whereby Kintner could assume a new, clandestine mission aimed at another attack of some kind against the infrastructure of Islam. That would certainly create an increased risk for other national treasures of France and perpetuate a conflict that had already cost all sides too much. If that were so, then it would be up to the Renseignement Interieur to stop it. When his headquarters received his report, they would conclude the same thing, he was sure. Well, first things first.

Chapter 3

Breuger walked out of the companionway and into the terminal. He went down to the main reception area and spotted the rent-a-car agency desk. They had a four-wheel-drive vehicle ready for him, a Ford SUV. He had requested it on the advice of the embassy, which had done some research to find out where the monastery was and the difficulty of getting there. Holy orders, by definition, needed some separation from the world in general and were usually located in secluded and sometimes very difficult-to-reach spots.

He took I-25 north to Santa Fe and turned onto Highway 84 toward a small place named Abiquiu. His instructions read that he would find the dirt road to the Benedictine Monastery a mile or so past the Ghost Ranch retreat house, an unostentatious setting now turned seedy with trailers and shacks for a Protestant religious group of some sort. The surrounding desert terrain was strikingly beautiful, the place made famous through the paintings of Georgia O'Keefe. As yet, the developers had not thoroughly ruined the view-shed, but they had started the process, their signs along the highway advertising "ranches" of five acres and ghastly overpriced houses overtaxing the meager resources of water and energy.

He drove past the turnoff twice before deciding that that must be it. It looked like a little-used ranch road, winding off along the sparsely vegetated dry washes, arroyos, and grazing lands. Only a few miles down, the road turned abruptly right along the high bank above the Chama River. The canyon walls were set back from the river by several meters on both sides, the lower level crowded with willow, juniper, and pine. The river wound gracefully through the surrounding land, the view unsullied by any man-made structures, power lines, telephone lines, or support shacks. The road was dry but still risky in places, with deep ruts, washouts, and potholes. It wound gradually down closer to the river until it was below the canyon rim but still a few meters above river level. The roadbed looked like it might become one big greasy mudslide in any sort of downpour. Wintertime travel was probably all but impossible. For fifteen miles, he guided the cumbersome vehicle along the road until, at a suddenly wide section at the base of the canyon wall, he spotted the church.

The creation of the famous architect George Nakashima, the church melded into and complemented the terrain, the high painted canyon wall serving as backdrop. Its dominant feature was the stark, vertical bell tower, surmounted by a cross and framed on each side by narrow strips of stained glass, which soared from ground level to the outward sloping roofline. Below, the top of the high brick wall that surrounded the church was punctuated with horizontal timbers in the fashion of the early Spanish missions. The adjacent buildings were of unobtrusive adobe stucco. The building off to the right had a small sign saying that this was the administration office. Breuger parked the SUV in front and then walked into the office and looked around.

"May I help you, sir?" The young man in a brown monk's habit and cowl stood up from his table, which served as a desk, and put aside his breviary.

"Yes. My name is Breuger. I have an appointment with your abbot, a Father Toriano, I believe. My embassy in Washington called."

"I am sorry. I gave the name of Father Toriano to the man who called from the embassy because he was our abbot until several days ago, but he has died and a new abbot has not yet been appointed. I have been doing the administrative chores until someone is sent by the head of our order. If I can help you, I will be glad to try. Please have a seat."

Breuger sat down, frowning. Surprises, even mild ones, were unsettling to him. The young man sat down and extended his hand across the table. Breuger grasped it briefly.

"I am Father Craig. Are you interested in reserving quarters, or are you just visiting for the day?"

"I am here to make inquiries concerning a Dr. Michael Kintner. My government has some mutual interests with the Holy See on a business with which we were led to believe he may be of some help. It concerns some antiquities."

Father Craig looked puzzled. Michael Kintner was pretty much a mystery to all of the priests and monks at the monastery, but their vow of silence had kept the gossip to a minimum.

"All I can tell you is that Father Kintner came to us about five or six years ago by special arrangement between the Benedictine mother house and the Societas Jesu in Rome. I never knew that he had anything to do with relics, or 'antiquities,' as you put it. We are principally a praying order, sworn to silence in all but essential matters, and Father Kintner kept to himself, as we all do. But he did seem to have a special relationship with Father Toriano. Anyway, he was called back to Rome after a couple of years here, and we never saw him again until a few weeks ago. He looked as if he had been in a fire or something, but when I asked the abbot if there was anything any of us could do to help him, he told me that he had come home to die. I didn't know what he meant, and I didn't press it."

"Well, what happened? Is he still here? You said it was your abbot who died, didn't you?"

"Yes." Father Craig crossed himself. "God's will is a mystery. Father Toriano was so concerned with Father Michael and the state he was in, and then he was taken first. But, as soon as the abbot's funeral Mass was over, Father Michael disappeared. He didn't even wait for interment. As far as I know, he never spoke to any of us before he left."

Breuger sat waiting for him to continue, but he did not.

"Can you tell me what sort of transportation he used—Did he call a taxi? Did someone pick him up? What?"

"He arrived in an old pickup truck, which he kept down by the maintenance building. It's gone, so I guess that's how he left."

"What kind of truck? Can you describe it?"

Father Craig hesitated. It seemed to him that this man was beginning to sound like a policeman—and a Frenchman, no less. There was something not quite right here. The church cooperated with the authorities, but when one of their own was involved, it was better to let someone higher in authority handle it.

"I'm . . . sorry, Mr. Breuger, but I think I'd better refer you to the mother house on this. I don't really have any useful information, but I am not authorized in any case to give out any personal information on anyone. I'm sure you understand."

Breuger stood up and put his hand out. "I understand, of course. Please excuse me. I will take my leave now. You have been most helpful."

He strode out of the office building toward the little gravel parking lot in front. He was annoyed with himself, because he had allowed himself to become too impatient. Now he would have to get his information somewhere else. But he had found out one thing he had intended to discover here: Michael Kintner was still alive.

* * *

Michael had crossed the last few remaining low mountain ranges west of the lake, and the country was becoming empty indeed. It had been two hours, and he had met no one on the highway. There were no ranch houses, no roadside businesses, not even any filling stations. It was as if the world had suddenly tired of man and had forgotten him entirely.

It ought to be easy to find someplace to pull off and make something to eat. It was obviously open-range country, with no fences of any kind. Up ahead, he spied a coyote lumbering across the road with that peculiar, slouching, go-to-hell gait they used to remind all other creatures that they were the ones who held sway here and would brook no argument. Michael smiled to himself, envious of such self-containment, of such utter confidence of their place in the world. He slowed and turned off the road in the direction the coyote had gone. It was a flat spot enveloped by high banks, a dry wash stretching off through the plain. If he decided to, he might spend the night here without worrying about someone spotting his campfire. He continued to drive up the wash for several meters and then pulled over to park the pickup next to the bank. He shut down the engine and sat in the truck listening for a long time. The silence was like a special kind of music. Prairie silence usually had some sound or other, if nothing but the wind. But here in the defilade there was absolutely no sound.

Finally, he got out of the truck and walked slowly off in the direction the coyote had gone, more to ease the tension than to explore. He had seen the whole of the countryside from the last rise he had topped, and there had been nothing. This was high country and had the same climate as if it had been hundreds of miles farther north. So even though it was spring, there were no flowers, no green grass or fresh shoots coming out of the ground. There was just an endless brown grayness spotted with juniper and piñon. The ground was not flat so much as it was a huge concavity falling and then rising gradually between the rows of rocky hills spaced ten or twenty miles apart. *No one could possibly live here,* he thought.

He went back to the truck, thinking about what he could fix to eat. He unlatched and lifted the topper door above the tailgate and then dropped the tailgate down to its horizontal position. Inside, the bed had a row of narrow cabinets on each side, the former owner having used them for tack and grooming equipment for his horses. Judy had asked a wealthy friend with a large horse farm outside of Middleburg if she could borrow one of his trucks for Michael, and he had insisted that Michael take it as a gift. It was ten years old, and there was no equipment on the farm that Judy's rich friend didn't have replaced every few years. To Michael, it had been a godsend, something he could use to take a last look around at the country of his birth before heading for Chama Canyon and his friend Father Toriano.

He opened the hinged top of the near cabinet on the left and looked inside. Before he left Washington, he had packed several items of canned goods, crackers, coffee, wine, a bottle of brandy, and items that were needed for camping outdoors or in. He took out the helmet bag with its many zippered and Velcroed pockets and sewn-on tag with the name *Warlock* embroidered on it. The last vestige of a long-ago previous life, one which he had been recently forced to revive, briefly but not entirely reluctantly. He opened the bag and brought out a can of hash and a plastic bag of crackers, and then, as an afterthought, he took out the bottle of cabernet sauvignon, with a wineglass wrapped in a hand towel. *A touch of class,* he thought wryly, *in any adversity.* He reached back into the cabinet, got out matches and tinder for a fire and then the blackened skillet and cup, and laid them on the tailgate. When he had all his implements laid out, he took the folding entrenching tool out of the cabinet and walked away to look for a place to make a fire.

He picked out a spot close to the bank a few meters from the truck, unfolded the little shovel, and began to dig a small pit for the fire. It was then he heard the first short whinny of a horse some ways off. He stopped digging and stood up, listening. Then there was a louder whinny, more like a scream of pain. He threw down the shovel and began walking up the wash toward the sound, looking for a place where he could climb the bank and look around.

He found a shallow gully and clambered up it to the top where he stared off into the gathering dusk. About two hundred meters away, he spotted movement, a small figure walking back and forth in an agitated gait as if trying to get to something out of reach. He began walking rapidly toward it, almost in a jog, about as fast as he could safely go on this terrain. The closer he got, the more the figure looked like a girl. Then he could see the long dark hair and slim silhouette, but she still hadn't seen him. Finally, he was close enough to shout at her and yelled a "hello" to her so she wouldn't be frightened. She stopped pacing back and forth, turned, and watched him all the way until he came close. He could see that she was not very old, perhaps not more than sixteen or seventeen. She was wearing a straight-brimmed, flat Spanish riding hat, her dark hair left to hang down to her shoulders. She had on an embroidered vest, white shirt, and jeans. Her boots were of the English riding style. She started walking toward him, and he stopped.

"What's the trouble, miss? I heard a horse, sounded like he was in some—"

"Sir, please help me. My filly was bitten by a snake. She panicked and fell down into the wash. I can't get her up, and I can't leave her. Is there any way you can . . ." The young girl was breathless, obviously scared but determined not to get hysterical.

"Wait a minute. Let me have a look."

He stepped over to the edge of the wash and looked down. The horse was lying on her side against the shallow bank, the dirt skidded loose where she had slipped down into the wash. She was pawing with her outer hoof, digging at the dirt as if trying to dig her way back up. He climbed down and approached her, speaking low and soft. He rubbed his hand over her neck and flanks and shoulders. She was obviously in pain, showing the whites of her eyes with her ears pinned and trembling violently. She seemed to calm a bit under his touch, and he leaned down close to her face and gently breathed into her nostrils. He kept this up for some time until she no longer associated the strange man with her pain. Then he went over her front legs, feeling for the swelling from the snakebite, which the girl said she had suffered. He found it low on the right foreleg and looked intently at it to see if he could see the points of penetration, but he could not. He stood up and looked over at the girl, who had followed him down into the wash.

"I don't think we should try to move her. We need to keep her warm and get a compress on that wound. I'm going back to my truck to get some water and cloth for a compress and a couple of blankets. I'll also look for some wood for a splint. You stay here close by her and keep stroking her and talking to her to calm her down and keep her from struggling. Can you do that?"

The girl looked up at him, the tears streaming down her face, and nodded. Then she knelt down by the filly and began to stroke her neck. She heard him climb the bank and walk away. She began to sing softly to the horse, some lullaby, and kept rubbing her all over. She did not notice the passage of time, and it seemed to her as if the man had not been gone long when he returned with what he needed wrapped in blankets and slung from his shoulders with woven nylon cords, the type known as parachute cord. He came back down into the wash and began laying out his stuff. In a few minutes, he had a fire going with a stew pot full of water heating on a rock beside the fire. He brought the blankets over to the filly, and he and the girl laid them over her horse. She was no longer struggling, but she was still breathing heavily and trembling. When the water began to simmer, he dipped some cloths into it, took them out, and let them cool so as not to dilate the blood vessels. He brought them over to the horse and wrapped them around her right foreleg over the swelling. He secured the cloth with a short bungee and stood up.

"I don't know of anything else to do for her. I don't want to try to incise the wound, because of the swelling and the possibility of infection. We need to keep loosening the bungee cord every so often so as not to restrict blood flow. I decided not to splint the leg because it might agitate her. Can you think of anything else we should do?"

She looked up at him from where she was kneeling by her horse and wiped her face with her kerchief where her tears had dried. For the first time, she noticed the condition of his skin and hair and decided that it might be discourteous to mention it.

"Sir, I don't know how to thank you. I don't know what I would have done."

She got to her feet. She looked at what he had brought from the truck and noticed that he had also brought some food and a bottle of wine. She started to smile.

"Looks as if you thought of everything. Do you usually camp out with wine and napkins?"

He smiled back at her. He knew she was going to be pretty stressed out over her horse and decided on the way back to his truck that he would cook her some supper. He brought the wine for himself but guessed she was old enough for a small glass. It would help her to calm down also, he hoped.

"A habit I acquired while I lived in Europe. I thought a small glass also might help you . . . Do your parents allow you to have wine?"

She stood up a little taller and gave a mock shrug.

"I'm eighteen. I guess I can drink it when I like."

"Eighteen."

"Well . . . in September I will be."

"That's what I thought. Okay. Do as you wish. But just one glass. I don't want to move your horse until—by the way, what's her name? And what's your name?"

"My name is Magdalena Morales. Mother calls me Maggie. And my filly's name is Selena. After the full moon. She's almost the color of the moon. What's your name?"

He hesitated. He wasn't sure he wanted to give his name to anyone. But this young girl required honesty.

"Please call me Michael. I can't believe you are out here alone. I haven't seen any signs of life for two hours. Where is your home?"

"My uncle's ranch house is about two hours' ride from here. It's nestled in between the two buttes you can see on the far mountain range to the west—when it's light enough. I'm not allowed to go out riding this late, but I was upset and angry and just took off without telling my uncle." She looked as if she were about to cry again.

He decided not to press her further. She was already upset enough. He went over and checked the compress. He loosened the cord for a couple of minutes and then reapplied it. He turned back to Maggie.

"I'm going to keep this up all night, so when you get sleepy, go back up the arroyo to my truck and bed down in the back. It's carpeted and covered, and there are blankets. For now, let me get some hot food in you—and a tiny bit of wine—and you can bag it whenever you want."

An hour later, Maggie had gone back up the arroyo and was already asleep in the back of the truck. Michael was still tending the fire, watching the filly, and occasionally looking around for the presence of snakes like the one that had laid the little mare low. It was going to be a long night. He couldn't be sure whether the horse would survive. His experience with horses extended only about as far as what he had picked up while riding with Judy and attending events at Ashburn Farm with the hounds-and-stirrup-cup crowd. He was treating the horse much as he would have a human in similar circumstances. He didn't know if it would be enough.

* * *

Judy looked around at her house with an appraising eye for the first time, it seemed, in weeks. It looked terrible to her. She hadn't even thought of housekeeping chores during her long depression over Michael's death. Now, the mere suggestion that he might still be alive had given her new life. But there were things about the Frenchman's visit that disturbed her. His story about Michael being mentioned in terrorist communiqués and about trying to prevent further attacks didn't quite add up. She had been involved, either academically or professionally, with defense issues for most of her life, and few nuances of it escaped her. The man from the French embassy, whatever he was, was certainly not a diplomat. That left one other possibility. She opened the top of the desk in front of the sitting room window and took out a black notebook she had stuck in a small drawer. She opened it, found what she wanted, and began to punch in a number on the desk phone. Very shortly, a woman's voice answered.

"Extension six one four one. How can I help you?"

"This is Dr. Judy Weiss. Please have Mr. Thomas Valence call me. He has my private number."

"Thank you, ma'am." The line went dead, and Judy hung up. The protocol for calling any of the thousands of vaulted offices around town was pretty much the same. Stupid little game, really. Product of the Cold War.

Her phone rang almost immediately, and she picked it up.

"This is Dr. Weiss."

"Judy, this is Tom. Good to hear from you. Someone told me you had been ill. Nothing serious, I hope?"

"Thanks for calling me back, Tom. No, I've just had a virus for a while. This off-and-on spring weather, I suspect. Tom, I need you to check something out for me, quite unofficially, of course. I don't take the king's shilling anymore, as you know. You think you could—"

"Absolutely, Judy. Someone who has held your position keeps her clearance as long as she wants it, you know that. How can I help?"

"Yesterday, a man from the French embassy paid me a visit. He wanted to talk about Michael Kintner—you remember him, I know. He was the man who headed up the Vatican's military response to the terrorist attacks."

"Yes, I do indeed. He also led that assault team into Pakistan's nuclear arsenal, didn't he? Or was that someone else?"

"That's the man. Well, he was seriously hurt in the explosion in the Sistine Chapel, when the pope and all those people were killed. He wasn't supposed to live for more than a couple of weeks. I saw him briefly just before he went off to live out the few days he had left with a friend of his in New Mexico. That was the last I heard of him until this Frenchman came to see me.

"Anyway, this man tells me point-blank that the French have been picking up communiqués from the terrorists mentioning Michael's name. And he is worried that this portends in some manner a new terrorist attack. Is any of this tracking with you?"

The phone was silent for a few moments.

"Judy, what was the name this man from the French embassy gave you?"

"Henri Breuger. And he certainly didn't strike me as a diplomat."

"He's not. He's . . . listen, Judy, could you come over and visit me at my office in the OEOB? I'd like you to debrief me thoroughly on this conversation you had with Monsieur Breuger. Can you do that?"

"Well, is what he said true? Is our apparatus picking up any—"

"We're on an unsecured line, Judy. I have some more questions of my own also. Tomorrow okay?"

"I look forward to seeing you. Been a long time. Good-bye."

Judy hung up and sat still, thinking about what it used to be like in the White House as the president's national security adviser, the endless briefings, meetings, intel reports, sitrep reports, intelligence analyses, and assessments. Tom Valence had always been one of the reliable ones, a minimum of rear-covering and a maximum of honest appraisal. He had been deputy for Middle Eastern Ops at the CIA back then. He had probably moved up a notch in the new administration. She knew if there was anyone who could make sense of this, it would be Tom. He was also the one who could do something about it.

* * *

Michael was putting on the last of the compresses, thinking that it might be beneficial for the horse to let its immune system work on its own for a while. The sun was about to clear the eastern ridge of rocky hills. He stood up and started over to the fire to reheat some coffee when he heard the engine, very faintly, to the west of the dry wash where the three of them had spent the night. He decided not to go back to the truck and wake Maggie just yet. Her filly was resting quietly. He climbed up the bank and looked off to the west. A small cloud of dust was visible far out on the desert, indicating a vehicle of some sort. He stood and waited for it to get nearer, if it was headed for them.

"Good morning, Michael." Maggie had quietly come down the wash and climbed up the bank behind him. She stood looking as fresh as a daisy, as young teenagers always did. He turned to her and took her hand. It was cool and soft but with just a little toughness from the reins.

"Morning, Maggie. I was about to reheat some coffee when I heard that." He pointed over his shoulder at the dust from the vehicle out across the desert. "I expect that will be someone from your family. We can get some proper care for Selena if it is."

She peered around him at the distant dust and then looked up into his face.

"You saved her life, Michael. It's like you were an angel from heaven or something."

"I may be a lot of things, Miss Morales, but an angel isn't one of them." He smiled and let go of her hand. He started back down into the dry wash. He went over to the filly and took off the two blankets. She wasn't trembling anymore so the fever had likely abated. He got his half-full water container and poured some of it into the stew pot. He carried the pot over to the horse and slipped the rim under her nose while he lifted her head enough for her to drink, if she wanted to. She eagerly sipped down what she could, and the rest just trickled through her mouth onto the sand.

He stood up and looked down at her. He didn't know if he should try to get her on her feet. He remembered from somewhere that livestock with no broken bones seemed to heal more quickly if they were on their feet. Maybe the safe thing to do was wait for the people from the ranch, if that was who they were. He climbed back up to the top of the bank where Maggie was and watched the vehicle getting nearer. In just a few minutes, he could make out the outline of a jeep.

"That's one of my uncle's jeeps, I think." Maggie didn't exactly seem overjoyed at the prospect of someone coming to get her. Michael thought it was probably because she expected to be in some hot water with her uncle. She didn't seem to him like a seventeen-year-old in her reactions to things. Something had made her mature for her age.

The jeep drove up to within a few meters and stopped. Four men got out of it and started toward them. One of them carried a rifle. They were all obviously ranch hands but were well outfitted, unlike some of the help on meager ranches.

The man who had been driving was a tall, deeply tanned man who could be easily identified as the leader. The others hung back slightly while he went up to the girl.

"Miss Morales. I guess you know the colonel is half out of his mind with worry, you taking off like that. He's had us out most of the night looking. You all right?"

Maggie hesitated. It seemed to Michael that there was something—he couldn't guess what—like a tension between them.

"Yes, I am, Bob. Selena got bitten by a snake. I saw it taking off across the ground—a sidewinder, from the way it moved. She just freaked and threw me before she fell down into that dry wash. She would have died if it hadn't been for my new friend here who found us." She turned, took Michael by the arm, and brought him forward.

"Michael, this is Bob Sutter, my uncle's foreman. Bob, this is Michael."

Michael stuck out his hand, but the foreman ignored it and stood looking at his face.

"What's wrong with you? You got something we could catch?"

"No," Michael said, dropping his hand down. "Do you?"

Sutter's jaw hardened, and he took a step toward him.

"This is Morales graze, buddy, as far as you can see. You mind telling me what you're doing on it?"

"Bob, stop it," said Maggie. "I just told you he saved Selena's life and maybe mine as well. He stayed up all night looking after her."

Sutter looked down at the girl. He knew the colonel set great store by her, and he knew better than to get her upset. But he had the instinctive mistrust of strangers that was endemic to the isolated parts of the American West. Plus, there was something strange about this man, in addition to his battered appearance—an air of controlled hostility or even belligerence. He couldn't put his finger on it.

Maggie had noticed it too, when, just as the jeep was pulling up, she had seen Michael step back and away from her as if expecting some kind of trouble—not at all like the gentleness he had shown her from the moment she had met him.

"Sorry, Miss Morales. I guess I forgot my manners." He turned his head toward the stranger again and stuck out his hand. "My thanks for taking care of her—what was your name again?"

"Michael," he said, shaking the foreman's hand. "You don't need me anymore, Maggie, so I'll be on my way. Let me get my gear—"

"Nonsense, Michael. I want you to come to the house. My mother and uncle would never forgive me if I didn't bring you back so they could thank you for what you did."

He stood and thought about it for a long moment. He didn't know if he could trust himself in polite company, the way he felt. But maybe it would be okay for a short while.

"Okay, Maggie. For just a little while. Then I've got to be going. I'll get my truck and come up here and follow you in. Someone's going to have to stay behind with the filly, though."

"My boys'll bring her in slow, after they check her. Don't worry about her, Miss Morales," said Bob. "Get in the jeep, and I'll drive you back to the house."

Michael gathered his gear and walked off back down the wash. He glanced back once and saw Maggie in agitated conversation with the foreman. She probably was trying to get him to let her stay behind with the horse. But he had his orders, no doubt.

A half hour later, the two vehicles, the jeep in the lead, were headed toward the distant range, glowing a faint orange in the early morning sun. Two buttes projected out from it at a slight angle to the south. No cattle were in evidence, but on this sparse graze, the cattle would have to have miles of land from which to get enough nourishment. It crossed his mind that, in a place like this, it might be possible to live out his life safe from his pursuers, whoever they were—if they even existed. He hadn't seen them for a couple of days now and was beginning to hope that he might have shaken them off his trail.

* * *

Judy Weiss walked into the foyer of the Old Executive Office Building and got into line for one of the three security desks. A young man standing behind the balustrade, which served as a visible barrier to casual entrance, saw her and came out through the gate to where she was.

"Dr. Weiss, I am here to escort you up to Mr. Valence's office. Here's your visitor badge. I have already cleared you through."

They walked through the gate and down the marble-floored hall for a few meters and then turned up a winding, ornate staircase. Judy had always liked the nineteenth-century ambience of the building, one of few still in use by official Washington. It was inefficient and hard to heat, but it contained many vaulted areas protected by high-technology electronic screening.

When they came into Tom Valence's outer office, he was there to meet them, having been alerted by the secretary, who had surveillance video on the wall beside her. He came forward and took her hand.

"It's really good to see you again, Judy. I've missed your being at the briefings, straightening us out when we got too far off the mark." He grinned at her, remembering how her incisive questions had withered many a brave briefing officer. But she had always been imminently fair and had more than once come to his defense during tense episodes at the White House.

"It's good to see you too, Tom. Thanks for seeing me on such short notice. I know what your schedule is like." She grinned back at him, feeling a kind of poignant comfort at being back in the halls of power, if it could be called that.

After settling themselves down in Tom's conference room, the coffee poured and the amenities over with, they got down to business.

"I did some checking up on this character Breuger since we talked. He's been involved in some very scary stuff. Bit of a loose cannon, too, even for the notorious Renseignement Interieur. Also, I had the NSA send me their data on recent al-Qaeda communications. They haven't finished their analysis of it, or so they said, but Michael Kintner's name had been mentioned. I guess the NSA didn't want to commit themselves to another agency until they had their bases covered."

"Some things never change," said Judy. "In what context was Michael's name mentioned? Is he a target?"

"The excerpts they gave me were pretty vague. But I inferred from them that they believe Michael's death was staged by the Vatican. They seem to have concluded that the purpose was to give him cover for the bombing of Mecca. And there was one even more puzzling sentence—let me read from this: 'We have discovered him and have him surrounded,' which, if he is dead, seems a bit peculiar."

"But no one knew he was going to New Mexico, Tom, except me. How could they—"

"Where exactly did he go in New Mexico? Ought to be a simple matter to check."

"He was going back to Christ in the Desert Monastery in Abiquiu, to see a friend of his from when he did a sabbatical there, or whatever they call it. The doctors said he had a few weeks to live, at most. I got Jack Taylor to give him a pickup from his farm to use, and I assume he drove down there in that."

Valence sat staring at the wall. There was a painting hanging there of the battle of Saratoga, the Revolutionary War battle for vital access to the Hudson River. But it was another, no less critical battle that he was thinking of.

"Judy, I propose we do two things to start with. First, we need to get somebody down to New Mexico to check this out. Then I need to get the data on that truck, you know, model and make, license number. Just in case he still is alive. Since Jack knows you, maybe it would be better if you called him or his farm manager to get it. A call from the CIA could start something public, and we don't want that, do we?"

"All right, Tom. Listen, when you get something definite on Michael, could you call me? I hate to interfere with your busy schedule, but—"

"Don't worry about it, Judy. You have saved my rear end more than once in that shark tank they call the White House command center." He stood up. In spite of his disclaimer, he really didn't have enough hours in the day to do the routine stuff, let alone special projects. But if the former national security adviser was interested, then it could only be a short while until the current White House staff were involved. He took Judy's hand and pressed it briefly, and she quickly left the conference room. Her escort was waiting to take her out of the building.

Driving back to Georgetown, Judy couldn't shake the impulse to keep taking deep breaths. Was it really possible? Was Michael still alive? Could he have really been responsible for the bombing in Mecca? That wasn't the man she knew and loved. Her thoughts went back to the first time she had met him, in her office at the White House:

The man standing in front of her desk reminded Judy of what she thought might be a recruiting poster for fighter pilots. Clear-eyed and tall, with sandy, close-cropped hair and angular features marred only by a scar in the left eyebrow—he looked nothing like what she expected from a Vatican envoy. There was also his detached, peaceful expression—nothing like the ingratiating, nervous smile of a European diplomat about to pick your pocket. That had been the session when they started negotiations for the United States to provide the Vatican with assistance in the areas of defense and intelligence equipment. On impulse, she had invited him to her house for dinner—as a courtesy, she told herself.

They had had wine on her patio before dinner, and she suddenly became very aware of the intimacy of the setting.

"Mike, I just realized that this . . . situation . . . might be making you uncomfortable. If I have breached any sort of protocol the Catholic clergy have about being alone with people of the opposite sex . . . I mean . . ." Good God, *she thought,* what am I saying? I sound like a schoolgirl. *She became even more flustered.*

Mike laughed out loud. "Don't worry, Judy. This isn't the fourteenth century. Besides, I was married before losing my wife during the September eleventh terrorist attacks."

Then it was Mike's turn to be flustered. What in the name of sense did he say that for?

Mike busied himself with the wine and fruit and cheese, while Judy busied herself in the kitchen from time to time. Finally, she announced dinner was ready and they went inside. Two hours, four courses, and parts of two bottles of fine French wine later, they relaxed in the drawing room, warm and comfortable, with some napoleon brandy.

Judy was curled up in her comfortable chair, her shoes off, and Mike had sat down on the plaited rug in front of the gas-log fire, staring at the flames. Neither of them spoke for a time. He looked over at Judy. What a vision she was. He didn't think he had drunk too much wine. And he hadn't even thought about a woman, about sex at all, for such a long time. Then he remembered a line from The Razor's Edge *and grinned.*

"Okay, Michael, what is that evil little grin about, you should pardon the expression?"

"I was just remembering something Somerset Maugham once wrote. 'It's easy to be a holy man on a mountain.'"

Judy got up out of her chair and came over to sit down against Michael.

"Well, if it makes you feel any better, I'm tempted too. But you're bound by vows or something, aren't you?"

Yes, *thought Michael.* I'm bound by vows or something. *What was he doing here? What made him think he could come here and behave like a normal human being? But that is exactly what I am, he thought.* Everything else notwithstanding, I am a normal human being. And I am back in reality. *He turned to Judy and kissed her. A long time.*

The night was all it promised to be. With Judy, Mike rediscovered that the love of a man for a woman was as intense a spiritual experience as one could achieve outside that of God. He felt no explanation was necessary, for himself or for Judy.

For her part, Judy felt as if she had just made love for the first time in her life. She had had more than one partner in her life, of course, but had had precious little occasion for sex lately. Her longtime boyfriend from college had been there for her sometimes in the past, but he had grown so distant and preoccupied in later years that his lovemaking had become little more than perfunctory. But Michael had made her feel as if she were the only woman on the planet, that she was somehow the key to his very existence. She had been at first startled, and then excited, and finally, amazed at his intensity, which was coupled with a tenderness she had never seen in any man.

* * *

Henri Breuger sat down at the desk with which he had been provided at the French consulate in Albuquerque. He would have much rather been enjoying a respectable cognac in his hotel, but he felt his information was too valuable not to share immediately with his superiors.

The secure phone on the desk buzzed, and he touched the contact button.

"Monsieur Breuger, the Washington embassy contact you requested is on the line."

"Merci." He waited for a few seconds until he heard a click. Then he began to speak to the senior Renseignement agent in America.

"Commissaire Valmaux, I have found that there is every likelihood that Kintner is still alive. If he is and the al-Qaeda are right about him, then he could be on some other mission for the Vatican. Assuming worst case, another escalation could be in the offing. We cannot allow that to happen, do you agree?"

"If all your suppositions are correct, Inspecteur, then we would have to prevent it, at any cost. But I must check this out with Paris. It may take a day or two, but stay close by so I can pass on their instructions."

"Very well. But in case I am right, I am going to need some more information about Kintner and his mode of travel. I would like to request electronic surveillance of the house of Dr. Judy Weiss, 1211

O Street in Georgetown. I strongly suspect that she may start her own investigation after what I told her."

"You are probably right. But I doubt she would use her private phone for these kinds of things."

"Commissaire, it has been my experience that the higher the rank of government officials, the less attention they pay to security. And have your agent record everything, no matter how trivial."

Breuger broke contact on the secure phone. He would have much preferred to contact Paris on this himself, but the bureaucracy in the Renseignement Interieur was no different from any other government department. Anyway, he would have to wait.

Chapter 4

The ranch house was built in the old hacienda style. The compound was very large but nestled comfortably between the two buttes, which gave some protection from the weather. The barns, bunkhouses, and stables were located well away from the compound, but the buildings for all other support activities were inside the adobe wall. There was a small chapel located inside the wall, but the front entrance faced outward, so that people could enter without coming through the compound. There was a private entrance for family located near the sept. The entrance to the main house faced east, away from the rocky ridge. A *ramada* contained some carefully cultivated cacti and manzanita, and a large *fuentes* was in the middle of a circular driveway, the water splashing out of the bowl onto the white stones at its base.

As Michael drove through the arched front gate behind the jeep, he could see a small group of people standing on the tiled floor of a portico in front of the main entrance to the house. He stopped a few meters behind where the jeep had stopped and waited in the truck. A man in Spanish riding breeches and boots strode across to the jeep. Maggie got out, and he hugged her to him. Maggie stood with her arms down by her sides, waiting until he let her go. He stepped back after a moment and looked at her. She stepped around him quickly and went to embrace the woman who stood just behind. The woman was tall and blonde and was wearing very dark sunglasses.

Even from a distance, she looked very pale and wan to Michael, as if she had some illness.

Maggie spoke briefly to the woman and then turned and pointed at Michael in the truck. All three of them started walking toward the truck, and Michael got out and waited until they reached him.

"Sir, I am Colonel Lorenzo Morales. I'm told I owe you the life of Maggie's filly and perhaps hers as well. *Muchisimo gracias. My heartfelt thanks.*" The man stretched out both his hands, and Michael stuck out his right. For just an instant, Michael felt a flash of recognition. Morales was a tall man with aquiline features and the air and demeanor of an aristocrat. He was every bit the epitome of a European officer and gentleman. Michael was sure he knew him, but how could he, when he had never even been to this far, out-of-the-way place?

The woman offered her hand also, and Michael took it. "I too am grateful to you—Michael, is it? I am Maggie's mother, Jean."

"You owe me nothing," said Michael. "I just kind of babysat them both through a tough night."

"Oh, so I'm just a child who needs a babysitter?" Maggie laughed a little bell-like laugh and went over to hug him. Then she hooked her arm in his and looked up at him. "You have to stay with us for a while, Michael. You don't want to leave until you know Selena is okay, do you? Besides, I'd like to get to know you better." She giggled again, but Michael thought he saw the colonel's face darken slightly. There was that flash of recognition again.

"Yes, I insist you stay, Michael," said Colonel Morales. "We don't get many guests out here, and I would consider it a great favor if you would stay."

"Do you ride, Michael?" asked Jean. "We have some fine Andalusians you could choose from. I know Maggie would love to show you around the ranch."

"I've ridden some back east. I have no riding apparel or appurtenances, though."

"I'll take care of that," said the colonel. "Come on inside. My men will bring in your gear if you set it out for them."

"That's all right. I just have the one bag." He opened the door to the cab and brought out his rucksack. A house servant waiting nearby quickly stepped over and took it from him. The four of them and the servant walked back toward the front door. As they passed the jeep, Michael went over to where Bob Sutter was standing.

"Thanks for finding us, Mr. Sutter. Sorry about the misunderstanding."

Bob Sutter stared hard at him, making it obvious that he still didn't like his looks. He took his hand but just slowly enough to convey his mistrust, if that was what it was. Then he got back in the jeep, started it, and drove off.

As they crossed the portico into the cool darkness of the interior, the colonel turned and looked at Michael.

"What was that all about? Did Bob give you any trouble?"

"No. I think he was just concerned for Maggie's safety. I don't blame him for that."

They continued on into the sitting area, Maggie still hanging onto Michael's arm. The colonel stopped and told the servant where to take the bag, and then he told another to bring refreshments. He turned back to Michael.

"By the way, I know this sounds unlikely, but I can't get over the feeling that we have met before. Is that possible, do you think? What is your family name?"

"My name is Michael Kintner. But the furthest west I have been is the monastery in Abiquiu, New Mexico. So we wouldn't have had an opportunity to meet, I don't believe."

Colonel Morales stared at him unbelievingly.

"My God, is it possible? Michael Kintner? I couldn't see the resemblance before, Comandante, but now . . . I led the assault on Ambon, Indonesia. You wanted to come along, but I wouldn't allow it, even though you were my superior. Don't you remember, sir?

Clark Air Base, in the Philippines, you were there on a preinvasion inspection tour."

Michael closed his eyes, slowly and painfully, at the remembrance of it. How could this have happened? The last thing in the world he needed right now was to have all that come back to him. Was this just one more thing sent to torture him?

"Yes, Colonel, it is a clear but very unwelcome memory. You were commanding a mixed special operations force of Spanish and French troops. You had resigned from the Spanish army to do so. But you told me your home was in—Where was it? *Toledo, España*. What are you . . . and your family . . . doing here?"

"*Madre de Dios*, you have a memory, Comandante. Yes, Toledo was my home, but I resigned from the Keys army when I got word from my family in Spain that my older brother Alfonso had died. That was almost two years ago now. Our family is an old one, as are our traditions. It was expected that I would protect my brother's family and lands if some tragedy befell him. But what happened to you? I am sorry; I mean no disrespect, but your face and hair . . ."

Michael involuntarily reached up and touched his face. He had not looked in a mirror for some time, but he knew what he must look like—the white hair and the peeling skin, he remembered all too well.

"Well . . . it is still very painful to talk about. Perhaps we could defer it to another time?"

"Certainly, *sin duda*, my apologies, sir."

"Colonel, you would be doing me a great favor if you would call me Michael."

"Yes, of course, Michael. But there is no question now; you must stay here, for as long as possible. *Mi casa es suya*. It is an honor."

He didn't know what to think. This was clearly too improbable to be a coincidence. He didn't really believe in coincidences anyway. Was it the hand of God? And if it was, was it grace or penance? As a Catholic, he knew they were sometimes the same. What was it

Dom Aelred Graham had written? "There is a salutary fatalism in the Catholic doctrine of grace and free will." Certainly, there was fatalism.

"I am afraid my stay must be short. I am not well, and it will not be long before I will be in hospital for good."

The three looked at each other. Maggie's eyes were starting to widen as if she were about to cry, and her mother and uncle were at a loss as to what to say. He hadn't said so directly, but they knew he had implied that he was dying. Michael realized he had said too much.

"Please don't look so stricken. I will be fine for a while yet. No one ever knows about these things, right?" He didn't know why he had lasted this long, but his symptoms hadn't abated much. If it was a hiatus of some sort, it really changed nothing, and he didn't want to die with people hovering about him. If he had, he would have stayed with Judy, whom he loved, and not sought out strangers.

"If you would show me where I can freshen up and change, I will join you later, if that is all right."

The servant showed him back to his room, and he sat down on the bed, silently going over in his mind the words that had been spoken. Why had he told them those things? Maybe Morales wouldn't have recalled him to mind if he had just kept his mouth shut. And he hated pity. Why hadn't he been allowed to die when the doctors said he would? He wished Father Toriano had not died so quickly after his return to Chama Canyon and the monastery. And who exactly was it that was following him? He knew al-Qaeda wanted him dead, but why didn't they just wait? If they had found him at Christ in the Desert, they must have known he had gone there to die. But al-Qaeda didn't think like normal people. He had briefly thought earlier that this might be a safe haven, if only temporarily. But if they found him here, then all their lives would be in danger. Maybe he could just slip away after it was dark.

* * *

With a slightly melancholy trepidation, Judy dialed the number on the phone and waited for the inevitable: "Good morning. 'Hail to the Redskins!' This is Mr. Taylor's office. I am Ruby. How may I help you?"

"Hello, Ruby. This is Judy Weiss. I see you're still spouting the propaganda. Is Jack available?"

"Why, Dr. Weiss, it's been awhile! Glad to hear from you. I'm afraid Mr. Taylor is going to be away a few days on business. He does own some corporations other than the Washington Redskins, you know."

"Yes, I am well aware of that, Ruby. Maybe you can help me. Jack gave a friend of mine one of his pickups from the farm in Middleburg a few weeks ago. I need to have it brought back here now that my friend—well, he doesn't need it anymore. Can you get me in touch with the farm manager? I assume he'll have the data I need on the truck."

"Yes, ma'am, be happy to. His phone number at the farm is 502-6740."

Judy hung up and dialed the number.

"Taylor Farms. This is Tony."

"Hello, Tony, Judy Weiss here. How have you been?"

"Pretty good, Dr. Weiss. Haven't seen you around lately."

"No. Busy with some other things. Listen, Tony, you remember the pickup you let my friend Michael Kintner have a few weeks ago? Well, he doesn't need it anymore, and I'm going to have it brought back. Can you give me the make, model, and license number? I'll need them for the driver."

"Sure, Dr. Weiss, but there's really no need. Mr. Taylor told me to replace it, and I have."

"Well, let me have the information anyway. I need to check on where he left it and alert the locals, in case the registration is out of date."

Judy could hear him rifling through his card files.

"Here it is. Ford F-150, white, Virginia license GRI-1377. Looks like the registration is still current, though."

"Thanks, Tony. Hope to come out for a ride soon. Say hello to Sue Ann."

Judy hung up the phone and sat still, remembering the few but happy experiences she and Michael had enjoyed at the horse farm. Then she remembered again the morning after her first evening with Michael at her house in Georgetown:

In the morning, as they were having their continental breakfast on the patio, it was Judy who finally broached the subject that had been in the backs of both their minds.

"Michael. I am going to say something that may not seem logical or proper. But I am going to tell you what I feel. This cannot be the end of it for me. And unless I have lost all my judgment about people, it can't be the end of it for you, either. What are we going to do?"

Judy was looking at him as if he, and he alone, possessed the key to the future of the world. She was not used to this feeling. She could not remember a time when she hadn't felt completely in charge of her destiny. Now, this.

Michael set down his cup and looked back at her.

"Judy, we are going to do precisely what our feelings tell us to do. I have never subscribed to a strictly rule-based religion, and I don't believe there are any rules for loving each other, save the most important one— love, itself. The human race has not many redeeming qualities, but one it does have—love—makes all the rest pale by comparison.

"I discovered a number of important things during the years I was in the desert. One is that to love God for hope of salvation or out of fear of punishment is not to love him at all. Obeying man-made rules is

not true salvation. It is love, more than anything, that is the ultimate expression of the inner person—especially the kind of love that expects nothing in return. It drives out every other negative emotion. Besides life itself, love is the greatest gift."

He searched her face for a sign that she understood. And he saw it.

They stood at once and went to each other. They held each other tightly for a very long time.

* * *

The French embassy had a long-term lease on a high-rise office building in Rosslyn, Virginia, just across the Potomac River from Georgetown. A man in one of the offices was making a note of the date and time of a telephone call displayed on a digital LCD screen. It appeared to be what he had been told by his superior to listen for.

* * *

Tom Valence handed the folder across his desk to Agent Ken Russell, who was standing on the other side. Ken had been in the CIA for some years, but his appearance was that of a blond, blue-eyed college quarterback. The caricature many people had about an intelligence operative—that of an aging, dissolute misfit, established with the help of movie characters—was far from reality. They were generally an elite cadre of covert warriors, and Ken was one of them.

It was fairly unusual for a CIA agent to receive background information directly from the chief of operations, and Ken was more than a little curious—and a little nervous, as well. Getting briefed at this level usually meant that more than one agency was involved. And that meant tiptoeing around the federal statutes as if they were eggs.

"Everything we have on Kintner is in here, Ken. I've asked Jerry Owens down at Quantico to prepare a similar file for comparison.

When you meet with him, see if there are any contradictions or conflicts between the FBI and the CIA data. I'd much rather do this electronically, but, in spite of all the Homeland Security hoopla, our systems still aren't compatible. I think they like it that way, to be frank. But, anyway . . ."

"Sir, who's going to be in charge of this operation? I don't much like the idea of dragging along after one of those glorified cops."

"The official answer is the FBI. But you're responsible only to me, and you take orders directly from me. There's high-level interest in this, or soon will be, and your boss, Sam Clancy, and his boss, Gary Matthews, have agreed to stay out of it. We'll let the FBI chase around after the vehicle that was identified to us by the people at Taylor Farms. But I want you to look for something else. I want you to watch for any incident, no matter what it is, that smacks of al-Qaeda. You've been chasing these ragheads long enough to be able to smell them, if nothing else. If they are after Kintner, as I believe, there are bound to be people who get in their way and pay the price. You get my drift?"

"Yes, sir. But from what I already know about Kintner, he's not too patient with folks who get in his way either."

"Exactly. There may already be some casualties of this pursuit, if that's what it is, and they would probably be on someone's police blotter. That's another area where the FBI is going to be a big help. You insist to whoever your counterpart is over there that data scans are run hourly on the area in question. Anything that looks like a candidate, you check it out personally, you read?"

"Yes, sir."

"Another joker in the deck is that we have good reason to believe that the DCRI has involved itself in this. A man named Henri Breuger. You recognize the name?"

"Yes, sir. I've seen one or two examples of his work. He's very good."

65

"All right, then, let me summarize the recent data for you. The file tells you when and where Kintner was thought to have been last—Abiquiu, New Mexico, the Benedictine monastery there—I forget its name. You check with the prior or the abbot, or whatever they call it, and start with whatever information he gives you. My guess is, if he left there alive, he would head west, to the least populated area he could find. If he is dying, that would seem to fit his behavior profile. If he's not, he may do the same thing just to disappear from view. The official announcement of his death that the Vatican issued might have at least two possible meanings: First, it could have been to protect Kintner's privacy for his last few weeks on earth. Second, it could mean that Kintner was never actually in the Sistine Chapel, and the Vatican lied to conceal the fact that he was the one responsible for bombing Mecca. If so, he may have been given another mission. He would be the logical choice for a follow-up. That is the assumption the intercepted al-Qaeda communications appear to be based on."

"That leaves me with the question of what you want me to do when I catch up to him. If I get to him before the al-Qaeda people do. You want me to do the ragheads' work for them and terminate him?"

"Not before we find out what his new mission is, if there is one. Because the Vatican could always send someone else if Kintner is stopped."

"Well, if the stories are true about his capture and interrogation in Pakistan, we may not get anything out of him. If he could withstand what those little sweethearts did to him—"

"Maybe. But there is a third possibility, which I didn't put in the file, because I thought you might like to draw your own conclusions after you read it."

Ken Russell stared at the director. *Just like in Afghanistan and Iraq,* he thought. There always seemed to be something that had no official credibility left out for the operative to stumble over. He had hoped Valence wouldn't turn out to be another one of those bureaucrats, but it looked as if he was.

"Pardon me, sir, but you can't leave me hanging like that. What do you have in mind?"

Valence squirmed in his chair. He realized he shouldn't have mentioned it, but maybe it was better to tell Russell.

"Okay. Let's assume these first two possibilities are wrong, and by some fluke, Kintner survived a radioactive dirty bomb blast in a closed building. Let's assume further that he was the one who bombed Mecca—in retaliation for the destruction of the Sistine Chapel and the death of the pope—and he did it without Vatican knowledge or approval. As the commander of the Keys troops, it would have been easy for him to commandeer an airplane and fly it into Saudi Arabia, especially after hostilities had formally ended."

"Well, that doesn't seem too far-fetched to me. It might have happened just like that."

"Yes, it might. But then, why is he still alive? There were only three people who survived, and the two of them who have since died lasted only a week. And they were much farther away from the blast than Kintner."

"Well, who can say? Does it matter? A few weeks, more or less . . . He's not long for this world, in any case."

Valence sat still, not saying anything. He couldn't bring himself to say it.

"Oh, no," said Russell. "You don't actually mean you think he is under some sort of 'divine' protection."

"Yeah, maybe. Now you know why it isn't in the file."

* * *

Michael walked into the dining room wearing some fresh clothes he had fetched from the truck. They were the same kind of dungarees and Windsor shirt he had had on earlier, but these were at least clean. The colonel rose from where he was seated at the head of the table and gestured to the empty chair on his right. Maggie was sitting next to it, and Jean was opposite, still wearing her dark glasses.

"Ah, Michael, you are here by me, if you please."

Michael sat down, and then the colonel sat and picked up his glass.

"Before we begin, let us raise a toast to our guest and to absent comrades in arms."

They all sipped from their glasses, even Maggie.

"And to a very gracious family, my thanks for your hospitality."

They all drank from their glasses again and set them down. Involuntarily, Michael glanced over at Jean, and she noticed it. He saw she looked even more drawn than she had earlier, outside. She was a striking woman with short, wavy blonde hair; a full mouth; and an aquiline nose, but, because she was still wearing sunglasses, he could only guess at her eyes. He wondered briefly exactly what the relationship was between her and her late husband's brother. Why, he wondered, hadn't she and Maggie inherited the ranch instead of Lorenzo? He was pretty sure American law would have permitted a very strong challenge in the courts to such an irregularity. A surviving brother taking over a property might be a tradition in Spain, but it was very unusual for America.

"Please forgive my glasses, Michael. My eyes are sensitive to desert glare, and they sometimes get swollen."

No one said anything for a moment. The servants came in with the trays of food and served it up in silence. Then Maggie spoke up, more to relieve the apparent embarrassment than because she had something to say.

"Uncle Lorenzo tells me that you were the leader of the Ninth Crusade, Michael. I remember when it was in all the papers. I think I was about twelve years old, and all I could think of were the stories of knights and jousts and battles for ladies' honor from the novels.

It sounded so romantic! Like the stories of King Richard Lionheart. He led one of the crusades, didn't he?"

"Yes, the Second. But I'm afraid the reality was quite different, both for King Richard and for me. It's one thing for warriors to slaughter each other; they choose their profession and know what to expect. But when you see the refugee camps, the crippled and starving children, the desperate women trying to feed and care for them, it's not very romantic."

"But romantic or not," said the colonel, "there are times when taking the sword is the only alternative, even for Christian gentlemen. There are some things that are not to be borne. Don't you agree?"

"Yes. I believe you must be referring to St. Augustine's 'just war,' or St. Bernard's entreaty to the pope on behalf of the Templars—all are apparent justifications. But there is one other thing, mentioned even in the oldest of the 'romance' novels, *Queste del Saint Graal.* Even in the balance of God's mercy and justice, there are some actions by men that put them beyond redemption. Not a very popular idea in the politically correct church of today. But it doesn't alter the truth of it."

"Yes," said the colonel. "One needs only to look at the ruins of the Sistine Chapel, Notre Dame Cathedral, St. Paul's Cathedral—"

"And the ruins of Mecca," said Michael. "Let us not forget that."

The little group was quiet for a long time. Then Maggie spoke up again.

"Were you an actual knight, Michael? Did the pope actually . . ."

Michael didn't say anything. His mind was far away, watching the huge fireball enveloping the Grand Mosque, the thousands of people gathered in it for Ramadan all incinerated in seconds.

"Yes," interposed the colonel. "His title was *Caballero Comandante, Ordo Sacer Clavium Sancti Petri,* Knight Commander of the Sacred Order of the Keys of Saint Peter. They called us the troops of the Keys. We came from all over the world, in millions. Of course, they would only take the ones who already had current military training. I don't know what the actual number chosen were. I suspect Michael could tell us."

"It was never more than about two hundred thousand. And we had the latest military equipment, purchased from many European countries but mostly from the United States."

"Do you remember, Comandante, when I showed you the bombs we got from the Americans, the ones they call the MOAB? The ones we used to clear landing zones in the jungle?"

"Yes, indeed, I do. I was flying one of the C-130s that cleared the way for your regiment on the Ambon raid. At your suggestion, as I remember."

"What does MOAB mean, Uncle Lorenzo?"

"The American Air Force says it means 'mother of all bombs,' but it really stands for massive ordnance air burst. It is a fuel-air mixture causing massive fires and overpressures and wipes out everything within a couple of miles, if it is large enough. I think that is the one that was used on Mecca."

Michael picked up his napkin from his lap and laid it on the table.

"I am sorry to leave so fine a dinner so early, but I guess I was more tired than I thought. Please excuse me." He got up and left the room slowly without another word.

The three at the table sat quietly, remembering what he had said earlier about going into hospital for good. Jean sat still, looking in the direction in which Michael had just left.

"What do you suppose is wrong with him, Lorenzo? Was he hurt in the war?"

"We heard stories about his being captured and tortured in Pakistan when he led a raid against their missile fields. I guess it could be that. After I left the army of the Keys, there was another report that he was killed in the bombing of the Sistine Chapel, along with the pope, after the war was effectively over. If he was there, in the chapel, he most certainly would be dead. I don't suppose we will ever know what really happened. And I am not going to ask him." Maggie got up from the table quickly, the tears streaming down her face, and ran out of the room.

* * *

Breuger looked at the fax from the embassy. He had been called back into the Albuquerque consulate an hour ago to look at it. It contained a summary of the surveillance data on Judy Weiss's phone calls and his relayed instructions from Paris. It was better than he had hoped. He was to be given a free hand to stop Kintner any way he wished, so long as it could not be connected to France. That sort of thing was a specialty of his.

Then there was the data on the truck, which surveillance had provided. The best way to use that data to track down the location of the truck was to let the American police do it. He picked up the nonsecure phone on the desk and dialed the New Mexico State Police. After listening and talking to three recordings, he obtained a real person.

"This is Lieutenant Stryker. How may I help you?"

"This is Gerard Montfort of the French consulate in Albuquerque. My vehicle has been stolen. I wonder if you can help me?"

"Yes. Give me the info on your vehicle, please—and the circumstances in which it was stolen."

"It is a white Ford pickup, ten years old, Virginia license plate GRI-1377. It was taken from the parking lot behind the consulate, 200 Torrejon Street, Albuquerque. It has been missing for three days. I delayed reporting it because I thought my friend was using it, but he was not."

"You said a Virginia license plate? Why didn't you have diplomatic plates?"

"I bought it from an American friend only a few days ago. I have not yet received new plates."

"Very well. What is the VIN number?"

"I'm afraid I don't know."

"It will be on the registration slip you got from your friend who sold it to you."

"I'm sorry, but that was stolen along with the vehicle."

"Well, we're going to have to have that to identify the vehicle when we find it. Call your friend or the county where he lives in Virginia, and get it from there. In the meantime, I will put out an APB and start the search. Give me a phone number where you can be reached."

"The consulate number, 242-1000. Will the bulletin cover all adjacent states as well?"

"Yes. That is our procedure."

"Thank you for the assistance, Officer."

He hung up and sat still, wondering what his next move should be. He hated to just sit and wait. Maybe now would be a good time to look at some maps and decide which way Kintner was probably headed. He walked out of the secure office and went down the hall to the office of his DCRI counterpart. There was at least one agent in virtually every embassy and consulate.

"Marcel, if you wanted to run and hide in this part of the country, where would you go?"

"You mean to stay hidden or hide as you run?"

"Both."

"There are places out here where one can hide forever. The Americans call the Four Corners area the best hiding place there is. Many wanted men have disappeared there over the years, from the accounts in the newspapers. It is where the states of New Mexico, Arizona, Utah, and Colorado join."

"What makes it so easy to hide there?"

"The geology, the terrain. It is a vast area of twisted strata, volcanic wastes, canyons, huge rock formations—and then there is the fact that most of it is on Indian reservations. They are policed by the natives. And I suspect they could not care less about white fugitives."

"Can you show me on a map?"

"There's a large one of the whole country on the consul's wall. He is away just now, so we could use that."

They went down the hall, and the consul's secretary let them in the office. On the side wall was a large map that showed major terrain features and roads as well as cities, states, and counties. Marcel pointed out the area he had mentioned.

"This section here," he swept his hand over the map, "is practically empty except for the few administration buildings and dwellings of the Navajo, Ute, and Apache native tribes. And the road traffic is nil, except for the federal highways between the Anglo cities. Are you planning to go out there?"

"Yes. You saw the fax from the commissaire in Washington. I gave the data on Kintner's vehicle to the state police. They will be calling here if they find it. But that could take a long time. I want to start looking for Kintner in the meantime. Show me on the map where you think I should start the search."

Marcel pointed at a spot about fifty miles north of Santa Fe.

"The monastery at Abiquiu is about here. As a first guess, I think he would head straight west on the county and state highways, through the Apache and Navajo reservations. He would have to stay north of the area around the Grand Canyon to avoid the tourists. That leaves only the highways north to Utah or northwest to Nevada. Now, there's a place to hide. It's probably the emptiest state in the country. I drove through it once on federal highway number 50, and I once went three hours without seeing a soul."

"What about the mountains, up north in Colorado? There must be many places up there . . ."

"You'd think so. But it's still early spring, and there would be a fair amount of snow. Also, the Colorado mountain highways are always jammed with tourists, even in winter—the ski areas, you know."

Henri studied the map in silence. It was stunning how much unused space there was in this country. It was hard enough to find someone in Europe, but this—it seemed impossible. Well, he'd just have to put boundaries on the problem somehow and make his decision. It was pointless to stay here.

"I am going to assume you are correct in your guess, Marcel. I will get some supplies and pack the SUV I have rented and start out early tomorrow. You have the number of my cell phone, I assume, since you provided it to me. Call me immediately if the embassy forwards anymore information—especially on any new al-Qaeda communiqués. If the police find Kintner's truck, which I doubt, call me about that also. And on anything else that is pertinent, of course. I suspect the American government will become involved, if it hasn't already. The CIA can't operate here legally, but the FBI will certainly take some action. And that means local police involvement. Do you have adequate surveillance of their communications?"

"Yes, all the Homeland Security channels and those specific to city and state police communiqués. But I am only one man. I will need some help."

"Then get Washington to send you some. And call me when they get here."

"You must keep me informed, as well, Henri. You know the embassy will need something to report to Paris. That is, when there is something to report."

"Yes. As soon as Kintner is confirmed dead, one way or the other, I will tell you."

* * *

"General Kane, Dr. Judy Weiss is on the line. Would you like to speak to her?"

"Absolutely. Maybe she's calling me up to tell me what I'm doing wrong in her old job. Put her through."

General David Somerset Kane was one of those rarities in official Washington, a talented and powerful man who possessed a truly humble attitude. His career had started with graduation from the Air Force Academy and had taken him through three wars, two against Muslim jihadists and one against the Serbians who had been killing Muslims. He had also managed a doctorate in mathematics. At the Pentagon, he had been known as a man who was intolerant of incompetence but even more intolerant of his own failings—at least of those things that he regarded as his failings. And he was a practicing, confessional Catholic.

"Judy, it's a pleasure to hear from you. I hope you are well."

"Thanks, David. I hope I am not interrupting something. I know there's more than enough work to keep you busy in that office."

"Always glad of an excuse to talk to a friend. What's on your mind?" Of all the people whom he had known and worked with in Washington, Kane remembered Judy as one of the most reasonable and ethical, especially when compared to the alley-cat morality of the average government stooge.

"Actually, my call is more about business than our friendship, which I value. You bent over backward to help us out when we were enmeshed in that nuclear blackmail dustup with the Pakistanis. I hope you will never forget how grateful the president and I were for that."

"Just doing my duty, Judy. This new president could take some lessons from the old, if it's not too disloyal to say so."

"No, I know what you mean. Something has come up, which you may already know about but which I needed to talk to you about in any case."

"I'm intrigued. What's up?"

"I received a visit from a man sent to me by the French embassy a few days ago. He was inquiring about Michael Kintner. I believe you remember Kintner for his part in the raid on the Pakistani missile fields, among other things. Anyway, my visitor said that the French had information that al-Qaeda believed Kintner to be still alive and maybe plotting another strike against Islam. Of course, I was thunderstruck, to put it bluntly. Do you know anything about that?"

The line was silent for a long moment.

"Have you spoken to anyone else about this, Judy?"

"Yes. Tom Valence. I just called him out of force of habit. He was one of our best sources of advice while I was on the White House staff. He told me who my visitor really was, and I started to get scared. After I had time to reflect, I realized I probably should have called you first. I apologize for that."

"No, that's perfectly understandable. Who did Tom say your visitor was?"

"An agent of the DCRI. A man named Henri Breuger."

"Yes. I see what you mean about getting scared. As far as I know, the government of France has made no official statement or request on this to the state department or to the White House. That's reason enough to be concerned. But I thought Kintner was dead. The official pronouncement from the Vatican said so."

"Well, he may be, David, for all I know. But someone doesn't think so. If the suspicions of French intelligence are right—"

Kane's mind was racing in the abrupt, brief silence in the conversation. He remembered Judy's incisive intellect for what it was, a shortcut to the heart of any dilemma. This appeared to be one of those insights for which she was famous.

"Judy, I think we need to get to the president on this right away. Worst case, we could be in a new terrorist war before we knew what happened. Those guys never give up, do they?"

"No. To say nothing of the French."

"I'm going to set up a meeting in my office after I have a chance to talk to Tom Valence and Dick Dowling over at NSA. Will you be around for a few days?"

"I'm at your disposal, David."

"Good. I need to get to the president on this, but I have to have my ducks in a row first. And, by the way, Judy, for God's sake, don't talk to anybody else about this before then. If anyone gets to the president before I do on this, she's going to have someone's head on a pike, and it will probably be mine."

* * *

Ken Russell sat next to Jerry Owens in front of a large LCD screen at the FBI lab in Quantico. Owens had never worked with Russell before, but he knew of him from his colleagues in the FBI who had—and they were all very complimentary of his ability and discretion in interagency matters. Owens was dark and a good deal older than Russell but was every bit as fit and trim.

They were looking at the first scan of recently reported violent crimes on police blotters throughout the Four Corners region. Most of them involved drug-related cases, about half of them fatal, and there had been arrests in about a third of them. The computer technician who was running the scan for them had her own small screen to one side.

"Sonny, clear all except for the ones with no arrests. And display all the details."

The technician, a redheaded young woman with a computer science degree from Stanford, quickly brought up the requested data.

After a few minutes of reading, Jerry had zeroed in on the first interesting candidate.

"Look here, Ken, this homicide in—what is that? Kaibito, Arizona, Navajo Indian reservation."

"Yeah, I was just reading that. Four rounds, nine-millimeter hollow point. Victim had just strangled a woman. Sounds like it could be some *ménage-à-trois* or something, doesn't it?"

"Yeah, there was another woman there, but she claims the killer was a complete stranger, someone who just came in from off the street or wherever, it sounds like. Drugs on premises, still in transport package. Probably not our guy. What do you think?"

"Let's come back to that one. Let's get through the rest of the list."

After a few minutes, they had eliminated all of them except one other.

"Okay, let's see," said Owens. "One probable drug or sex-related killing, one state trooper wasted on a remote stretch after apparently stopping a speeder. No suspects, no arrests. I think the speed-trap murder is worth looking into. The other—I don't know."

"Sonny, could we see a map of the areas where these two occurred?" asked Russell.

In an instant, Sonny had a topographic map displayed, showing both sites, which she annotated with small arrows. The two sites were only about thirty-five miles apart, the police killing on US Highway 89, north of Tuba City, Arizona, and the cantina killing on State Road 98. The two highways converged forty miles farther north in Page, Arizona, the site of the Glen Canyon Dam and Lake Powell. Russell and Owens looked at each other.

"Too close for a coincidence, don't you think?" said Owens.

"Yeah. How close in time did these two homicides happen?"

Sonny brought up a corner window with the statistics on the two crimes listed.

"The deputy was killed about twelve hours after the cantina shooting," said Owens. "If it was the guy from the cantina who shot the deputy, he sure didn't get very far in twelve hours, did he?"

"No, and he wouldn't have been running in that direction anyway. He would have kept heading northwest, it seems to me.

That's the direction of the Utah badlands. If he had headed south, he wouldn't have left the reservation for hours, but Utah is only about a thirty-minute drive from Kaibito."

"So, what's your guess? Could they be the same guy?"

"No," said Russell. "My guess is that, if they are related at all, the guy who shot the deputy may have been chasing the shooter in the cantina."

Chapter 5

Michael opened his eyes and looked at his watch. Two in the morning. Amazing how he had nearly always been able to wake up at whatever time he chose. He supposed that his military background and his years in the church had combined to create the skill. He sat up in bed and listened.

Everything was quiet. He stood up and went into the bathroom to complete his ablutions as quietly as possible. Then he came back out, got his rucksack, and began to pack it. When he was through, he looked around to see if he had left anything. Seeing nothing, he reached under the pillow on the bed, got out the Sig Sauer, and shoved it in his belt. He picked up the bag and stepped out into the hallway. Still no sound. He walked out onto the portico and saw his truck where he had left it, twenty meters or so to his left by the fountain.

As he walked around the graveled driveway, he caught some movement in the compound. He stopped and stared in the direction he heard it. A man was walking from the side of the main house toward the side entrance in the wall, the gate facing the bunkhouses. He could just make out who it was—Bob Sutter. Now, what would he be doing coming out of the house at two in the morning? He could think of only one explanation, and it wasn't pleasant. But which one? The mother or the daughter?

He stood there in the driveway, listening to the fountain. This wasn't his business. He didn't feel like a priest anymore. How could he, after what he had done? And even if he did, what right did he have to interfere? But the more he thought about it, the worse it became in his mind. If it were the mother, maybe she had been unfaithful to Maggie's father with Bob Sutter before he had died. If so, that put something of a question on the death itself. And it may have involved both Maggie's mother and Bob Sutter.

Then there was Maggie. The thought of Sutter with the pretty little seventeen-year-old disgusted him. Well, even so, it was none of his business. What could he possibly do to help? Sutter obviously didn't like him and didn't want him there. And he had had an instant dislike for the man also. He remembered his own first reaction when Sutter had walked up to them at the dry wash. He had quickly stepped away from Maggie and been ready to defend himself. Now, why had he done that? His own instincts in such situations were rarely wrong. Then, when he had seen Maggie and Sutter arguing as he was going toward his truck, he had assumed they were arguing over the horse. But maybe it had been some other, more personal matter. Then he knew he couldn't just leave Maggie to the mercies of this man, if there indeed was something between them. He would have to stay long enough to find out what was going on. At the very least, he might have to have a talk with the colonel.

He decided to go back in and see if he could at least find out who Sutter had been with. He dropped off his bag in his room and walked down the hall, which was still dimly lit from a lamp at the end. The bedroom door opposite his had been open earlier, and the decor inside had obviously reflected Colonel Morales's tastes. The bedroom next to his was probably Maggie's and the next one Jean's. He would take a look into each. He quietly opened Maggie's door and looked inside. He could make out some frilly little cushions, a large stuffed animal, and other things that smacked of a girl. Then he could see Maggie's form under a sheet on the bed, her small foot stuck out from under it over the side of the mattress. He stepped back and softly closed the door.

He continued down the hall to the next door, and as he came closer, he could see a light on under the door. He didn't want to risk the noise of a knock, so he just opened the door and went inside.

Jean was sitting naked on the side of her bed, her head in her hands. At the slight noise, she raised her head and looked at Michael. She sat very still, neither moving nor saying anything. Her left eye was bruised and swollen, as he had suspected. He turned and started to leave.

"No, don't leave yet. What the hell are you doing here?" She stood and started walking toward him as casually as if she were fully clothed. Michael could see a bottle of tequila, not quite empty, on the bedside table.

"I apologize for intruding. I was taking a walk outside, when I saw Bob leaving. I was concerned that he might have been bothering Maggie, so I decided to check. Did he give you that eye?"

She stopped about two feet away, swaying slightly, from the liquor, he guessed. She was in good physical shape, lightly tanned all over. He wondered if her sunbathing had been all that private from the hired help.

"No. Lorenzo gave me that the last time he caught us together. He always beats me up when he finds out. It's strange; he never offers to beat up Bob. All he does is threaten to kill him if he ever catches him at it."

Michael remembered a great deal about Lorenzo, and he could not conceive of any circumstance under which he would strike a woman. But Jean was in no shape to give a reasonable account of the situation.

"Well, from what I know about the colonel, I would take that threat seriously, if I were you."

She turned around and started walking back toward the bedside table. She picked up the bottle and a glass and poured a drink. Then she turned back to him.

"Care for some? No? Then I will." She took a large swallow. "By the way, what were you going to do if you had found Bob had been with Maggie? Beat her up, like Lorenzo does to me?"

"I'm not sure what I would have done to Bob, but I don't beat up women. I'm surprised the colonel does, though. I thought I knew the man pretty well, from the short time I spent with him. Why would he care who you slept with?"

"Because I am his late, lamented brother's wife, I guess. Spaniards have a peculiar sense of honor. About some things, anyway. I was ready to provide all the comforts of wedded bliss to Lorenzo when he first came here. But he wasn't buying. Some medieval notion about it being incestuous, even after the brother is dead."

"Yes," said Michael thoughtfully. "I believe Henry VIII used that excuse when he got his first divorce."

"What?" Jean looked at him, a confused expression on her face.

"Why didn't you fight your case in the courts? I'm no lawyer, but I'm pretty sure American law would rule in favor of your getting at least a piece of your husband's property."

Jean sat back down heavily on the bed. Then her head snapped up, staring at something behind Michael.

"Because she did not dare." Colonel Morales had quietly entered the room behind him. "If the police had involved themselves, they would no doubt have found out the same thing I discovered."

Michael turned all the way around and took a step back, unsure what the colonel's intentions were. Morales took his eyes away from Jean and looked hard into Michael's face.

"It did not take long after I came here to see what had happened. She and Sutter had covered their tracks pretty well, I'm sure they thought. It seems my late brother had caught these two together, just as I did. And they made sure he could not do anything about it."

"That's a lie!" screamed Jean, throwing her glass at Morales. "You trumped the whole thing up so you could keep the ranch!"

Morales regarded her quietly and evenly.

83

"Put on some clothes and at least act as if you were a fit mother to your daughter before our guest." He turned back to Michael. "Come with me, Michael. There will be some coffee in the kitchen. There are some things I need to explain. Out of the hearing of this trollop."

Michael followed the colonel out of the room and down the hall toward the kitchen. He wished he had not come back.

They sat down at the kitchen table after pouring their coffee from the carafe on the warmer.

"I apologize for your having to see this. I have tried to keep it away from Maggie, and, to her dubious credit, Jean has also. How did you get involved?"

"I was outside, taking a walk. I saw Sutter leaving, and I was afraid he might have been bothering Maggie. So I decided to check. I realize this is none of my business . . ."

"No, your instincts were honorable. And you did what any decent man would have thought to do. If all this were happening back in Spain, I also would have done the honorable thing and killed them both. But in America, they would call it murder. Perhaps they would have in Spain, also, but they would have made allowances."

"What did you mean about explaining some things?"

"When I came here, I was prepared to arrange for Jean and Maggie to take control of things at the ranch whenever I had satisfied myself that they could do so. A woman alone with a young daughter trying to rule over a small empire would have been daunting, even for Americans. But as I was examining the accounts, I saw that after my brother's death, there had been some large withdrawals in favor of the foreman, Bob Sutter. Naturally, I became suspicious, and I began to ask some questions of the servants, of the vaqueros, and of the priest who comes here to say Mass once a month. Father Guitierrez of course could not say anything about information he had got from the confessional, but he warned me to be very cautious in my dealings with Sutter.

"It was then that I went to see the county coroner who had done the autopsy on Alfonso. He had ruled an 'accidental' death by gunshot—a rifle shot, of all things, in the right temple. He said he had no evidence to the contrary. But Alfonso was an expert in weapons. In my family, all the sons were expected to master both the sword and firearms. Anyway, I confronted Jean with these facts and told her I was prepared to have the body exhumed and the case reopened. She begged me not to, for the sake of her daughter Maggie. I relented but warned her that I was going to stay until Maggie was of age, and then I would see to it that the lands became hers. I also warned her about going near Sutter ever again. And she agreed. But, as you saw, her promise means nothing."

"Why didn't you dismiss Sutter? As long as he is here, this situation . . ."

"Because I am not prepared to let him get away with murder, for that is surely what it was. I have been biding my time, looking for the right way. And I have no way of knowing that he wouldn't come back and do harm to Maggie, or even to Jean."

Michael sat quietly for a time, thinking about everything he had been told. However this situation played out, Maggie was bound to be hurt. And maybe Colonel Morales had underestimated the danger to himself, although he was not a man who made decisions based on fear. He knew that much about him from the war. He stood up.

"I think we both could use some sleep, Colonel. I think Maggie is lucky to have you around. Let me think about it. I believe I may be able to help in some way. Anyway, *buenas noches*."

"Buenas noches, Comandante."

As Michael walked back down the hallway toward his room, he thought about what Morales had just said. It all rang true to him, but he had a feeling there were some things the colonel wasn't telling him. As he got closer to his bedroom, he thought he saw Maggie's bedroom door close.

* * *

Henri Breuger picked up the cell phone from the console and answered it.

"This is Breuger. What is it, Marcel?"

"I have had another call from the Washington embassy. The DGSE have picked up some more al-Qaeda communiqués. They believe they have picked up Kintner's trail again. They mentioned a place, it sounded like Kaibito. I looked it up. It is a small town in Arizona on the Navajo reservation, about fifty kilometers from the Utah border on Highway 89. Do you see it on the map?"

Breuger pulled off the highway onto the shoulder and stopped. He picked up the map from the seat and looked at it.

"Yes, I see it. It's about two hundred kilometers from my present location. Anything else from the intercepts?"

"There was mention of some trouble with the local police. And they also mentioned some kind of surveillance of their own . . . of police channels. What do you make of that?"

"It's obvious the ragheads have been taking lessons in electronics. I should have got a scanner myself before coming on this trip. Have you got one in the consulate?"

"Yes. But we rarely use it."

"Well, keep it on from now on, and listen for any news of Kintner's truck from the state police. Did you put in the request for additional help from Washington?"

"Yes. They are sending two men down right away. They should be here tonight."

"Very well. I am headed toward Kaibito. There may be something I can learn there. *Au revoir.*"

Breuger studied the map awhile longer and then drove off down the highway. Two hours later, he pulled into the little reservation town of Kaibito. He drove slowly down the main street looking for a police signpost or car. Then he spotted a dusty, beat-up car with a red light mounted on top, parked in front of an unmarked storefront. Through the dust on the car door, he could just make out the words "Navajo Police." He pulled over and parked beside it. He looked inside his wallet for the right identification and pulled it out before going inside the building.

He paused just inside the door to accustom his eyes to the darkness after the scathing light outside. There were a couple of desks, each with a jumbled mass of undifferentiable papers and dirty coffee cups. One man stood against a soft-drink machine drinking a soda. He was paunchy and tall, well over six feet. He wore a uniform shirt with a shoulder patch and a badge pinned to the pocket. His trousers were faded jeans, the legs tucked into the top of cowboy boots. The other man was almost a copy of the first but older and sat with his feet propped up on a desk. Breuger turned toward him.

"Good day, Officer. My name is Gerard Montfort. I am a member of Europol. Here is my identification." He took out the card and handed it to him. The seated officer took the card gingerly and looked at it as if it were a snake.

"First time I seen one of these. Looky here, Billy." Billy came over and looked at it.

"Damn if it ain't. Europol. I be damn." He handed the card back to Breuger.

"Heard about you guys. Never seen one. What're you doin' out here? You lost?"

"I hope not." Breuger put his card away. "I'm assisting in a drug case the American FBI is investigating. There are some international implications, of course. May I ask a question or two?"

The seated man took his feet down from the desk, stood up, and put out his hand.

"I'm Charlie Onehorse. This here's Billy Antelope. I guess you must be with them two that was here yesterday."

Breuger shook his hand and then Billy's.

"Yesterday? Were they foreigners?"

"No. FBI. Ain't you with them?"

"Oh, yes. I am indeed. Did they already ask you about the foreigners?"

Billy stepped away and retrieved his soda from where he had left it on the other desk.

"Nah, they was askin' about the killings over at the cantina. Could o' been a foreigner, though. Witness said the killer was a man she never seen before, looked like he'd been in a fire or somethin'. Anyway, it looked to me like it might have been mixed up with some kind of drug deal. Eddie Chavez was known for dealing. Had been a long time. That was the man that was shot. He'd just wasted little Betty Whitejack who never hurt nobody that I know of."

Breuger waited for him to say something else, but he didn't.

"Well, if my colleagues in the FBI have already interviewed you, I won't take anymore of your time. Sorry I missed them. Did they say where they were headed?"

"No. They just asked some more questions about the killer, his vehicle, and where he was stayin', stuff like that. But we didn't know nothin' else. You goin' after him too?"

"No. I was looking for some others, foreigners, as I said. Middle-Eastern types, perhaps. Have you seen any?"

"Hard to say. Ragheads, Hispanics, Indians—we're all dark people. Lots o' them around here." Billy grinned.

"Well, thank you again. Good-bye."

Breuger went outside and got back into his SUV. *So the American government has involved itself at last,* he thought. This lonely area was getting kind of crowded.

* * *

Judy Weiss sat down after the president did and looked around. It had been awhile since she had been in the Oval Office, but it felt very comfortable to her. Seated on her left, next to the president, was

General David Kane, and opposite was Tom Valence of the CIA and Dick Dowling of the NSA. On her right sat Jerry Owens, deputy director of the FBI. The president spoke first.

"Well, David, interesting memo you sent me on today's meeting. Very mysterious, though. Are we getting into another mess with the jihadists?"

"I hope not, Madam President. But there's still a lot we don't know. I thought we ought to come to you now, even with all the unknowns, so there wouldn't be any unpleasant surprises later."

President Hilton looked at Judy.

"Judy, it's very nice to see you again. I wasn't aware that you were still involved in foreign affairs."

Judy's face started to redden. She was hoping they would be able to avoid any partisan politics in this affair, but she should have known better. She had never been on friendly terms with Senator Hilton, but then the senator had not had many close friends of any type. Judy doubted that Catherine Hilton would gain many friends as president.

"I am not, Madam President. This situation landed in my lap, so to speak, and I felt it my duty to make your staff aware of it. But if my presence here is inappropriate, I would be glad to leave."

"No, please stay. For a while yet. Tom, I understand you were the first Judy called. I don't remember seeing anything about it in any of your reports to me."

"No. At first, it seemed to be a relatively inconsequential event. It is certainly unusual for the French embassy to send an agent to White House advisors, former or current. But it sounded to me as if they were just trying to tie up some loose ends about the late war. I am not in the habit of sending up fragmentary reports to the White House before I understand what the situation is."

Good old Tom, thought Judy. Nobody had ever been able to bully him. She wondered how long he was going to last under this new president. Routine presidential appointments usually didn't reach down to the level of the director of operations of the CIA, but he was SES and served at the pleasure of the chief executive.

"Madam President," said Kane, "forgive me for interjecting here, but I had hoped to make clear in my memo that this was strictly a preliminary, exploratory meeting. We won't be asking for any executive decisions today—that is, unless you feel it is necessary."

Hilton looked at Kane with a wry expression.

"Yes, David, I fully understand the purpose of the meeting. You must be patient with me. I am still getting a feel for the capabilities of my departments and agencies." She turned her flat, heavy-lidded gaze toward Owens.

"Jerry, are you involved? Have you taken any action yet that I should know about?"

"Yes, Madam President. I have the FBI looking into the matter, trying to determine if the man Kintner is still alive and, if he is, whether he is involved in any further planned actions against the jihadists. I have been working this in concert with Tom and his people. This seemed necessary in light of what appears to be an interest by al-Qaeda in Dr. Kintner."

Dick Dowling spoke up.

"There seems to be little doubt of their interest in Kintner, Madam President. Our intercepts contain at least five unmistakable references to him and his putative responsibility for the bombing of Mecca."

"So, this is just a quest for revenge? They want to kill him—to get even? If he isn't already dead."

Kane could see that President Hilton still wasn't grasping the import of what she was hearing, but everyone else in the room knew that what they might be looking at was a resumption of the string of horrific acts of violence which had characterized the recent holy war.

"The danger, Madam President, as we see it," said General Kane, "is that at this point, we must assume that the al-Qaeda communiqués could be right. The Vatican might have faked his death and sent him on the mission to Mecca, and, quite possibly, he might have a mandate from the Vatican for a follow-up action of some kind. If that is true and if he carries such a mission to completion, it might set the stage for a massive resumption of hostilities."

"I, for one," said Tom Valence, "happen to believe that Kintner carried out the bombing without, and maybe even in spite of, their wishes. If he did it at all."

"Thanks, Tom," said Hilton. "I am not so ready to absolve the Catholics, if you'll forgive the pun, but what if he intends to take some action on his own with or without permission?"

"That's why we need to get to him," said Owens. "And fast . . . before the terrorists do. We need to know what he knows. That's the best way for us to take some preemptive action against any more violence."

"Well," said Kane, "he certainly is in no position now to take any similar action. He doesn't have access to the arsenal of weapons the church built up for their Crusade. Doesn't our intelligence indicate that they're disarming as rapidly as they built up?"

"It does," said Valence. "That's why I think this is just some more al-Qaeda paranoia. And, if Kintner was in the Sistine Chapel explosion, as I believe, then his days on the earth are numbered."

President Hilton sat quietly, tapping her fingers on the armrest of her chair. After a few moments, she spoke again. "Well, I believe we have to go with worst-case assumptions at this point. Put as many resources on this as you need, Jerry. Nobody should be able to come into the United States for an assassination, no matter who they are." She looked at General Kane. "David, set up a meeting for me with Secretary Rawlings and tell him that preparatory to that meeting, he should meet with the papal nuncio and officially convey our concern on this matter and that we are going to insist on the full story behind all this. I want this to remain *sub rosa* for now. But I want the truth from the Vatican, if they even know it."

"What about the French, Madam President?" asked Valence. "They have a DCRI agent after Kintner, as well."

"Yes, I was getting to that. I don't want this to turn into a dustup over how many secret agents we have in each other's countries. But tell Rawlings to meet with the French ambassador and let him know we won't stand for any French cowboys running around shooting at American citizens." She paused.

"By the way, Kintner is an American citizen, isn't he? I know that current law permits dual citizenship, but did he have to give it up during the late war?"

"I don't think so," said Kane. "I believe both President Baird and the pope insisted he keep both citizenships for political purposes. But one thing is clear, right about now, Kintner is a man without a country."

* * *

FBI Special Agent George Bronson was driving the car. He had been handpicked by Jerry Owens at Langley to be point man on the "Kintner chase" as they euphemistically put it. Ken Russell was in the passenger seat. To Ken, Bronson seemed well-informed on the case, and he could detect no reluctance in him to cooperate fully on the assignment. It was also somewhat comforting to Ken that Bronson bore a remarkable resemblance to a heavyweight boxer.

The Ford sedan was fitted out with two-way radios for four different frequency bands, each with hundreds of channels, and two scanners, one of which was dedicated to cell phone frequencies and one for selectable radio frequency bands. The radio transmitters were the secure "frequency-hopping" kind, which were reprogrammed at intervals by satellite-linked transmitters at FBI operations in northern Virginia.

"You read the same dossiers I did on Kintner," said Bronson. "That killing back at the cantina just doesn't sound like him. Two naked broads and a drug dealer get into a tiff, and a guy walks in out of the blue and wastes the guy? Please."

"I know what you mean. But look at it this way, he hears some woman screaming, and he investigates, and the guy who is strangling one of the dames goes after him. What would he do? What would you do, for God's sake? It could be him. I think it is."

"Yeah, I guess you're right. I can see why he would go around packing heat also. After what he went through during the war . . . Why do you suppose he got himself involved in so many tactical missions? He was the Crusade's supreme commander, wasn't he?"

"Yeah. Knight commander. Sounds like something out of a Charlton Heston movie, doesn't it?"

"Yes, but why did he do it? Makes no sense."

"There was something in the dossier, struck a chord in me. The reason Pope Thomas selected Kintner to head up the military order. He had written a book while at a monastery, a book on *The Just War*. I was amazed to learn that there is Catholic doctrine on such a thing."

"I'm not surprised. I'm a 'victim' of the Catholic school system. They've got answers for everything."

"Yes, I guess they have to answer every question in some way. Anyway, I went to the Langley library and got a copy of it. He had some interesting things to say. One was that the leaders responsible for authorizing and conducting a war should be at comparable risk as the warriors are. That's pretty revolutionary, wouldn't you say?"

"Yeah. Be a lot fewer wars that way, wouldn't there?"

They both chuckled and sat quietly for a while, wondering exactly what kind of man they were chasing.

They entered Flagstaff, and Bronson drove directly to State Police Headquarters. They were expected and Troop Captain McNally laid out the files on a table for them to read. He sat down at the table as well.

"I made these copies for you to take with you if you want. The facts as we know them are pretty straightforward, but there are a couple of things we can only guess at. About a hundred miles north of here on US 89, at 0415, Trooper Miles Wilson pulled a speeder over and called it in, per procedure. A 1993 Chevy minivan, New Mexico license plate CRX-664. He left his mic keyed on his shoulder strap and approached the vehicle from the rear—"

"Is that standard procedure? Leaving his mic keyed? Ties up a channel, doesn't it?" asked Bronson.

"No. Trooper discretion. It was four o'clock in the morning on a deserted stretch of highway. Made sense." McNally waited a moment and continued, "He asked for the driver's license and registration, and the dispatcher said she heard a muffled response in some kind of foreign language."

"Lots of Hispanics around," said Russell. "I guess that's pretty common."

"No, all of the troopers and my staff speak Spanish. Pretty much have to, if you know what I mean. I'll play the recording for you, if you wish. The transcript is in the folders I made for you."

"Yes," said Ken. "I would like to hear it. That okay with you, George?" Ken knew the FBI had the lead on the investigation, by federal law, and he wasn't about to pass up the opportunity to reassure Bronson on that point.

George agreed, and a couple of minutes later, they were listening to the recording.

"Station, Unit Five. Stopped speeder, US 89 North. Looks to be a 1993 Chevy minivan, New Mexico license CRX-664. Stand by."

They could hear the sounds of a car door opening and closing, followed by the crunch of gravel.

"May I see your license and registration, please?"

An unintelligible mumble was followed by a shout from another voice, angry and loud.

"Get out of the vehicle! All of you! Hands in the air!"

They heard sounds that could be doors opening, mechanical clicks, and scuffing sounds.

"Put it down!"

Automatic rifle fire, two single shots, and then more automatic rifle bursts followed. They heard doors being slammed, more unintelligible shouting, and tires spinning in gravel and then the sound of an engine receding, all overlaid with faint requests for backup and then silence.

"That's it," said McNally. "Either of you recognize the language?"

"Yeah," said Ken. "I do. Arabic. Lots of profanity, the second voice telling the first to stop acting like a coward and shoot the son of the devil. Stuff like that."

"What did the trace on the plates tell you?" asked Bronson.

"Not much. Purchased from a used-car dealer in Albuquerque about a month ago. Registered to a Manuel Ortega, address at a hotel in the east end of town. Records show a driver's license in that name, same address, issued six months ago."

Bronson turned to Russell.

"Headed in the same direction as our boy." He turned back to the captain. "I wonder if you could check for any recent traffic stops on a white Ford pickup, Virginia plates?"

"As it happens, we got an alert from the New Mexico police on just such a vehicle two days ago. The reason I remember it is we got an alert on the same vehicle just yesterday from your headquarters, Agent Bronson."

"What? Are you sure?" Bronson couldn't understand why he hadn't been given the same information by his headquarters—an unacceptable oversight, as far as he was concerned.

"Yeah. The first alert reported it stolen from a member of the French consulate in Albuquerque, a man named Gerard Montfort, I believe it was. But the FBI alert said the driver was wanted for questioning in connection with a federal crime. Sounded very peculiar."

Bronson and Russell exchanged glances.

"More peculiar than you know, Captain," said Russell. "Gerard Montfort is a known alias for an agent of the French intelligence service. I think he may be using the state police to find the man the FBI alert referred to. Contact the New Mexico State Police, if you would, and tell them the report was phony and under no circumstances are they to pass on any information on the vehicle to the French consulate."

He looked at Bronson.

"This pretty much confirms our information about Breuger, George. I guess you and I have some secure calls to make."

They thanked the captain, collected the folders, and left.

Chapter 6

Michael lay awake for a long time, thinking about the encounter with Jean and Lorenzo, and then lapsed into a fitful sleep. Swirls of images swam through his mind, constantly changing, shifting just as he thought he recognized something or someone. Then he saw the face of Colonel Morales:

"We are scheduled to deploy on transport helicopters to the USS Kittyhawk *tomorrow morning at 0400. Five hundred troopers. We'll be accompanied by two squadrons of helicopter gunships, mostly Apaches and a few Comanches. The* Kittyhawk *will steam south to the Molucca Straits and be on station by 1700. Just before dark, at 1845, three AC-130s will each drop a ten-thousand-pound 'daisy-cutter' on positions suitable for landing zones. Our troops will be dropped off at the LZs and make their way down the mountain to the city of Ambon. Our target priorities for destruction are number one, the loading docks for the amphibious craft Indonesian soldiers use for infiltrating into the Southern Philippines; number two, army barracks and installations that protect and support the infiltration operations; number three, all targets of opportunity of a military nature, and, if time and circumstances permit, two mosques."*

"Mosques? What's the reason for that?"

"All the Christian churches in Ambon have been destroyed, sir, and at least a thousand Christians killed. I felt the Christians still left alive

needed some encouragement, and the Muslims needed a message. Do you object?"

"No. No objection. I want to be in the lead helicopter and accompany you on the assault. Will that be a problem?"

Michael sat straight up in bed, breathing hard, his heart pounding. *What was that?* he wondered, the image and the words already beginning to fade. He lay back down, waiting for the spasm to pass. He ran his hand over his face involuntarily and then wiped his hand on the sheet, as he had done for weeks, shedding steadily the skin that grew fitfully there. He looked down. There was no dead skin. He rubbed his face again but still no fragments of tissue came away. He started to wonder what it meant, but he was too tired to ponder it and fell back into a doze and then a deeper sleep. Then the images came:

"Sorry, Comandante, I cannot allow it. Have you ever trained or fought in the jungle? Especially mountainous jungle? My men and I have been training for months with the negrito people, who are born, live, and die in the jungle. They have taught us as much as they can, but I still lose troops every week out there. Let me give you a picture of what it's like. Triple canopy, two hundred feet high, little or no sunlight, even at high noon. The jungle floor never dries; it's slick with slime and so slippery that you cannot even stand up on most of it. When you slip and fall, you grab a vine and it breaks into razor-like ribbons, which cut through a leather glove and slice your hand to the bone. You can be walking along a trail and step off a hundred-foot precipice, which a moment before, you couldn't even see. The jungle floor is full of holes, covered over with vines and leaves. When you step on one, you are in a deep pit full of vipers, scorpions, and insects, too many to even name, and each with its own special poison. No fresh water, except on leaves. Fruit, most of which will kill you with one bite a half hour after you eat it. Are you getting the picture, Comandante?"

The knocking on the door became insistent. At first, he thought it was still in the dream, but then he realized it was happening now. He groaned and raised his head from the pillow, still wet with sweat.

"What is it? Who's there?"

"It's me, Michael. Maggie. Get dressed and come down to breakfast. I'm taking you riding today, and we need to start early because of the heat."

He swung his legs off the bed and sat up. He still had his jeans on.

"Okay, Miss Morales. Orders are orders."

She pushed open the door slightly and stuck her head in, grinning.

"Right you are, good sir. A lady can command a knight, can't she?"

He groaned again.

"Let me get showered and made presentable for court, milady. I'll be at table in ten minutes."

Maggie closed the door and stood just outside it, wondering. He had looked different—not much, just not quite as . . . *injured*, if that was the word. She dismissed it and went back toward the breakfast room and patio.

True to his estimate, Michael came into the breakfast room ten minutes later and walked out onto the patio, where breakfast was being served. Colonel Morales and Maggie were there, but Jean was not. Morales rose to meet him.

"Good morning. I must say you are looking very well this morning, Comandante. You must have needed your rest."

"Thanks, Coronel. I feel better than I have in weeks, for some reason."

"I will leave you with Maggie, as I have already eaten. I will go and have some riding gear and boots put in your room. I think you and I are about the same size." He put his foot alongside Michael's and drew it back.

"Please excuse me, both of you. I will see you when you return." Morales walked quickly back into the house.

"The men who brought her in say that I should be able to ride Selena today, if I only let her walk or canter and not too far. Your treatment must have worked well on her."

"Nothing special, really. She is young and strong, and the snake may not have had time to inject very much poison. I have not worked with horses for a long time."

They both ate quietly, chatting about trivial things until they had finished. Maggie left to go down to the stables, and Michael went back to his room and put on the riding apparel the colonel had left for him. He had also left a hat for him, which fit pretty well. Then he walked down to the stables where Maggie was waiting. Selena nickered softly when she caught sight of him. Next to where she stood, the groom was holding the halter of a young roan gelding, already tacked.

"I hope you don't mind my picking out a horse for you. Selena is used to the gelding. Mother usually rides him when we go riding together."

Michael mounted up just as Maggie did, and the two of them rode off stirrup to stirrup in the direction of the dirt road, which led from the hacienda to the highway. The road was somewhat elevated above the terrain to the east, on the upswing of the generally concave shape of the plain between the far mountain ranges.

"Selena looks in pretty good shape, Maggie. How does she seem to you?"

"She seems fine. The highway is about three miles away. Why don't we canter a bit and see how she takes it?"

Michael started to kick his horse into a canter, when he saw Maggie rise slightly in her seat and heard her say, "Canter." So he did the same. After about fifteen minutes, they brought their horses to a walk again.

"I hope your uncle and I didn't wake you last night. We both were having a cup of coffee in the kitchen, talking over some things."

Maggie looked at him. She studied him for a long moment, unsmiling.

"If you're asking me if I overheard what you said, why don't you say so?"

"Sorry, Maggie. I saw your door close as I was going back to bed. Your uncle wants to protect you from some things—"

"I know what the colonel wants to protect me from. And my mother too. I am not a child, and I am not stupid."

They rode on in silence for several minutes.

"I know how dangerous things are, Michael. Not for me, but for my mother—and for my uncle also."

"How long have you known about . . . Sutter?"

"If you mean about what he did to my father, I have known since shortly after his death. The way my mother and Bob acted afterward was just shameful. Then I thought about what hadn't seemed right all along—that Daddy would accidentally shoot himself. It was ridiculous. My father taught me to handle weapons, and he was a stickler for safety. It just wouldn't happen the way they said it did."

"What did they say happened?"

"The three of them were out hunting antelope, riding through the foothills a few miles south of the hacienda. They brought my father back over his saddle. They said my mother's rifle jammed, and my father handed his own rifle to her. When she tried to grab it, it almost slipped from her hand; my father pulled it back toward him, and it accidentally discharged. Mother said the finger of her glove got caught in the trigger. The whole thing sounds just stupid."

"Your uncle said he was shot in the right temple. That doesn't sound plausible."

"No. Nothing about it sounds 'plausible,' as you put it. Anyway, long before it happened, I could see how Mother and Bob acted when my father wasn't around. Until my father's death, I believed it was just a flirtation. That's what I wanted to believe, anyway."

"What do you think is going to happen now? You heard what your uncle said."

"Yes. But I don't believe my uncle will kill him. I hope Bob will just leave of his own accord. I have tried to talk to Mother about it several times, but she won't listen. She pretends as if nothing is wrong. I don't know what will happen."

She put her face in her glove, and Michael could see she was sobbing. He stopped his horse, took Selena's bridle, and stopped her too. He stepped down, grounded his reins, and walked around to help Maggie down. She put her face into his chest and continued to weep silently for a long time.

Michael continued to hold her. From where they were, they could see the highway turnoff about a mile away and below them. As he held her, he saw a vehicle turn off the highway and stop just short of the cattleguard. It was a red pickup with a black grill.

* * *

Breuger pulled his SUV off the highway and answered the cell phone.

"Yes, Marcel, what is it?"

"The request for more men has been honored. I now have twenty-four-hour coverage of the police channels. And I have someone to assist you, should you require it."

"I have always worked alone, Marcel. But you may send him on an alternate route to look for Kintner, if you wish. What else?"

"More intercepts. DCRI have not been able to complete their analysis, but here it is: 'Kintner has led us to the other. Also suspect other parties involved in search. May need more resources.' That's all they forwarded to me."

"What 'other'? Have the al-Qaeda better intelligence than we?" Breuger sat and thought about it for a while. "Marcel, pass the word to Paris; ask them to compile a list of all the Crusade's major combat commanders. Ask them to try to determine if any on the list have been linked to other direct attacks on the infrastructure of Islam during the late war. And see which ones are in the United States. Have you got all that?"

"Yes. So you suspect that they are chasing more than one person?"

"I believe that is the only interpretation of the intercept that makes sense. It is only logical that they would try to avenge themselves on everyone in the Crusade who so much as shot at a mosque." Silence. "And, Marcel, see if Paris has intercepted anything else that has referred to 'more resources.'"

"Very well. The agent I am sending to help is Elise Marquette. Do you know her? I will need a rendezvous point for her also."

"Yes, I remember her. She acquitted herself very well in that mess the CIA stirred up in Pakistan, when they blundered in on the surveillance we had set up for Osama. Tell her to meet me in Ely, Nevada, in three days. I will send you the GPS coordinates later on today. And tell her to look for a green Ford SUV, New Mexico plate number 4415. *Adieu.*"

* * *

Monsignor Robert Bohemund sat listening to the intelligence briefing from an operative of the intelligence apparatus that had been set up for the Crusade commanders during the war with Islam. Even though the standing army had been all but disassembled, the apparatus dedicated to gathering and analyzing data on jihadists was still at full strength. The apparatus had been set up with the assistance of both American and French intelligence, the latter of which Bohemund was a former member. They still exchanged data with other countries, especially those that had been active partners in the war: the Americans, the French, and the Israelis. The briefer was nearing the end of his presentation.

"The latest intercepts sent to us by the American NSA refer to another person who may be the next or may even be the primary target of the terrorists. As it happens, there is a former commander of a combat brigade in Indonesia who is in the United States. I believe you may know him, Monsignor Bohemund. As most of you here know, Monsignor Bohemund was Knight Commander Kintner's deputy in the hostilities. Monsignor, do you recall a Colonel Lorenzo Morales?"

Bohemund looked around the dimly lit briefing room, trying to assess the impact which the briefing might have had on the listeners. Most of the people there were surrogates or principal assistants to the men who had been most actively involved in the Ninth Crusade. There was Monsignor Brendan Culligan, secretary to Cardinal Leo Abrusco, the president of the Council on Justice and Peace. And there was Msgr. Francisco Archuleta, assistant to Cardinal Bocelli, the Vatican secretary of state. And there were others of a somewhat less powerful stripe.

"I remember him very well. His brigade performed brilliantly, especially on the initial raid on Ambon. He came under some criticism for destroying some mosques in addition to his military targets. But he had explicit authority to do so. Father Kintner was there during the raid."

"What?" said Culligan. "Michael authorized that?"

"Yes. Colonel Morales pointed out that the Indonesian Christians on Ambon had undergone particularly appalling atrocities. All the Christian churches had been destroyed by the Muslims and over a thousand Christians slaughtered. Morales felt that the Christians still left alive on Ambon needed some encouragement and the Muslims needed a message. Michael agreed. He told me later that there was also the psychological effect for the Keys troops. Perhaps it would help focus their attention on what this was really all about. They came there to put things right for the people being persecuted for their faith. That was something worth dying for."

"Wasn't there an element of revenge in all that, Robert?" said Archuleta. "Not strictly in accord with Holy Scripture, was it?"

"No, Francisco, it wasn't. But you will find that very little in war is strictly in accord with scripture. Reprisals, counterattacks, whether you call them revenge or not, are common tactics in warfare. I happen to think Michael made the right decision. There have been no more attacks on Christians in Indonesia since that night."

The group was quiet for a time. Then the briefer spoke again.

"That is all I had planned to say today. Are there any questions?"

"I would pose a question for all of us here," said Bohemund. "Are we not obligated to some extent to try to find out if Kintner is still alive and try to do something to help him? And also Colonel Morales?"

"Well," said Msgr. Archuleta, "the Holy See has not changed its position that Michael was killed in the Sistine explosion. Reversing that position may not be in the best interests of Holy Mother Church."

"Unless Holy Mother Church is willing to sit on her hands and watch two of her most dedicated servants get slaughtered by the jihadists. If you'll forgive the expression."

"Can we even be sure that Michael is still alive, Robert?" asked Culligan.

"Look. I was there, at the Israeli air base at Har Megiddo, when Michael took off with the C-130 loaded with a ten-thousand-pound hyperbaric bomb. Of course, I had no idea where he was going with it, but I saw him, and he was very much alive. That was a week after the Sistine explosion. Now, I understand and agree with Cardinal Bocelli's decision at the time to declare him deceased to offer some possible protection for him. None of our doctors gave him more than two weeks to live, and everyone wished that he could die in peace.

But he must be still alive; even the French believe it is true, and so do the Americans. President Hilton even said as much to the nuncio. Isn't that true, Francisco?"

"Yes, it is. And the American president is also insisting that we revise our position. Cardinal Bocelli is under some pressure to give all the details to the Americans. They have evidently committed themselves to finding Father Kintner also."

"Well, isn't it clear?" said Bohemund. "We've got to involve ourselves as well. We are all aware from these briefings these past few weeks that al-Qaeda, probably the French, and maybe even the Americans all want Father Kintner dead. And now Colonel Morales will be on the list. We cannot sit by and see this happen."

"But that would require decisions by Cardinal Bocelli and Cardinal Abrusco and maybe even Pope John," said Archuleta. "This could lead to new hostilities between the church and Islam."

"With respect, Msgr. Archuleta," said Bohemund, "the new hostilities may be said to have begun. And they will get a lot worse if we allow these assassinations to occur."

The group was silent, stunned by the realization that what Msgr. Bohemund had just said was true. Then Msgr. Culligan spoke again.

"I am prepared to go to Cardinal Abrusco on this. But I will recommend that we send someone to talk to the American authorities, before we 'come clean,' as the Americans like to say. I believe one of President Hilton's closest advisors, the national security advisor, may be the one to approach. I remember the Vatican press extolling him as a good Catholic, when he was appointed. What do you think, Robert?"

"I agree, Brendan. But it will really be up to Cardinal Bocelli. Are you ready to make a recommendation to him, Msgr. Archuleta?"

Archuleta squirmed in his chair. He thought he knew what Bocelli's reaction to involving the Holy See in more hostilities would be. And that might certainly occur if they sent someone to America. So they would have to be careful whom they sent. He knew the Americans for the hardheaded lot they were, and an ordinary diplomat would have his head handed to him. They needed someone who knew al-Qaeda and who knew Father Michael Kintner well.

"All right. I will go to the secretary. And I think sending someone to talk to the American national security advisor may be a wise step. We need, in any case, more information before we reverse our position on Father Kintner. But choosing the right person to send is critical. I will recommend that we send Msgr. Robert Bohemund."

* * *

Michael took his arms from around Maggie, and she stood back, beginning to get her composure back. He helped her back aboard Selena and walked around to his horse. He mounted and reached over to the scabbard on Maggie's saddle and withdrew the rifle. He laid it across his own saddle and cradled it in his left arm.

"Maggie, I need you to do me a favor without asking any questions. Will you do that?"

"Yes, of course, Michael. But if there's something wrong, I'm sure I can—"

"No, please, Maggie. This is important. Take Selena back to the stable. Don't rush her, but take her straight back. I will be along in a little while."

Maggie hesitated just for a moment and then neck-reined Selena around and headed back at a canter. Michael watched her over his shoulder until he was sure she was on her way back, and then he turned and looked down toward the distant truck once more. The deep, ineffable dread came back to him, more intense this time, almost bordering on terror. It was an unfamiliar feeling but unmistakable. He was at once confused and disappointed in himself, because he had never experienced terror in combat, either before he became a priest or after. He knew the effect fear could have on clear thinking and the ability to act quickly and rationally. That was the motive for getting Maggie away. He simply did not know if he could protect her—or himself. But what was the ancient adage? "Act bravely and true courage will come to you."

He urged his horse forward at a walk.

Nothing and no one moved at the truck. There was a thin overcast, just enough so that there was no reflection from glass or metal. He could see clearly enough to shoot, if necessary, but he was still too far. He hadn't handled a rifle in some time, but one never forgot. When he was about a half mile away, he could see that the windshield and side windows were darkly tinted—an unlawful modification almost everywhere. *Who are they?* he wondered for the hundredth time. If they intended to kill him, they had had many chances on the road before now. What were they dogging his trail for? Even he didn't know where he was headed.

He pulled up short and sat his horse. The truck was still a good quarter mile distant. Still no movement. Then he slowly rode forward at a walk, watching the cab intently for any movement. Finally, he stopped a few yards short and dismounted. He walked around to his left, trying to see through the dark tinting of the windows. He continued on around the back. The bed had a topper on it, but the windows were just as black as they were in the cab. He came back to the driver's side, grasped the door handle, and pulled it. The door came open smoothly, and he caught sight of a pair of legs in jeans and boots. The driver didn't move. Michael stepped up even with the seat and saw Bob Sutter sitting there, unmoving. His left temple had a two-inch hole clotted with blood. No one else was in the cab. Michael reached up and took his wrist, which was dangling down beside the seat. There was no pulse. He let the arm drop, and Bob slumped to his left and fell out of the cab. He landed on his left side and lay there. His right temple had a small, neat hole, obviously the entry wound. The blood appeared to have clotted some time ago. Michael looked inside the cab, but there was no sign of blood or tissue anywhere. He walked back to the rear of the vehicle, opened the topper door, and looked inside. Empty. He continued around the truck to the passenger door and opened it. He opened the glove compartment, and it too was empty. The key was still in the ignition.

Michael gazed all around the area but could see nothing but terrain—rock and chaparral cactus, a few junipers, and piñon. Nothing about this made any sense. Whoever had done this was nowhere in sight. He felt he shouldn't leave Sutter's body here. But this was a crime scene. The police were not going to be happy if he moved the body.

He walked back to his horse, who was snorting and nervous from the smell of carrion. He climbed aboard, still cradling Maggie's .30-30, and started back toward the hacienda.

When he arrived back at the hacienda, Colonel Morales and Maggie were waiting outside the front gate in one of the ranch jeeps. He dismounted, and they got out of the jeep. Maggie ran up to him.

"Michael, what happened? I wouldn't let the colonel go after you because you said you—"

"Something bad has happened, Maggie." He turned to Morales. "Do you own a red Dodge pickup, Lorenzo?"

"No. We own a couple of Fords and a Chevy. And some jeeps. Why? What's happened?"

"Bob Sutter is dead. Shot through the head. I discovered his body when I rode down to the pickup, parked just off the highway at the cattleguard."

"What pickup?" asked Maggie.

Kintner looked at her. They had both seen it surely. It was the only vehicle in sight, in plain sight. Then he remembered. She had been weeping in his arms when he saw the truck pull off the highway. And he had sent her away almost immediately. It was quite possible she hadn't seen it.

"I saw it pull off the highway just before I sent you back. I thought I had seen it before, and I thought there might be trouble.

But when I went down there, Sutter was the only one in the truck, and he had been dead for some time. Or so it appeared. He couldn't have been driving when he was shot, because there was no blood in the cab. I guess whoever drove it there managed to jump out and put Bob in the driver's seat in the short time that I watched you go back."

"Let's go inside," said Morales. "I will call the sheriff, and then we'll drive down to meet whoever they send."

Morales went inside, and Maggie and Michael waited by the jeep. One of the hands came over to take the gelding back to the stables, and Michael handed the rifle back to Maggie.

"Maggie, are you sure you never saw the truck? It was in plain sight . . ."

"No, Michael, I'm sure. But I still don't see how someone could have driven it off the highway and then jumped out and run off without you spotting him."

"No. I don't understand it, either. I only watched you for a minute or two, to make sure you were out of danger."

"But why would you think I was in any kind of danger? Who did you think was in the truck?"

Michael just shook his head. He wasn't sure of anything.

"I don't know, Maggie. These last few weeks, it seemed as if someone was following me. I saw the same truck, same red color, same black custom grill, a half dozen times. I finally decided that I was just being paranoid. But then when I saw it again today, I just panicked, I guess. My mind hasn't been very clear since the—well, for a long time."

Morales came out of the house and walked over to the bunkhouse. In a few moments, two cowboys followed him out of the bunkhouse, got into one of the jeeps, and drove off down the road toward the highway. Morales came back to where Maggie and Michael were standing.

"The sheriff says for us to stay here. I told him I was sending two men down to guard the body. It doesn't take long for the scavengers to gather out here. Buzzards, crows, coyotes. The prairie keeps itself clean."

* * *

The sheriff's car drove up to within a few yards of the group of people standing by the front entrance to the compound and stopped. The sheriff got out from the driver's seat and his deputy from the other side. The two cowboys Morales had sent out earlier pulled up in their jeep in back of the sheriff's car and got out. The sheriff was a bit overweight, and his face showed a lot of years in the hot Nevada sun. His deputy was young, tall, and fit. But there was a grim look to him in spite of his youth. He looked as if he would fit in nicely either as the subject or object of law enforcement.

* * *

Jean was standing on the portico when she saw the sheriff's car coming up the road. She started walking toward where everyone was standing, outside the compound's main entrance. There was an awful feeling of dread deep inside her. Last night was still a vivid and bitter memory—another assignation with Bob and another confrontation with Lorenzo. She didn't know what either of them might do. She had watched unbelieving two years ago as Bob had shot her husband dead. They had both decided that it had to be done, but she hadn't quite believed that she could bring herself to go through with it. Then Bob had just done it. Now she was trapped by the memory, the guilt, and the certainty that one way or another, someone else was going to get killed.

She walked up to the group and stood next to Maggie, away from Lorenzo. She wondered why Maggie was holding her rifle.

The sheriff walked up to the little gathering. "Howdy, Colonel. Nasty little present someone left down there. Who's this?"

"This is Michael Kintner, Sheriff, the man who discovered the body."

"What body?" asked Jean, a touch of hysteria in her voice.

Maggie looked at her.

"It's Bob Sutter, Mom. Michael found him shot dead down at the turnoff."

A sound of choking came from her throat, almost like a growl. She grabbed the rifle from Maggie, pointed it at the colonel, and tried to pull the trigger, but the safety was on.

"You bastard!" she screamed. She looked down at the rifle and pushed the safety off with her thumb.

In the small hesitation, Michael leaped toward her, but she fired just as he came between her and Lorenzo. Michael caught the round in his chest and dropped heavily to the ground. The sheriff was fumbling with the flap on his holster, but his deputy had already cleared leather and fired his revolver. The .357 magnum bullet left a neat hole in Jean's right temple, and a pink cloud exploded from the other side of her head. She slumped quickly and bonelessly to the ground.

* * *

For what seemed like a long moment, no one else moved. Then Lorenzo dropped quickly down by Michael's side, putting his arm under his shoulders and feeling for a pulse on the carotid artery. He could feel nothing. He kept kneeling there for a moment, watching the red stain spreading on his shirt under the open jacket. Maggie stood frozen, her tight fists against her mouth to keep from screaming, as she looked from Michael's body to her mother's. The sheriff walked up and looked down at Jean's body. He glanced back at his deputy, still brandishing his Colt Python and shook his head. Then he knelt down, picked up the spent shell casing from the rifle, and put it into a plastic sandwich bag.

The colonel stood up and motioned for his two cowboys to come over.

"Jed, you and Frank carry Kintner's body up to the infirmary. Then come back for . . . Maggie's mother." He had almost referred to her as "the woman," but then he remembered what Maggie had just lost.

He stepped closer to where the sheriff was standing.

"What are you collecting evidence for, Sam? Is there any doubt what just happened?" he said wryly.

"No. No doubt about what happened here. But I found a fresh .30-30 shell case down at the turnoff. Not ten feet from Sutter's body. I think it might be a good idea to have the state lab do a comparison."

"What? You think Maggie's rifle was used to kill him? You're crazy."

"Well, you got any other .30-30s on the place? I'll have a look at them if you do."

"No. The rest are .30-06s. My late brother preferred them, as I do. They are much more powerful and versatile."

"Does anyone else besides Miss Morales ever use the rifle?"

"No. Well, Michael had it when he found Sutter. But no one else that I know of."

The sheriff stood thinking about what he had heard. There was a lot more to all this than met the eye, he was sure. And he figured Colonel Morales knew it all. But just exactly how this man Kintner figured into everything, he couldn't guess.

"I guess we'd better do a test for gunpowder residue on Kintner's hands and clothes. Do you know of any reason he might have had to kill him?"

"That's ridiculous. Kintner is an old friend. He only arrived here yesterday. He had never met Jean or Maggie or anyone else on the ranch. Plus, he is . . . well, he would be unlikely to murder anyone. He was a priest."

The sheriff's eyes widened. Damned if this didn't have all the twists!

"All right, then." He turned to his deputy, who was still standing with his revolver raised in the air. "Hey, hipshot," he said sarcastically, "call for another ambulance and two, uh . . ." He didn't want to say "body bags" in front of the girl. "Something to put around the deceased."

"Right, Sheriff. Body bags." He went back to the car.

"Sam," said the colonel, "is there any reason why you couldn't just give a sworn statement to the coroner about the deaths of my late brother's wife and Michael Kintner? I am from an old European family, a traditional Catholic family. Autopsies are avoided whenever possible. I would like to have our family priest say their funeral Mass here, at the ranch, and inter them both beside my brother. As soon as possible."

The sheriff nodded and looked back at his deputy. He drew his finger across his throat to cancel the call.

Maggie had knelt down by her mother and was still there, but she hadn't touched her. She just kept staring down at the wound in her head, as if hypnotized by it. The two cowboys had come back from the dispensary and stood just behind Maggie, waiting. The colonel walked over and knelt beside her.

"Maggie," he said softly. "Maggie, it's all over. You must come with me now. Back to the house. There's nothing more we can do here."

Maggie slowly turned her head and looked at him.

"Yes, Uncle Lorenzo. It is all over now."

As they stood up and started back toward the hacienda, Lorenzo looked back.

"My thanks for your understanding, Sam. By the way, what are you going to do with the red pickup? It doesn't belong to the ranch."

The sheriff looked puzzled.

"What red pickup would that be, Colonel?"

Chapter 7

Ahwadi knew it would not be long now. There would be a wait while the others from the cells in Phoenix and Salt Lake City got here. But he and his men had already done the hard work. Now came the pleasant part. They would not escape them here. Now he had both sons of Satan in one place. The devil Kintner and the Butcher of Ambon. He had known that, if they were patient, Kintner would lead him to the other. His men, always impatient, wanted the quickest way, just shoot him on the highway. But then they might never have found the Butcher.

"Lord Ahwadi," said Suleiman, his second in command, "there was something else on the scanner. It mentions Kintner by name. Come listen."

They both came out of the motel room where they had spent the night and went over to the white Chevy van. Ahwadi opened the rear door and went inside where the man on radio duty was sitting in front of some very modern equipment. He and Suleiman sat down.

"What is it, Ali?"

"It is the channel of the sheriff of Wheeler County, Nevada, Lord Ahwadi. The same which reported the shooting of a man on a ranch. I will replay it for you."

He put a time code into the digital playback and waited.

"Sally, this is Deputy Scalf. Sheriff needs another ambulance out here. And two more body bags. The Morales woman just wasted a man named Kintner, while she was trying to kill Colonel Morales.

Then I shot her before she could kill anybody else. Damned good shot too. Got her right in the . . . Wait a minute. Sheriff says to cancel the call. Did that other ambulance get back yet? Did the coroner call?"

"No, Deputy. What's the sheriff planning to do with them other two bodies, if he ain't sending 'em back to the coroner?"

"Don't know. I'll call you back. Or the sheriff will. Out."

Ahwadi shook his head, muttering.

"Mother of all bad fortune! Now we will never get revenge on the devil Kintner. I would have never given him such mercy as he just received. The way of Allah is inscrutable."

"But we still have the Butcher, my brother. He will pay for both their sins. The motel clerk told us where the ranch is after we picked up the first call from the sheriff. It is less than an hour back the way we came."

Ahwadi sat deep in thought. This was not right. Allah would not allow his enemy to get off so easily. There had to be something more. Maybe there were others, family, perhaps, or maybe even some American agents. He knew they were coming. His own cell in Albuquerque had picked up the calls from the FBI to the state police. Perhaps it would be better to wait. But then, how many were they sending? Surely, for such a one as Kintner, it would not be many. But the Butcher of Ambon was there. He must be killed before the American agents arrived.

"Suleiman, alert the Wahabi action officer at the consulate in San Francisco. Ask him to try to find some more operatives to send to us in case—well, in case we need them. If he doesn't have anyone, then contact the Yemeni consulate in Los Angeles. There is no way to know when the American agents will show up, but they will."

* * *

George Bronson hung up the secure phone and turned to Ken Russell.

"You're going to love this—another intercept from the al-Qaeda network, claiming that a sheriff or someone has killed Kintner. Happened at a ranch south of Ely, Nevada. Headquarters is in contact with the Nevada State Police, trying to pinpoint the location. They want us to return to Phoenix. Mr. Owens says the White House has promised him as much as he needs to find Kintner. He's sending out two armed Blackhawk helicopters and a dozen more agents from Quantico. He's coming with them and wants us all to be there when he lays out a plan. He also said the NSA intercept from our little hairy friends indicated they're putting more people on this thing too."

Russell sat still, thinking about what Tom Valence had said to him before he left Washington. If the NSA knew about this, then the DGSE knew, too. And if Breuger was as close to this as he thought, the DCRI agent would have a clear field while the FBI did its "planning."

"George, I think another delay like this could let these other people get in and do their thing before we even get all these troops of yours deployed. A couple of days and this could be over and we'd be standing here with our faces hung out."

"I know, but what can I do? Owens is my boss."

"Well, he's not mine. And Breuger is someone I know, at least by his reputation and record. I've been dealing with people like him for a long time. I think I would like to go after him while you and the others sit down there in Phoenix and plan."

Bronson made a wry face and scratched his jaw, trying to decide.

"Ken, I could get in a lot of trouble for this, but . . . Let's do this. I'll call the Phoenix office back and get an update on police calls. If there's anything more on the trouble at this ranch in Nevada, you go up there in my car, and I'll get the state police to give me a ride back to the field office. If not, you come on back with me. Okay?"

"All right. Let's see what they've got."

A few minutes later, Bronson was on his way back to Phoenix in a state police car and Russell was headed north toward a ranch in Nevada.

* * *

Breuger shut off the cell phone. No easy answers had been forthcoming. Marcel had got nothing from the New Mexico State Police since he had called them. It was likely the FBI had involved itself, and their communications security was much better than that of the local police. He was on his own again, depending on his own wits as he had done many times before. In many ways, he preferred it that way. One thing he did have, however, was a list of former commanders who had served under Kintner and their probable locations. The DCRI had done its work well on that request, at least. There were only three in the United States, and only one of those was anywhere near here—Colonel Morales, who had commanded a regiment in Indonesia.

He took out the map again and studied it. In this part of the country, there were few alternative routes of travel. If his earlier assumptions had been right, Kintner would have had to travel either this federal highway, number 50, or number 93. And they both converged toward the town of Ely. It was the only town in a hundred miles that was large enough to have a law enforcement base of operations. There had to be a sheriff's office there. That was where he would get his information.

* * *

"How come you just left them bodies there, Sheriff? That ain't exactly procedure, is it? You're always harping on—"

"Listen, genius. Procedure ain't everything. Sometimes you have to use your head. You remember by any chance when Jean Morales's husband was killed, about two year' ago? Well, when his brother showed up, he began asking a lot of questions about it. Accidental death by rifle shot ain't exactly a common occurrence in this part of the country. Unless it's some damn fool from Texas up here hunting. I asked a lot of questions myself but never could get any kind of proof. Did you see how that woman reacted when she heard Bob Sutter was killed? She was sure the colonel had done it. What does that tell you?"

Deputy Scalf sat with his face screwed up as if he were in pain. Then he got it.

"You mean ol' Bob Sutter and Jean Morales? God a'mighty, that means they probably killed her old man. And the colonel found out about it."

"Ah. There is a brain in that gourd after all. Yeah, that's what I figured too. But the only .30-30 on the place belongs to his niece. She ain't but seventeen or so. I don't think Colonel Morales is the kind of man to put a thing like that off on a young girl and his own niece to boot. Not that I would have blamed him for shooting Sutter. I might've done the same thing myself under the same conditions. But I would have done it with a heavy-grain shell from a .30-06. And that's what I think the colonel would have done. Blowed the son of a bitch's head off."

"Well, what about that guy Kintner? Could he have done it?"

"Yeah, he could have. He would have been my primary suspect. But why would he? The colonel ain't the kind of man to get somebody else to do his killing for him. It's possible that Kintner, being his friend, might have done it on his own. As a favor. But that don't make any difference now, does it?"

The sheriff and his deputy sat for a while, each with his own thoughts. Then the sheriff spoke again.

"Anyway, I think I'm going to have the state lab compare those two shell casings. Just for grins."

* * *

Michael looked at the face of the man he held in his arms. Blood was still seeping from his mouth, his ears, and his nose. But his face had relaxed into peace. His pain was over. Michael stood up and slowly looked around at what was left of the chapel. He seemed to be the only person standing. Far back, he saw figures trying to make their way through the smoke and flickering flames toward the altar. They were wearing what appeared to be yellow plastic from head to foot. On the front of their overalls was a peculiar but familiar symbol, with a word beneath it: Radatio—*Radiation. Michael remembered what had happened at Notre Dame Cathedral. He wondered how many generations the Sistine Chapel would be unrepairable and uninhabitable.*

He felt strong hands take hold of him and ease him down onto a stretcher. He felt only numbness, heard only moaning, saw only the blackened ceiling, as his consciousness left him.

* * *

Michael groaned and tried to open his eyes. There was a pain in his chest like nothing he had ever felt. It felt as if a sledgehammer had hit him there. He tried to roll over, but he couldn't do that either. He waited, his heart pounding like a trip-hammer. Finally, his eyes began to focus. He was in a small, brightly lit room. There was the smell of alcohol and blood and something resembling gunpowder. He turned his head away from the wall and saw a woman's body lying on a wood and canvas army cot—like the one he was on. He swung his legs off the cot, slowly and painfully, and looked around. He saw some glass cabinets, medical supplies, surgical instruments, and bottles of something.

He looked down at his chest, where the pain was. His shirt under his jacket was soaked with blood on the left side. He took his right hand and carefully folded back the flap of his jacket. It felt heavy. He reached into the inside pocket and brought out a thick little book he had forgotten was there, a volume by St. Thomas à Kempis, a fifteenth-century monk, his favorite reading. A rifle bullet had penetrated the book and the round protruded a half inch out the back, covered in blood.

He carefully eased the jacket off his right arm and then off the left. He took off his shirt and laid it on top of the jacket. He stood up slowly and made it up to the sink at the end of the room. He looked in the mirror and saw the shallow hole the bullet had made in his chest just above his heart. It must have broken a rib, maybe even splintered it. But the heart was beating fairly strongly. Maybe the shock of the bullet had stopped it, at least for a while. He had read of boxers who had their hearts stopped by single blows to the chest. His head was swimming, and he still had to strain to focus. He opened the glass door of one of the cabinets and took out some thick wound bandages, the kind issued to medical corpsmen for their battle kits. Handy things to have on an isolated ranch, he guessed. He turned on the hot water faucet and let it run. He used a couple of the bandages to blot out the wound with hot water. He found a tube of antibiotic salve with an analgesic mixed in and applied it to the hole in his chest. Then he taped one of the bandages over it. He started looking for some surgical-grade antibiotic, but there was none in any of the unlocked cabinets. As he was standing there, still in a haze, trying to decide whether to force one of the locked cabinets, Colonel Morales walked in.

"My God! Michael! I thought you were dead! How . . . What . . ."

Michael managed a faint smile.

"The old 'holy book in the pocket' trick, Lorenzo. Look at that." He pointed over to the cot where the book lay on top of his shirt and jacket. Lorenzo walked over and picked it up.

"*Madre de Dios*! A charmed life—*sin duda*—without doubt." He laid the book back down. "Michael, I don't know what to say. I felt your pulse; there was none. And then when I saw the blood and bullet hole over the heart, I just assumed . . . Well, thanks be to God you're all right. I suppose you saw poor Jean." He turned and looked at the pathetic figure on the other cot. He went over to one of the cabinets, got out a thin cotton blanket, and pulled it over her body and face.

"I don't have a very clear memory of what happened, Lorenzo. Who shot us?"

"I'm afraid she shot you, Michael. By mistake. She was aiming at me. I guess you were fortunate she had Maggie's little thirty-thirty with the low grain load. The deputy killed Jean with his three fifty-seven." He stopped and got a peculiar look on his face. "You know, Michael, in all my years in the army, I never had anyone take a bullet for me. I owe you my life, my friend."

Michael went back and slowly sat down on his cot. He put his head in his hands. "Do you remember the old legend of the unrepentant sinner, Lorenzo? The one whose sins were so great that Christ doomed him to wander the earth until the Second Coming? That's who I feel like. No death for Michael, no release for Michael—and no forgiveness, either."

Lorenzo walked over and stood in front of him, his hands on his hips.

"I am surprised at you, Comandante," he said, "that you—a priest—would forget the greatest virtue a man can have. Self-sacrifice. Christ himself was the greatest example." He picked up the small volume from the cot and held it out to him.

"Look. Look at the title on this book. This is the book that for two hundred years outsold the Bible in Europe. Look at it."

Michael took the book and looked at it involuntarily. He already knew the title well, *My Imitation of Christ*.

"Now, stop feeling sorry for yourself for ten minutes and let's figure out what to do. You need to know a couple of things—first, the sheriff found a spent shell casing down by Sutter's body, a thirty-thirty. Maggie has the only thirty-thirty rifle on the place, and I think the sheriff is going to send the two casings to the state lab for comparison."

"The two casings?"

"The one from the road and the one from the round Jean shot you with. He also knows you were carrying Maggie's rifle when you found Sutter's body. You see what this means?"

"Yes, but . . . What about the red truck? Is he going to try to trace it? That has to figure into his thinking, doesn't it?"

Lorenzo looked at him steadily.

"The sheriff found no red truck, Michael. Only the thirty-thirty shell, lying ten feet away from Sutter's body."

Michael shook his head.

"I guess the only thing for me is to stay dead. It simplifies everything for everybody."

"You just may be right, Comandante. Suppose the lab finds that the two shells were fired by Maggie's rifle. I certainly will not sit by and see you go to prison for something you didn't do. And even if we could prove you didn't, that would not make things much easier. That would put her under suspicion. You begin to see?"

"I had already thought of it, Lorenzo, as improbable as it seems. But I will go to prison before I see her made a suspect."

Lorenzo sat quietly for a moment and then spoke again.

"I told the sheriff that I wanted to keep you and Jean here, so that a quick funeral Mass can be said and the two of you interred in the family cemetery. He seemed satisfied with that. You seemed to be his only suspect, so, with you dead, he can call the case solved. He may be a casual sort, but he's a smart old bird. I don't think he wants this to go any further either."

"What do you propose?"

"The obvious. I will have Father Guitierrez come out and say Mass over two closed caskets, and I will have them interred the same day. One will be marked with your name. And by that time, you can be miles away. Do you agree?"

Michael sat still. Twice now, he had been declared prematurely dead. Maybe whoever was following him would give up. But there was another danger.

"Lorenzo, there is something I must tell you. It may be that I am paranoid, but I believe al-Qaeda has followed me from the day I left the monastery in New Mexico. I think that they are whom the truck belongs to. The nonexistent red truck that only I can see, apparently. But if I'm right, and they trace me here or have, as I believe, already traced me here, then you and Maggie could be in great danger. They must know who you are. The Arab newspaper, *Al Jazeera*, called you the Butcher of Ambon. Do you remember?"

"I remember, Comandante. And I regarded it then, as now, a badge of honor. They may find I am not so easy to kill."

"What about Maggie? She can't stay penned up here the rest of her life, afraid to step foot off the ranch. Is that the life you want for her?"

"No. And it's not a life I am going to live, either, one of fear and trepidation. We just fought a war to make sure no Christians have to live that kind of life anymore. But whether you leave here alive or dead, it's a risk I must take."

Michael stood up unsteadily.

"All right, then. But I suggest you contact the FBI right away. You owe Maggie that much. And—if I may presume further on your hospitality—do you think I could swap my truck for one of yours? If I am being followed, it's pretty clear they know what I'm driving."

"Yes, of course. I have a new Ford 150, blue, with Nevada plates. And it has a topper. I will put the registration in the glove box. I will leave enough of your gear in your truck to avoid suspicion if the sheriff manages to think of looking at it. And I will make sure your new one is fully supplied and equipped. I will do it myself, so the *vaqueros* do not have to answer any questions the sheriff may have. I will also put some medical supplies in it. You may have a charmed life, but it's one that needs lots of attending to." He smiled slightly. "Do you have a weapon?"

"I have a Sig Sauer nine-millimeter."

"I will give you one of my .30-06s with plenty of ammunition. And a Glock ten-millimeter. You may not need it, but if you do, you won't want for the means to defend yourself."

"Thank you, Lorenzo."

Lorenzo locked the door to the infirmary when he left. About an hour after dark, Michael heard the door being unlocked. Lorenzo came in, handed him the keys to the truck, and led him out to where it was parked. Michael climbed in the cab and looked back at him.

"*Adios, mi compadre,*" said Michael. "*Vaya con Dios.*"

"*Adios, Comandante. Vaya con cuidado.* Take care, my friend."

* * *

Breuger had spent the first half hour just driving around through the streets of Ely, Nevada. He could easily have done it in fifteen minutes, but he wanted to get a cautionary look for any suspicious vehicles. It had once been a prosperous mining town and was having some resurgence because of new techniques for extracting ore. It had a very mixed population, from what he could see, but nothing much different from any other lonely western town. He drove back to the sheriff's office he had spotted earlier, parked, and went in.

A pleasant-looking woman with red hair and a sunburn sat at a desk with radios stacked in a tier on a wall shelf just above the desk. She got up when he came in and went forward to what looked like an administration desk.

"May I help you, sir?"

"Yes. I am looking for the ranch of a friend of mine, a man from Spain, a Colonel Morales. I wonder if you could help me. This country all looks the same." He forced an embarrassed smile.

"Oh, yeah. Rancho Santiago. Biggest ranch in the state, some people say. Are you inquiring about the killings?"

"The killings?"

"Yeah. Just yesterday. Three in one day. Never seen the like in this town. Not in about a hundred years, anyways. Their foreman and the lady who owned it, or used to own it, and a stranger, some friend of the colonel's."

A man came out of one of the inner office doors. He was wearing the uniform and badge of the sheriff's department. He was tall and dark and not very pleasant looking.

"I'm Deputy Scalf, mister. Was there something you wanted? Sally, why don't you go about your business and stop blabbing about department business."

Sally got a miffed look on her face. She went back to her communications desk and sat down. Breuger turned to face the menacing-looking man, assessing him instinctively, and was not impressed.

"Yes, Deputy. I am trying to find an old friend, and the lady was kind enough to offer some help. I wonder if you could give me some directions to the ranch of Colonel Morales?"

"Just exactly what do you want with him?"

"That is a private affair. But since you ask, I was invited to stay with him for a while. I have come a long way to see him."

Deputy Scalf screwed up his face as he usually did when he was trying to figure something out.

"He had another visitor just yesterday, a man named Kintner. You wouldn't happen to know him, would you?"

"As a matter of fact, I do, from some years back. I would look forward to seeing him again."

"Well, you missed your chance. He was shot through the heart yesterday. Now, let me ask you one more time. What's your business with the colonel?"

Breuger was very still. He had not expected this news. This changed everything. Or did it? He had better go have a talk with Morales. He turned and started out of the office.

The deputy grabbed his left arm from behind. Breuger grabbed his wrist with his right hand and wheeled around, twisting the deputy's arm up and behind his back. He pushed up on the arm, twisting it in the socket, and pushed the man's head down to the floor. Then he drew back his left fist and put a straight karate chop into the back of his neck. Scalf went limp and unconscious to the floor. Breuger stood up and calmly walked out of the office. Sally sat dumbfounded, frozen in her chair. The whole episode had lasted about four seconds.

He had all the information he needed, for now, including the identity of the "stranger," whom the clerk had said was a friend of Morales. He would go find a motel somewhere in town and wait for an extra day before proceeding further. There might still be police or FBI at the ranch investigating the killings the woman had spoken of. He found a motel and pulled up in the parking lot. He checked his GPS receiver and called Marcel. When he had him on the line, he brought Marcel up to speed on the killings and gave the coordinates from his GPS to pass on to Agent Marquette. He got out and went toward the motel office to check in, thinking about the best way to use the considerable talents of Elise Marquette in this hectic chase.

* * *

Ken Russell was watching the GPS receiver on his dashboard as it ticked down to the turnoff to the ranch. At about a mile to go, he looked ahead and spotted what looked like a turnoff to the left. There was no traffic and hadn't been for the last hour. He slowed and turned off up the road. A small sign just past the cattleguard was beautifully lettered in faded red and gold: *Rancho Santiago*, and underneath it the registered brand, the letter M with a line through the middle. The bar M, Russell guessed. He drove on up the gradual rise, and as he got to the top, he noticed a car had pulled off the road behind him about a mile back. He drove on over the rise, pulled off the road, and stopped. He popped the hood, got out of the car, and raised it. Then he stepped over to the right front fender and waited, his hand on the HK ten-millimeter under his coat.

A few minutes later, a banged-up Chevy SUV topped the rise and slowed to a stop just opposite Ken's car. A man got out and walked over to where he stood. He was an old man, wearing black trousers and jacket and scuffed black brogans. He had on a Roman collar.

"Are you in trouble, my friend? Can I be of some help?"

After a moment, Russell relaxed and closed the hood. He came around to where the old man stood.

"No, Father, just checking. Thought I heard something funny with the engine. Are you headed for the ranch?"

"Yes. A sad duty, but one which I am honored to perform for the family. I am saying the Mass today for the repose of the sister-in-law and the friend of Colonel Morales. I am semiretired, but I still say Mass at the rancho for the Morales family, as I have done for fifty years. Are you attending, my son?"

"Did you say 'repose,' Father? You're saying the funeral Mass?"

"Yes. Very sad business. Death of any kind is always a loss for the family, but . . . to see them killed in such a violent way, it makes one doubly sad. If you are a friend of the family—"

"No. Just here on some business. I didn't know there was to be a funeral. My business can wait, I suppose."

"Well, you are welcome to attend, I am sure. I will speak to the colonel. What is your name?"

"My name is Russell, but the colonel doesn't know me. I will come along, though, and pay my respects, if that is all right."

The priest got back into his vehicle and drove on toward the ranch. Russell followed in the FBI car. When they drove into the hacienda compound, Colonel Morales was waiting, having seen their approach from the cemetery where he had been checking on the two excavations made by his men. One was next to his brother's grave and the other in a lonely corner, away from the other graves of the family. The priest stopped, got out of his SUV, and walked up to Morales. Ken stayed in his car, waiting to be invited to get out. The colonel was saying something to the priest that apparently he didn't expect. It seemed to Ken that he registered surprise and then stood shaking his head, as if the colonel had just given him more bad news. After a couple of minutes, the colonel walked toward his car and Ken got out.

"Are you from the FBI?" Colonel Morales fixed him with a hard stare.

"Yes, as it happens, sir, I am a liaison. But I didn't mean to intrude. I will come some other time if you—"

"No, no. That is all right. I didn't expect you so soon after my call. You are welcome to wait or attend the Mass, as you prefer."

"Thank you." He held out his hand. "My name is Ken Russell, sir. And I'm sorry for your loss."

"Yes, yes, a great loss. My late brother's wife and my good friend from some years ago. From the late war. Come inside. There are some refreshments." He turned and walked back toward the house.

Russell waited just a moment, looking around at all the buildings and terrain, filing it away. Then he followed Father Guitierrez and Colonel Morales into the house. There were many expensive items in the decor, Ken noticed, but there was something else, something peculiar. All the lights were on, and the old-fashioned colonial-style shutters had been closed. Each of the shutters had a cross cut into them, not for religious purposes, but as rifle ports, to provide access for a wide field of fire, side to side and up and down. In Spanish colonial times, such defensive measures were necessary against the constant raids of Indian tribes. Some haciendas built in the last century still added them as reminders of the traditions and travails of the past. Could the colonel be expecting some kind of attack? And if so, from whom?

"We will have refreshments on the patio, if no one objects," he said. "I keep the rest of the house shuttered in the daytime against the heat. I was just telling Father Guitierrez, Mr. Russell, that my niece, Maggie, will not be joining us. She is . . . distraught . . . and I am letting her rest. Please come this way." He gestured toward the side patio, where two servants waited with wine, sliced fruit, and some breads.

After several minutes, with the three chatting about the weather and other trivialities, one of the cowboys who had been in the cemetery came up and stood, hat in hand, about twenty feet away. Colonel Morales got up and went to him, listened briefly, and then came back to the patio.

"Everything is in readiness, Father." He took the old man's elbow and guided him gently toward the little chapel in the corner of the compound, beside the cemetery. Inside the chapel, the colonel and Father Guitierrez genuflected toward the altar where the tabernacle was, and Colonel Morales went and sat in the front row of seats. The two caskets were closed and sealed. The priest walked up to the altar and bowed and then gestured to the altar boys, two children from ranch families, all of whom lived close to the compound. The church was almost filled with other ranch family members, and Ken walked all the way to the back row and sat down.

"In nomini Patris, et Filii, et Spiritui Sancti. Amen." The priest began the Mass, and some minutes into the ceremony, the altar boys began having some difficulty with the variations from the normal Sunday Mass, but Father Guitierrez was oblivious to their little mistakes. At the colonel's request, the homily was short, with little emphasis on Jean's role as wife and mother and mentioning only that Father Michael Francis Kintner had died in an act of self-sacrifice. After Communion, everyone in the church walked out to the cemetery and assembled around the two open graves where they waited for the *vaqueros* to bring the caskets out and put them on the ropes laid out beside the graves. The priest went first to the grave of Michael. He took the silver mace of holy water and sprinkled it on the casket, reciting: "Rore coelesti perfundat et perficiat animam tuam Deus."

The vaqueros took hold of the ropes beneath the coffin and lowered it into the ground. The wind freshened and stung the faces of the little gathering with sand.

"Sume terrâ quod tuum est, sumat Deus quod suum est, corpus de terrâ formatum, spiritus de coelo inspiratus est."

Father Guitierrez scattered earth from his hand three times upon the coffin. Then he proceeded to the other grave.

Ken decided to slip away from the proceedings. He walked out the main entrance of the compound and stood staring down the road as if he were trying to see something a thousand miles away. He hadn't bargained on running into something like this when he arrived at where Kintner had last been. Subconsciously, he had been expecting something, but it hadn't been this. He had never attended a funeral Mass before, and the sparse, lonely setting had set him to thinking about things he had no wish to recall. What in God's name was this all about? *Everything ends in death. But why do we spend so much of our lives trying to kill each other? Or to get ourselves killed?* Nothing made any sense anymore. Then, as if in mocking reply to his thoughts, he heard automatic rifle fire from somewhere in the direction of the highway.

* * *

The sheriff walked brusquely through the door and slammed it behind him.

"Sally, what the hell was that call all about? 'Officer down in your office!' Don't you know that channel is monitored by every lawdog in the county? First thing you know, we'll have the state police in here! You never use that phrase unless an officer has been shot or killed."

"Sorry, Sheriff, I didn't know what else to say. When I saw Lyle get punched out—"

"What? Punched out by who? Where the hell is he?"

Deputy Scalf came sheepishly out of the bathroom, holding a wet towel to the back of his neck. The sheriff walked over to him and stood about a foot in front of him.

"Can't I even make the rounds without you getting things screwed up? What the hell happened?"

"Sorry, Sam, I was interrogating this suspicious character when he caught me with my back turned and laid me out with something."

Sally rolled her eyes and turned back to her desk.

"What kind of suspicious character? Why were you questioning him?"

"Man come in, spoke with a funny accent, started asking questions about the killings out at the Morales ranch. Claimed he was just going over there for a visit, but he didn't know the way. Sounded mighty suspicious to me."

"You're not making any sense. Sally, were you here? Did he talk to you?"

"Yeah, Sam. He seemed nice and polite. Wasn't no Hispanic; sounded like he was French or something. Then Lyle grabbed him, and the man just laid him out."

The sheriff wiped his hand over his face, trying to restrain himself from grinning. Then he looked back at Scalf.

"Come on, Deputy; let's get out there."

They drove without talking for a while, with lights and siren, about eighty miles an hour. He tried never to drive so fast that he couldn't see cattle and stop for them. There were few fences out here, open range being the norm. Finally, the deputy got up his courage and spoke.

"Sheriff, I know you said yesterday you wanted to let this thing be, but there's something going on out there we ought to find out about. Just too damn many strangers in this, if you ask me."

"Well, I think you're right, for once, Lyle." His temper had begun to cool, and he was feeling a little sorry for his deputy. He had pretty good instincts, even if he was afflicted with a room-temperature IQ. The sheriff had never been satisfied with the coroner's report on the death of the colonel's brother; there had to be a connection with the current dustup, but he wasn't sure just what.

"I'm going to get to the bottom of this. I knew the colonel wasn't telling all he knew, but this puts a different light on it." He looked over at his deputy. "And this time, Lyle, for God's sake, leave your gun in the holster. If there's any trouble, you just follow my lead, all right?"

When they got to the turnoff to the ranch, the sheriff slowed just enough to make the turn without skidding out of control and then increased his speed again. Up ahead was a cloud of dust on the top of the rise where some vehicle had evidently passed. He still had his lights and siren going, because whatever was going on out here was likely already out of hand. He topped the rise and saw down below the same huge cloud of dust, stirred up by at least three vehicles that he could see—a green sedan, a brown Toyota, and a white van bringing up the rear. As he started to close on them, the van pulled abruptly off the road and then the Toyota, followed by the sedan. Men spilled out of each vehicle, running for the brush alongside of the road. He could see that at least a couple of the men were carrying weapons. He was closing fast, but he didn't want to get himself in the middle of them. He fishtailed to a stop a few yards short of the van, reached up to the overhead rack, and got his shotgun. Scalf drew his Colt Python and rolled out, running in a crouch toward a cluster of junipers.

The sheriff sprinted for the brush on the other side of the road and made it just as a spray of rounds from a Kalashnikov automatic rifle tore open his chest and stomach.

* * *

Colonel Morales jerked his head up at the sound and stepped back away from Jean's open grave. He quickly motioned for the two vaqueros to follow him and ran for the hacienda. He let them catch up to him.

"Get what men you can find and tell them to grab some rifles and ammo and follow me!"

He ran into the house, pulled open his gun cabinet, took out a .30-.06 and a box of 250-grain ammo, and ran to the front driveway. He saw that Kintner's truck was still parked in the loop, closer than any of his vehicles. He opened the door, saw that the keys were in it, got in, and started it up. As he cleared the main gate to the compound, he slowed and looked toward the bunkhouse. He saw that some of the men were already in two jeeps and coming toward him. He floored the accelerator and drove down the road. About a half mile ahead, he could see the black FBI car Russell had come in, also traveling at high speed. A mile farther on, Russell turned his car off the road at a flat spot and drove off into the brush, still at high speed. Morales couldn't see what was ahead of Russell because of the dust his car had raised. He figured the man knew what he was doing, so when he reached the same spot, he followed him but stopped a few yards off the road, got out of the truck, and waited for the two jeeps to catch up. He ran over to them and motioned for them to stay in the vehicles. There were four cowboys in each one, and they all had rifles. He spoke to the men in the trailing jeep first.

"Ramon, go back and block the road to the hacienda with your jeep, and then two of you get up on that ridge. Anybody coming up that way, shoot them down." He pointed toward the low ridge that ran the length of the road just to the west. "You other two pick some cover on each side of the road near the jeep and shoot anyone you don't know who tries to get past."

He went back to the other jeep.

"Paco, you follow me toward that black car. He's an FBI man, so don't shoot him. Park a good distance behind where I do and take an interval in a line between where I stop and the road. I'll be up with the FBI man. Anybody trying to get past you, cut them down. *Comprende?*"

"*Patron*, who is it? What's going on?"

"I think it is the same people who killed Bob Sutter. I don't know who they are or what they want, but I'm not going to let any of them leave here alive."

He got back in the truck and drove up to within a few yards of Russell's car. He got out and sprinted in a crouch toward it. He saw that Russell was squatting down by the side of his car, holding an M16 and waiting for Morales to catch up. When he did, they both rose and looked toward the line of vehicles parked alongside of the road. The sheriff's car was just behind them, its red and blue lights still flashing. Morales put his hand on Russell's shoulder.

"Can you see anyone from the sheriff's car?"

"Yeah. There's a body in the ditch just this side of it. I don't know if there was anyone else in it or not. I haven't heard any—"

A low, booming pistol shot came from the other side of the road. It was followed immediately by two long bursts of automatic rifle fire.

"That pistol sounds like the deputy's Colt. I heard it yesterday."

Russell looked at him quizzically, but Morales didn't say anything more.

"What do you think is going on, Colonel? Has this got any connection with Kintner's death?"

"Yes, I believe it does. Kintner told me just before he . . . died . . . that he thought he was being followed by some al-Qaeda operatives. I didn't believe him then, but I do now. I think you must know who Kintner is—was—don't you?"

"Yes, I do. How are your men deployed?"

"I have two on the ridge, two on the road, and four in defilade out to the left. I propose to move in on line until we make contact. That is unless you have called in an air strike."

Russell smiled.

"Well, if this had happened a day or two from now, I believe I might have been able to. But no, your plan is sound. I am going to try to make it to the sheriff's car, maybe link up with the deputy. Do you think there are any more people with him?"

"No. They pretty much travel by twos. Let's move out."

Morales gave a brief whistle and motioned to his men to stay low and move forward. The six men moved forward in a crouch, Russell veering out wider to the right to make an arced path toward the sheriff's car. They had moved in about fifty yards when they saw three men rise up and run low toward the squad car. Fire from right and left splattered the car and knocked out its lights. Two more automatic weapons opened up on the line of men with Morales, driving them into the dirt. *Smart,* thought the colonel. *They know their tactics.*

The colonel whistled again, and when his men looked at him, he motioned for them to move forward in a zigzag pattern by waving his hand in an "S" through the air. They knew what he wanted. Morales stayed where he was for a moment, waiting for someone near the road to show himself. One man rose up partway with his weapon, and Morales shot him dead. Another rose up immediately and fired in his direction, the rounds kicking up dirt only a few feet away. Morales shifted his position forward and to the right a few yards to wait for someone else to show. As he was moving, two men rose up with their Kalashnikovs, and a cowboy shot one of them. The other sprayed the brush along the line of Morales's men, but he couldn't tell if anyone was hit. He looked off to the right for Russell, but he couldn't spot him. He moved forward again, this time jinking to the left.

He raised his head and saw the three men who were trying to get to the squad car cross the road into a stand of juniper. He heard the deputy fire off three quick rounds, quickly drowned out by a long burst of automatic fire. Silence followed. The three men started running back across the road, and the unmistakable sound of an M16 cut them down. *Ole for the FBI!* thought Morales—if that was what he was.

But that left Russell exposed, and he knew he and his men had to close fast. He whistled loud and long, and he and his four men started running low, converging toward the area they were being fired upon from. Two hostiles rose up, several yards to the left of where they had been, and opened up. The cowboy on the left end of the line fell. The three others took careful aim and shot the two men who had just fired on their *compadre* and then went back to the dirt and waited briefly. Then they got up and began to run in their zigzag pattern again. *They would make pretty good soldiers,* thought the colonel. Maybe a couple of them had been.

Morales heard the M16 again but couldn't see anything. Then he saw two men run across the road toward the ridge, and three others rose and started running low toward the advancing line of cowboys, firing their weapons in short bursts, spraying the brush. Four .30-06s and an M16 opened up in response, and the three coming toward them jerked crazily and fell, some of them obviously hit more than once. Two more .30-06 reports from the ridge, and the two who had crossed the road fell. Then there was silence.

Chapter 8

The pain was getting much worse now, and he was becoming groggy with it and the darkness and the hours he had been driving. He spotted a wide place in the road ahead and pulled off into it. The colonel said he would pack a medical kit. He had better look for it and try to find some painkillers. He looked around the cab interior closely for the first time—tan leather upholstery, bucket seats, disc player, XM radio, even a GPS receiver. Morales evidently liked the amenities. There were some things in the seat to his right: a flat canteen and a cylindrical plastic bottle. He picked it up and read the label. Oxycodone. The colonel had thought of everything. He looked up and saw a .30-06 rifle in the overhead rack with a box of shells in a small compartment.

He took two of the pills and washed them down with water from the canteen. Then he got out to stretch his legs. He walked over toward the bushes and relieved himself and then decided to take a quick look in the back to see what else Morales had packed. He opened the latch on the topper door, raised it, and looked inside. Something moved in the darkness and then sat up. It was Maggie.

"Michael. Thank goodness you stopped. I am about floated."

"Maggie! What in the name of—? How did you get in there?"

"I saw Uncle Lorenzo unpacking some things from your truck and putting them in his, and I asked him about it. He didn't want to tell me, but finally he said that God had saved you from death by obstructing the bullet. I didn't know what he meant, but I was overjoyed that you were still alive. Then he said that he and you had decided to—well, you know. That's when I decided to pack a few things and stow away."

"But he'll be worried about you. What do you think he—"

"No, I left him a note in an envelope on my bed. I explained that—well, never mind that now."

She put her leg over the tailgate and climbed out.

"If you'll turn your head, I am going to take a break too." She grinned at him and walked off toward the brush. Michael closed the topper door and walked back up to the driver's door, away from where Maggie was doing whatever she was doing. In a few minutes, she was back. They climbed into the truck and drove off. Kintner wasn't at all happy that Maggie was along. When they got on his trail again, it was going to be all he could do to keep himself alive. And if she should fall into their hands—well, he couldn't bear thinking about that. Maybe he should just leave her somewhere and call Lorenzo to come and get her. But he knew she would feel betrayed. He didn't much blame her for trying to get away, at least for a while. But it might be out of the frying pan and into the fire for her.

"Maggie, what did you tell your uncle in the note? Did you tell him when you were planning on coming back?"

"No," she said, after a moment. "I'm not going back."

"But you know my situation. The people who are following me could catch up anytime. And I've already lived some weeks longer than the doctors in Rome gave me. There's no future for you here with me."

"There's no future for me back at the ranch either. I killed Bob Sutter. And now the colonel knows it too."

"What? I can't believe it. But why? I suppose you thought you had good reason, but was it worth ruining your life for?"

"My life was already ruined. At least back there. I knew about my mother and Bob. Even before Uncle Lorenzo showed up. What's worse, I had guessed that they were planning to kill Daddy and I wasn't able to do a thing to stop it. I guess I hoped they would never go through with it. Then they brought Daddy's body back from that hunting trip . . ." She put her head down as if she were about to cry but then raised it up again.

"Why didn't you go to your mother about it? Have it out with her, try to talk some sense—"

"I did. More than once. But I couldn't tell her about . . . You see, Bob had started coming into my room too."

"O, my God, Maggie. Couldn't you go to your dad?"

"He was already dead by then. And I-I liked him coming to me. I thought I was in love with him. And I thought he was in love with me. I blamed my mother for the fact that he hadn't taken me away with him like he promised. He kept saying that Jean was going to sell the ranch and split the money with him. Then we could go away together. I know it sounds stupid now, but I believed him."

Kintner sat very still. A slow anger was starting to build in him. Sutter deserved what he got; that was certain. If he had known everything earlier, he might have killed Sutter himself. He knew the colonel would have if he had known about him and Maggie. What made people like Sutter what they were? Then he remembered what he had thought after killing that man at the cantina. Creatures without souls. Were they born that way, or had they killed it in themselves? And did it really matter? People without redemption. Even Holy Scripture mentioned it in a few places, properly translated. At seminary, he was taught that the soul was that thing in humans by which God communicated with them. Not literally perhaps, as in Old Testament tradition, but through spiritual perception. If there was no link to God, then there was no soul. How could there be?

"How did it happen, Maggie? I was with you almost all the time I was at the ranch."

"It was the morning I overheard you talking with Lorenzo in the kitchen. I knew from what he said that he would eventually kill Bob. And I thought I knew what Mom would do if he did. That part almost came true, but you got between her and the colonel. I felt worse about that, in a way, then I would have if she had killed Uncle Lorenzo.

"Anyway, I waited until about an hour after you and Uncle Lorenzo went back to bed. Then I went over to Bob's quarters and got him up. I held the rifle on him and told him he was going to drive me down to the highway. Told him I had to talk to him, and if he wouldn't, I was going to shoot him. I don't think he really believed I would, but he got up and dressed, and we got in the jeep and drove down there toward the turnoff."

"What time was this? Did you notice?"

"I think it was about four in the morning. It was before first light. Neither one of us said anything on the way down to the highway. When we got down almost to the turnoff, Bob stopped the jeep. He told me this whole thing was stupid, and what did I think I was doing anyway? He said he wasn't going anywhere with me, that I was just a stupid little . . . something or other and that I had better give him the rifle so we could get back."

Maggie choked back a sob and then began again. "I shot him where he sat, and he just fell out of the jeep onto the road. I got out and went around to look at him. I saw the bullet hole, and I knew he was dead. I started to get scared. I couldn't think up any good excuse for what I had done. Then I looked around for the shell casing that I had ejected when I chambered another round. I had just done it instinctively, as Daddy had taught me. But I couldn't find it. So I just drove the jeep on back and left it where Bob always parked it. It was starting to get light, and I took my shirt off and wiped the seat and dashboard in case there were any blood spatters. But there weren't any that I could see. Then I went inside and got showered and dressed and waited for everyone to get up."

"So when we went for a ride after breakfast, you figured we would discover the body together and that would perhaps give you some kind of alibi?"

"That was what I had in my mind, but when we started to get close to where I had left him, I lost my nerve and started crying. I couldn't bear to look at him again."

Kintner remembered how he had felt, holding her while she wept there on the road. Then he remembered the red pickup. He really must have been delusional. Had he only imagined actually opening the truck door and finding Sutter? He supposed anything was possible. But what was he going to do with Maggie? Maybe she would get tired of being with him in a day or two. And maybe there was a way she could help him. When the radiation poisoning finally finished him, she could see to it that things were handled properly. He could give her some numbers to call. But for now, he had to get them both to someplace where they could rest and where he could figure out how he was going to keep running with Maggie to take care of.

After they were both back in the truck, he started it up and pulled back onto the road. In a few minutes, he spotted a highway marker. US 50 West. Perfect. He remembered reading once that the Nevada leg of this transcontinental highway was the loneliest in the world. He needed solitude, and he needed an outside chance of spotting anyone following. That should be a lot easier out here.

The eastern sky was getting lighter, and the painkiller was having its effect. But he needed some sleep.

"Maggie, did you get any rest in the back? Could you take over the driving for a while? I'm about to run off the road. Took some pills your uncle gave me."

"Sure. I feel okay."

He pulled onto the shoulder of the road, and they changed seats. Michael reclined the back of the passenger seat and closed his eyes.

* * *

Maggie pulled out and continued the drive. She glanced over at Michael. He looked as if he were already asleep. Good. Now she could act as if she were protecting him for a change. As she drove, she could feel the burden of the last several weeks lifting from her. It had been so long since she had felt anything resembling peace. Only a few months ago, she had enjoyed the many small, what some would call "girlish" predilections, which had pretty much dominated her life at the ranch. But she felt much older now. The tortuous experiences of her father's death, her mother's depredations with Bob, and her own had changed her irrevocably. Whatever had been left of her girlhood at seventeen was gone. She felt nothing but an aching sadness and the terrible loss of innocence and self-respect. She glanced back over to where Michael was sleeping. Something deep down inside of her stirred, something she didn't understand.

* * *

Michael stirred in his sleep and began to dream. The images were violent and confused, a mixture of his recent experiences in the Ninth Crusade but interspersed with scenes from some earlier time, as if they were a reflection not of this century but of a thousand years ago, the flash of sword and shield, the scream of horses and men in rage and agony, the hot sun scorching the blood-soaked sand. The screams merged into the high-pitched roar of his fighter jet, climbing out from the runway at Har-Megiddo to meet the Syrian MIG 29s attacking the Israeli armored divisions driving north from the Golan Heights.

Michael uttered a low groan and twisted in the seat. Maggie looked over at him, assuming that he must still be in physical pain from the gunshot wound. She slowed the truck and pulled over on the shoulder of the road, stopped, and cut the engine. There was no traffic, and she wondered if she should wake him or let his anguish run its course. Who was he, really? What was he? The fierce warrior, the gallant knight, the Jesuit priest? All of them or none? The burgeoning feeling of affection she was starting to have for him suddenly seemed out of place. How could she help him? How could she love him, when there were so many mysteries that she did not and might never be able to understand? She sat still for long time and then started the engine again and drove off.

* * *

Msgr. Bohemund walked down the steps from the Old Executive Office Building after his meeting with General Kane and got into his limousine. The driver got back into the car and turned to his passenger in the back.

"Will you be going back to the consulate, Monsignor, or to your hotel?"

Robert paused, trying to pull his thoughts away from the disheartening meeting with the national security advisor to the mundane details of what to do with the rest of his day. There was so much to decide and so little time to do it. He knew that if the FBI or anyone else got to Kintner first, there wasn't going to be anything he could do. His past experience with the DGSE before he had become a priest had taught him that preemptive action was always the better option. But against the forces already arrayed against Kintner, how could anyone, even with the resources of the church behind him, hope to succeed? Perhaps he should first make use of what the church had always insisted upon as the first step, *in extremis*—prayer. *Lex orandi, lex credendi:* Law of prayer is the law of belief.

"Take me somewhere I can pray in relative quiet, if there is someplace near, dri—I'm sorry, I've forgotten your name . . ."

"My name is Anthony, Monsignor. There are several nearby churches, but there is a special Mass being held today in the Crypt Church at the Basilica of the Immaculate Conception in northeast

Washington. Would you like to attend and pray at one of the chapels inside the church afterward?"

"I don't think so, Anthony. I need some quiet time . . ."

"The reason I brought it up, sir, is that it is a Mass for members of the Keys troops, at least for those in driving distance. We requested from the archbishop after the end of the Crusade if we might have our own Mass once a month, and—"

"Did you say 'we'? Were you in the order?"

"I was never out of it, Monsignor; none of us have left it, so far as I know."

Robert was taken aback; he had assumed that, with the general disarmament, most of the members of the Ordo Sacer Clavium Sancti Petri, the Sacred Order of the Keys of Saint Peter, had just reverted to civilian status. But now that he thought of it, how could they? The order had been established by the late pope himself, and it had never been disestablished. Once in Holy Orders, always in Holy Orders. That included him.

"In that case, take me there, by all means. There may even be someone there I know."

"They will all know who you are, Knight Commander. If you would like to concelebrate the Mass, I can call ahead and—"

"No. No, I wouldn't wish to interfere with the plans of the principal celebrant . . . By the way, who is he?"

"It varies from month to month. There are many priests in the order, as you no doubt know."

Robert was silent, remembering the masses he had said for the Keys troops in the forward areas of the conflict—in the Middle East, the Philippines, Indonesia—and how different it was from saying Mass for the faithful in times of peace, knowing that many there would never live to hear or attend Mass again. The more he thought of it, the more perfect it seemed. This must be the will of God, not a coincidence—that he would attend this kind of Mass before setting out once more to save the lives of Keys knights.

They drove in silence for several minutes, threading their way through the traffic of the federal area of the district toward the northeast and the Catholic University of America, which lay hard by the Basilica. He had been here before, but the sight of the huge cathedral on the top of the hill took his breath away. It had been built in the Byzantine style, with a huge dome at the far end, covered in blue, orange, and yellow mosaic tiles. The bell tower, with its soaring spire as tall as the dome, stood on the left front corner of the church, by the great center arch, which was as tall as the top of the building. Inset several feet inside the arch was a circular mosaic at the top, over an entrance, which was in a protruding foyer, the whole of it flanked by finely chiseled alabaster stone, mostly unadorned but trimmed with long recessed engravings culminating at the very top with statues of St. Mary. As they parked the limousine on the right of the building, the bells in the high tower began to peal, the sound penetrating, it seemed to Bohemund, to the depths of his soul.

They dismounted from the limousine and walked toward a side door at back, where steps were located leading down into the crypt. They reached the bottom of the stairs and entered into the lowest level of the Basilica. It was a large open space with a vaulted ceiling over walls lined with small chapels and open rooms in which departed luminaries of the church now reposed in stone biers. To the right was the entrance to the Crypt Church, flanked by the Chapel of Our Lady of Lourdes, commemorating the Marian apparitions to St. Bernadette, a fourteen-year-old peasant girl at the Grotto of Massabielle in 1858. On their way to the entrance to the Crypt Church, Bohemund stopped and looked again at the statue of the apparition that Bernadette Soubirou had seen—a lovely, ghostly lady standing among the rocks of a grotto, her hands extended outward in pity to whatever supplicant might chance to kneel there in the little chapel.

Robert saw his driver waiting at the door to the Crypt Church and quickly walked over to and through it. Inside was the very heart of the National Shrine. It was reminiscent of the subterranean corridors and chambers where the early Christians gathered in secret to celebrate Mass. The back of the sanctuary was replete with mosaics of ancient scenes and personages from the earliest times of the faith.

The wooden benches and kneelers were already nearly full. All of the attendees were men dressed in austere black uniforms trimmed in gold piping on the high, stiff collars, which bore on the left side crossed keys, one embroidered in silver and the other in gold. On the right side of the collar was an insignia of military rank, small gold stars for officers and chevrons for enlisted. Gold stripes adorned the trouser legs, with one on each sleeve, regardless of rank, and with a small cross just above it. On some of the men, the collar was interrupted in front by a one-inch white, stiff linen piece—the Roman collar of a priest.

Since Bohemund and Anthony were not in uniform, they decided to sit in the back pew, which they entered, and knelt down, each saying, as was the tradition, a private prayer for beginning Mass. The magnificent floor-to-ceiling Schudi organ to the right and behind the great white marble altar began the processional music, and the congregation got to its feet, standing at attention. As the procession of altar boys and the priests and deacons entered, Robert looked to his right at the processional, hoping to see if he recognized any of the celebrants. As he did, the principal celebrant turned his head and looked straight back at Robert. Both men widened their eyes in surprise at seeing the other. *My God,* thought Robert. It was Knight Colonel Shamus Sullivan, the command staff chaplain, who had been his aide-de-camp at Crusade Headquarters in Har-Megiddo. He knew him as a fiery orator, frustrated at not being allowed to fight with the frontline Keys troops. This promised to be interesting.

Robert looked down at the floor of the center aisle as the procession passed and noticed the cuffs of the priest's trousers. They were black uniform trousers. Behind him were a deacon and subdeacon, required for a solemn Latin Mass. They, too, wore uniforms under their chasubles, which were red—worn for the "memorial to martyrs" Mass. A small, double line of choir sang the "Gloria" in the monastic, Gregorian chant.

When the procession reached the front, the priest bowed before the altar, made the sign of the cross, and recited: "In nomine Patris, et Filii, et Spiritui Sancti. Introibo ad altare Dei. Ad Deum qui laetificat juventutem meam . . ."

Robert followed the Mass, glad of the opportunity to participate in a Latin rite dating back to the earliest years of the church, which, in the beginning, said Mass in Greek. It gave him a feeling of continuity, of connection with the ancients. He knew better than all but a few of the horrendous losses sustained by the Ordo Sacer Clavium Sancti Petri and knew that the "memorial to martyrs" was dedicated to those men.

The Mass progressed through the five elements. First, the "Gloria." In the Communion verse, Robert noticed a peculiarity. This was one of the parts of the Mass that varied and was particular to each Mass. In English, the gospel scripture was read as: "Yeshua says: People perhaps think that I have come to cast peace upon the world, but they do not know that I have come to cast divisions upon the earth—fire, sword, war," and also: "A vine has been planted without the Father, and as it is not viable, it shall be pulled up by its roots and destroyed." The quotes were similar to readings from the Gospel of Matthew, but Robert could swear that they were from the Gnostic Gospel of Thomas. If so, it was the rankest heresy to read them at Mass. He wondered if the archbishop of Washington had ever attended one of these masses. It seemed highly doubtful.

Then, the "Credo": "Credo in unum Deum, Patrem omnipotentum, factorum coeli et terrae . . ." The Nicene Creed was recited. Then: "Sanctus, Sanctus, Sanctus, Dominus Deus Sabaoth . . ." Father Sullivan then consecrated the Host: "Qui pridie quam pateretur accepit panem in sanctus ac venerabilis . . ."

During the dispensing of Communion, Robert remembered how it was taken on the battlefield in Syria, when the mournful sounds of battle could be heard in the distance and the smoke and smell of cordite permeated the air. What a contrast it was from this peaceful place in the crypt of a beautiful basilica. What a contradiction it had been, the rites of holy sacrament and the sound of men, women, and children being killed a few kilometers away. Yet, not a contradiction. What was the Mass if not a sacrifice, an oblation? He remembered a line from T. S. Eliot's *Journey of the Magi*: "I should be glad of another death."

Finally, the homily—and another shock, when, in the middle, Father Sullivan asserted: "Let us take a lesson from *Le Milieu Divin*, by Father Teilhard de Chardin: "However marred by our faults, or however desperate in its circumstances our position may be, we can, by a total reordering, completely correct the world that surrounds us and conduct our lives in a favorable sense. Diligentibus Deum omnia convertuntur in bonum. Quomodo fiet istud? The Christian attitude toward evil lends itself to some very dangerous misunderstandings. A false interpretation of Christian resignation, together with a false idea of Christian detachment, is the principal source of the antagonisms, which make a great many non-Christians hate the gospel. Let us also remember the words of the late, beloved Father Thomas Merton, an authentic Catholic mystic, that 'A theology of love cannot afford to be sentimental. It must seek to deal realistically with the evil and injustice in the world—not to merely compromise with them.' Always keep in mind that Holy Scripture is not a suicide pact."

Robert was dumbfounded. Was this another heresy? Now there was this homily, one based upon the ideas of Father Pierre Teilhard de Chardin, which were condemned until after his death, and those of Father Thomas Merton, a man about whom a friend of his once wrote that "Merton never quite acknowledged the fixed medieval line between the sacred and profane." Still, in the context of the moment and the recent history of strife with the Muslim world, it made sense.

In the concluding rite, Father Sullivan gave the blessing: "Benedicat vos omnipotens Deus, Pater, et Filius, et Spiritus Sanctus. Amen." And then he made his announcement, to Robert's further astonishment.

"Today, gentlemen of the Ordo Sacer, I am pleased to draw your attention to the fact that the vice commandant of the order, Knight Commander Robert Bohemund, has graced us with his presence. I trust that he will forgive me if I prevail upon him to offer us some words of his wisdom?"

There was no escape, so Robert rose and started forward to the podium. He racked his brain for something innocuous to impart to the Keys troops assembled—then an idea came to him, something he should have thought of before, an inspiration.

From the lectern, he looked around at his audience. In their faces, he saw much more than expectation; he saw hopefulness, just what he needed for his message.

"Knights of the Sacred Order of the Keys of Saint Peter, I bring you greetings and blessings of His Holiness Pope John and my own humble gratitude for your holy service to the kingdom of God. It has been too long since I have had an opportunity like this, but this is most propitious, since there exists a grave threat to one of our order, a threat, not just from the evil radicals of Islam, but from the secular governments that benefitted the most from your sacrifices. That man is none other than our commandant himself, Knight Commander Michael Francis Kintner."

A murmur started growing in the assembly, getting steadily louder while Robert waited for his words to take effect.

"I know that all of you thought him dead since the announcement from the Vatican several weeks ago. I, myself, thought as much. But there is evidence that he is still alive and being pursued by the remnants of that evil army that was soundly defeated by your heroic efforts. Even more disquieting are the actions of the governments of two of our recent allies, the United States of America and the Republic of France. They have joined in the search, and I fear may mean to capture or kill Knight Commander Kintner"—Robert paused a moment for effect—"unless we can find him before they do."

The reaction this time was even louder and more animated. Robert looked at Father Sullivan, seated on the opposite side of the altar. His eyes were wide and staring, a deep anger behind them. Good. Just what he was hoping for.

"I am asking most urgently that the ranking members of your— our—order contact Father Sullivan as soon as practicable so that I can dispense to all of you the details and circumstances of our plight. If there is a Keys network in existence—and after today I am convinced that there is—please extend my plea throughout it, especially to those who are in the western part of America, where we believe that Michael is being sought. We must find him first, or else all may be lost. I must mention, also, that we believe that the Muslim terrorists are also seeking the key commanders of the late war, the Ninth Crusade, in order to assassinate them as well. This must not happen. These terrorists themselves must be hunted down and killed, since that seems to be the only thing they understand and respond to."

He paused again and looked around. Some members of the assembly were rising to their feet, those with stars on their collars and the three celebrants of the Mass were also standing. All were beginning to move toward the lectern. Robert raised his hand for silence, and everyone stopped in his tracks.

"I wish to incite no panic and no untoward publicity. This must be kept among us, under the weight of our holy oath. But let there be no mistake—the Ninth Crusade is not over."

Chapter 9

After a few hours, Maggie was also beginning to feel sleepy and decided to pull over on the shoulder of the empty highway. She turned off the engine and sat back in her seat. There was nothing in sight that was an artifact of man other than the highway. She put her side window down so she could hear and feel the desert breeze. Far off in the distance were other slight sounds of nature—a roll of distant thunder, the sharp bark of a coyote, the muted scream of a falcon, the strangled dissonance of a raven. This had been her home for all of her youth, but she now felt it becoming distant, a fading memory of the painful and deadly perversions that had slammed the door to her childhood forever.

She turned her head and looked at Michael's face, relaxed at last in repose, from which the "raveled sleeve of care" had been "knitted up." It seemed certain to her that he was somehow the key to her future, beyond just the rescue from the recent events at the ranch. How easy it would be to love him, not in the hormone-driven obsession that she had had for Bob Sutter, but in a mature and caring way, that odd but undeniable mix of the instincts of lover, sister, and mother, which were the essence of the feminine mystery. It did not matter to her that he was a good deal older and experienced in things that were foreign to her. Her intuition held sway over whatever logic might be competing for priority. That was the way it should be.

Michael stirred and opened his eyes, looking straight at Maggie. The expression on her face was one he had not seen there before.

This was not a child looking at him, not even a youthful woman, but a woman wise beyond her years. Then the pretty face softened into an impish grin.

"I hope I didn't wake you. But the time has come to talk about sleeping arrangements for the night. As you can see, there aren't a lot of options."

Michael raised his seat back and looked around. It was growing dark, and from the dark thunderheads blinking on and off like light bulbs in the distance, it looked as if there might be rain in the offing. That meant a cold supper, among other things. He rubbed his hand across his face and noticed again that his skin had stopped sloughing. Maybe that meant more time—he hoped so. He shook his head to clear the cobwebs. The pain in his chest was now down to a mere discomfort, so he would not have to take any more of the drug for a while. He looked back at Maggie.

"Any idea where we are exactly? Are we still on Highway 50?"

"Yes. The signpost a few miles back said Reno was two hundred miles away."

Michael shook his head.

"I don't much like the idea of driving in the dark, especially with a storm coming. I suggest we take a desert bathroom break while we still can without getting drowned and set up housekeeping in the back, where all the provisions are. Okay?"

They both got out of the truck and walked off in opposite directions for a few paces. The wind was picking up now, and the sand stung their faces and hands. The bird calls were gone, and the only sound now was the wind, the dreadful wind, bringing the unmistakable smell of rain. After a few minutes, they were both back in the topper-covered truck bed, with the drop-down window latched. Each of them looked into the built-in cabinets on the sides and examined the contents. There seemed to be plenty of canned goods, pate and sausages, cheeses, some bottles of wine, and Michael's bottle of Kelt cognac had made its way back with

Lorenzo's help. There were also breads and crackers and condiments. Michael saw that Lorenzo had included another weapon, a Glock 10, and a supply of cartridges. He grinned slightly but agreed with the philosophy that if he were going to be killed, it ought not to be because he didn't have enough weapons and ammunition.

Maggie unpacked her side of the truck and started laying out the plates, crystal, and silver. When Michael saw it, he grinned again.

"You can always rely upon a European gentlemen's taste," he said. "An American would have loaded us down with paper and plastic and to hell with the aesthetics."

Maggie reached into the cabinet, pulled some other things out, and held them up.

"Look. Candles and holders. I didn't know my uncle was such a romantic."

"I really don't think romance was on the colonel's mind." Michael grinned. "But I know what you mean. In his mind, there is a proper way of doing things to which a gentleman or lady must adhere. No matter what the circumstances, the proprieties must be observed."

They laid out the meal, poured the wine, and sat back. Michael rose up to a kneeling position and crossed himself. Maggie saw it, put down her knife and fork, and lowered her head.

"Bless us, O Lord, and these thy gifts, which we are about to receive from thy bounty. In nomine Patris, et Filii, et Spiritui Sancti. Amen."

Maggie also crossed herself and looked at Michael.

"Sorry, I almost forgot. The proprieties. Sometimes I almost forget there is a God. He has seemed very far away for a long time now." Then she thought she remembered something. "Michael, after you were shot, I think I heard Uncle Lorenzo tell the sheriff you were a priest. Was he just trying to protect you, or are you really a priest?"

Michael didn't answer for a long time. Then he spoke.

"Sometimes, I'm not sure anymore. I suppose I am. But I haven't said Mass since that day in the Sistine Chapel—when Pope Thomas and a lot of others were killed—including me."

Maggie felt a tightness leap into her throat, and she swallowed with difficulty, trying to keep her voice even.

"But you're still alive—and it doesn't seem as if you're getting worse. In fact, you look better than you did when I first saw you, a week ago."

"Whether that is true or not, my life as a priest may be over. The things I have done could be beyond forgiveness. Even Holy Scripture admits to the possibility of being beyond redemption."

Michael turned his attention to the food and wine.

"Let's just think about getting away for now. Nothing else seems terribly relevant."

Michael picked up his glass and held it out, as did Maggie.

"A toast to the fugitives—May God forgive us and send us help."

They set their glasses down, and Maggie smiled again.

"Please overlook my remark about 'sleeping arrangements.' I didn't realize . . ."

"No, it's all right. I wasn't offended. I wasn't always a priest, you know. In fact, I once had a family. But they were killed on an airplane by the terrorists who attacked us in 2001."

"Oh, Michael, I'm so sorry . . ."

"No, don't be. A lot of people have died since then. Whatever thoughts I may have had about retribution are buried with the deaths I caused in the war. And grief won't help my family or me. A Zen mystic once said that 'when you embrace grief, you become one with grief; and when you embrace compassion, you become one with love.'"

"That's very beautiful. It sounds like scripture."

Michael smiled and turned back to the little dinner spread before them. "Lorenzo chose well with the wine, didn't he? Your uncle is a remarkable man."

Yes, thought Maggie. *And so are you, Father Michael.*

* * *

Suleiman had been near the crest of the ridge when he saw that their position was hopeless. He had found a hiding place among the rocks and waited for a long time, afraid that they might begin to search for survivors. But no one came. He had seen Lord Ahwadi fall and knew that he must save himself so that he could report what had happened. But the vehicles were lost to him. He was leery of the cell phone, because he knew how easily they were compromised. He also knew it would not be long before the American agents discovered their motel. Ah, yes. He needed to get back there because he was not sure there weren't some incriminating items left lying around. But it was a long walk back to the motel in Ely. And he must get there soon.

He could see the highway down below and headed straight for it. If he could catch a ride soon, it would be safe to hitchhike, because it would still be awhile before news of the battle was public. And he still had his handgun. It only took a few minutes, and he was on the highway. Allah be thanked, a small truck was headed toward him, going opposite to the direction he needed to go, but that did not matter. He stepped out into the middle of the highway, raised his arms, and began to wave them back and forth. The pickup slowed, the driver not alarmed, because it was a common and expected thing in this desolate country to help someone who needed it. When the truck stopped, Suleiman walked up to the driver's side, pointed his pistol at the old man in the seat, and pulled the trigger. Then he pulled open the door and dragged the lifeless body out of the cab and over into the mesquite brush by the side of the road, partially obscuring it. Then he got into the truck, turned it around, and headed back toward Ely.

It was after midnight when he got back to the motel. He drove in slowly so as not to attract attention. On the way to the back of the motel, he saw a naked man standing in the doorway of a room. And there was a woman standing in the shadows. He was not surprised. These Americans were a depraved lot. He pulled into a parking place beside his room and went inside. Had it been his imagination, or had the man in the doorway studied him for the instant that he was in view? Perhaps he had not been an American after all.

He started searching systematically for anything that might have been overlooked when they left yesterday morning. He had left strict instructions at the motel desk that no maid service was wanted. Some scraps of consumables were all he could find. He took his little notebook out of his pocket and looked up the phone number of the Embarcadero Hotel in San Francisco. For a moment, he was undecided about whether to use the room phone or his cell and then decided on the cell. The room phone would leave a record, but the cell would not be traced unless someone was actively scanning. That was probably not happening quite yet.

The phone at the consulate suite in San Francisco was answered almost immediately, in spite of the late hour. The clerk transferred his call to the action officer on duty.

"*Asalaamu alei kum.*"

"And may peace be upon thee, brother. This is Suleiman, in Nevada. The attack upon the Butcher of Ambon has failed. Lord Ahwadi has died. I am the only one left. I have no doubt that—"

"Wait. I thought that you were trailing the murderer Kintner. What is this of the Butcher? And what of Kintner?"

"The information we received is that Kintner is dead. But we were unable to confirm it. The Butcher had many armed men that we did not know of and thwarted our attack. We also intercepted some information that the FBI was sending agents to the place where the Butcher of Ambon lives."

"And what was the source of that information?"

"Our home cell in Albuquerque intercepted some calls from the FBI to the state police. The death of the devil Kintner was reported over the local sheriff's radio. Our cell in New Mexico cannot spare any more people to help us. And the cells in Salt Lake and Phoenix have already provided assistance. That is why I turn to you. If you can get me to San Francisco, we can put together a new plan."

"I will have to consult with Saleh, who is currently at rest. I will call you back on your encrypted equipment in the morning."

"The equipment was destroyed at the ranch. At least I had to leave it behind. But the agents will be here soon . . . Perhaps they are already on the way. I had to steal a truck to get away, and that will also be discovered soon. Can you send a plane after me? There is an adequate airport in Ely, and I can be waiting for you if you dispatch it immediately. Otherwise, I too am a dead man."

The phone went dead for what seemed a very long time. Then the action officer was back.

"Suleiman, I am sending an airplane from Reno. It should be there in less than two hours. It is a twin-engine Cessna with red-and- white markings, tail number N662. Be where you can meet it at the parking ramp. Understand?"

"Yes. And I am grateful to Allah and to—"

"Save your obsequy for Lord Saleh, Suleiman. You are going to need it."

* * *

It was just past midnight when Breuger heard two gentle taps on his door. He took his automatic pistol from under his pillow, rolled out of bed on the side opposite from the door, and waited. He heard a muffled click in the door lock and watched as the door inched open. But no one came in. He padded softly over to the door and peered out to the left and then right. As he looked, a decrepit pickup truck drove slowly past. He couldn't see the driver very well, but there was something familiar. Then he saw the slim figure pressed against the wall in the semidarkness.

"On m'a dit que vous vendez des articles Francais, Monsieur. Combien?"

"They are free to you, *ma cher* Elise."

"In that case, I will come in, Henri. Aren't you tired of showing off your shortcomings?"

Breuger looked down and remembered that he was naked.

"*Excusez.* I will put on some trousers, if you insist. We have a great deal to cover."

He went in, switched on the light, retrieved his trousers and shirt, and put them on. She followed him in and sat down on the desk chair. She saw the Courvoisier cognac and poured herself an inch of the golden liquid, inhaled the aroma, and then sipped it. Breuger came over and poured himself a considerably larger portion and sat down on the bed.

"Did you have trouble finding me?"

"No. Could have used a GPS in the old days, eh? No challenges anymore."

"That's what you think. How much did they tell you in Paris and Albuquerque?"

"I know about the recent al-Qaeda communiqués and the alleged killings at the Morales ranch. Have you been able to confirm that Kintner is dead?"

"No. But the evening news on the television reported some kind of pitched battle at the ranch—one day after the first three killings. Several men shot dead, including the local sheriff and his deputy. There was no mention of FBI agents, but if there are none of them there now, that will no doubt change."

"Was there any mention of the identity of the others who were killed?"

"Some of them were ranch employees—cowboys, I guess. But the announcer said the others were so far unidentified. My guess is that they were al-Qaeda."

Elise took another sip from her cognac. This was a lot more complicated than she had hoped. But it didn't seem to her as if any action could be taken until Kintner's death could be confirmed. And the question had to be answered: Had al-Qaeda been after Kintner or Morales or both? If either of them were still alive, they were certain to come after the other one. But she believed from what she had been briefed that Morales didn't represent the potential threat to resumption of hostilities that Kintner was assumed to be. So, if Kintner were dead, the interest the Republic of France had in this affair would disappear and their job would be over.

"We have to know for certain, Henri, who the dead are and who the survivors are. We cannot trust the news media; they are just going to parrot whatever the government tells them to say. And you know that the government agents are going to be swarming around here for some time to come. Does the FBI know about you?"

"I had to go and talk to the former national security advisor when I first arrived. It seems very likely she passed the details of our conversation on to the American intelligence community, wouldn't you say?"

"I would. That means I am the only one who can show up in public. But I am sure to be conspicuously French, even to the rustics who live around here."

She thought for a few moments, and Henri didn't speak. He knew she was good at improvisation. He wondered what she would come up with.

"I speak some passable Spanish, Henri. An out-of-work Hispanic maid wouldn't draw too much attention. I might show up at the ranch looking for work. That would let me hear the household gossip from the other employees. Bound to be some information there. What do you think?"

"I think you are a genius. You wouldn't even have to be an employee of the ranch. The sheriff's office and the coroner's office are likely to need some assistance with all those dead bodies. And that might get you close to the ranch employees. It is worth a try."

He sat thinking for a moment and then abruptly rose and headed for the door. Before he went out, he turned to Elise.

"I am going to check on something for a moment. Go ahead and freshen up and go to sleep in the other bed, if you like. We will talk again in the morning."

He left the room, closing the door behind him, and walked in the direction the pickup had gone. He found it, noted the room number by the parking space, and went to the office. The night clerk was still awake, watching TV.

"May I help you, sir?"

"Yes, if you please. I am Gerard Montfort in room 115. I was expecting a friend to arrive and check in before now. He said he had reserved room 121. Would you check to see if he has arrived?"

"Okay, but no one has checked in since I came on at eight o'clock." He looked at the registration file on the desk computer. "No, the people in room 121 checked in three days ago and haven't checked out. I checked them in. They also rented 123. There were seven of them. Don't know how they slept in two rooms. No accounting for taste, I guess." He looked up and shrugged his shoulders.

"No, that wouldn't be the ones I was expecting. They would have been Europeans."

"Well, they did have some funny accent. Not like yours, exactly. Kind of dark complexions too. Not too friendly, either."

Breuger stood very still, without expression, deliberately not reacting to what he had just heard. Now he remembered the face he had glimpsed as the truck had passed his room. It was only dimly lit by the instrument lights, but he had looked at that particular face many times in the Europol files and in the DCRI files as well. Ahwadi's deputy. Suleiman.

When he got back to his room, Breuger found Elise in bed. She lifted her head and looked at him.

"Anything wrong?"

"Yeah. We seem to have an interesting neighbor a few doors down. Probably the remnant of the gang that went after Colonel Morales and Kintner. I am going to pack my gear and stay up. If he leaves, I am going to follow. I will call you on my cell phone when I find out where he is going. We can join up somewhere later and compare notes. I suggest you start tomorrow with the clerk in the sheriff's office. She will know where you can get a job, either at the ranch or with the county. Get some rest. *Bonne nuit.*"

Agent Marquette closed her eyes. *No rest for the wicked,* she thought.

* * *

Jerry Owens looked out the window of the Blackhawk helicopter down at the ranch. A desolate but beautiful place. What a shame that even a place like this was not immune to the terrorist machinations. He looked over at George Bronson.

"Have you spoken to Russell again since the shootout, George? Any survivors?"

"Apparently not. But there was no way to be sure how many men were in the group that attacked the ranch. Some could have slipped away. We'll have enough agents to do a pretty thorough sweep after we get on the ground. Ken also said he had had a preliminary look at the electronic gear in the van they brought with them. He says there is some pretty sophisticated scanning equipment included. That would explain how they were able to stay ahead of us—among other things."

"What about Kintner? Was he able to confirm that he was killed?"

"Well, Ken attended his funeral, but he didn't get a look inside the coffin. Catholic Spanish tradition doesn't allow for opening the casket. But if the grave hasn't been filled in, we can get confirmation fairly easily. I just hope we don't have to get a court order to disinter. That would mean publicity, which might do more harm than good—whether Kintner is alive or not."

The Blackhawk started its descent onto the courtyard of the ranch house.

"Let's have a chat with Colonel Morales, before we do anything. I think he might agree that we ought to avoid anymore publicity and cooperate with us. And, believe you me, we're going to make sure this story doesn't get any further."

"That might be difficult, sir. The Nevada State Police have already taken over the crime scene from the sheriff's department."

* * *

Monsignor Robert Bohemund sat listening in something approaching awe as the story of the postwar Ordo Sacer organization unfolded before him. He had never even considered the possibility that the order would survive the Ninth Crusade in what sounded like a robustness equal to that which it had had at the height of the war. The Vatican had, to all intents and purposes, ignored it after the cessation of hostilities. The current Pope, John XXIV, had not disestablished it, probably as much from embarrassment at its existence as from uncertainty. The College of Cardinals certainly did not wish for any attention to be drawn to it. A military order of the Catholic Church in the twenty-first century? Ridiculous on its face.

"That's just an overview, Monsignor," concluded the briefer. Knight Brigadier Peter Janowiscz shut off the projector with his remote control and hesitated briefly in case his audience had any questions—which was a good bet, considering the expression on the monsignor's face.

Bohemund turned to Father Sullivan, who had borrowed the conference room from the chancellor of Catholic University for the purpose at hand, having implied that it was for only some minor administrative procedure. Even though the existence of the presumed "remnants" of the order were not treated as a secret, Father Sullivan, still titularly the command chaplain, had no intention of exposing the underbelly of the order to unwarranted publicity and criticism.

"I hesitate to ask, Shamus, but what exactly are the reasons for which this elaborate structure has been so carefully preserved? Are you expecting the resumption of hostilities?"

"Well, if you're asking as a representative of the Holy See, Monsignor, then my reply is that it is intended to ensure that care continues for the widows and orphans of the veterans of the Crusade."

"And if I'm asking as deputy knight commander of the order?"

Father Sullivan hesitated. As far as he knew, Bohemund had shown no interest in the welfare of the order since the war and probably had given little thought to anything other than his own ambitions at the Vatican, whatever they were. At least that was where his office was, and it was a safe assumption that that was where his interests lay.

"Then I would say that it exists also for such exigencies as that which has just occurred—the danger in which Father Michael Kintner finds himself. Isn't that why you asked to meet with us?"

Bohemund was silent for a long moment. An excellent answer, considering the possible sensitivities. Sullivan would have made a good Jesuit. But he also now knew that there was considerably more to this than was apparent.

"To be sure, Shamus, to be sure. Thanks for bringing me back on point. First, let me tell you what I know about the situation, and the knight commanders here assembled can begin to make suggestions." He looked around the table at some familiar faces and some not so familiar. The majority, judging from the gold stars on the high collars, had high rank, at the level of general officers. But only he and Shamus wore the Roman collar.

"Before coming here this morning, I received an up-to-date briefing from the president's national security advisor, General David Kane. Two days ago, there were three killings at a Nevada ranch owned by Knight Colonel Lorenzo Morales, whom you will no doubt remember led the raid on Indonesian Muslim positions at Ambon. Michael Kintner was reportedly one of those killed at the ranch. But this has not yet been confirmed."

The men at the table looked at each other and back at Bohemund. Brigadier Janowiscz, still standing at the end of the table, spoke first.

"Well, who did the killings? And what about Colonel Morales? Is he still alive? Were the al-Qaeda involved?"

"Morales is alive, but the killings two days ago did not involve anyone except people at the ranch. The wife of Morales's late brother and the ranch foreman were murdered for reasons that appear to be personal. Kintner was shot by accident, according to reports. But the next day, a contingent of al-Qaeda, which had been following Kintner, attacked the ranch. They apparently knew that the man they call the Butcher of Ambon was also there."

"If it was known that Kintner was being followed, why didn't someone take action? Why was this all kept secret?" asked Knight General Mark McConnell at Bohemund's left.

Bohemund tiredly passed his hand over his jaw.

"Lots of reasons, many of which I am not privy to. But it was mainly politics. The church had already announced Kintner's death, probably with some relief, hoping that Kintner alone would get the blame for the destruction of the Grand Mosque at Mecca. And once the intelligence agencies of France and the United States became aware that al-Qaeda were following him, they feared that Kintner or the Vatican or both were planning some follow-up action to resume hostilities. Unfortunately, that's the kind of paranoia that is endemic to all intelligence communities. I know this from personal experience."

Father Sullivan held up his hand to stop the questions.

"Please. Let's give Monsignor Bohemund a chance to finish with his information. But before you do, Monsignor, would you tell us which assumption is correct? Did Kintner act alone in the bombing of Mecca? Or did the Vatican order it?"

"As I told members of the Holy See only recently, I can only report what I was told and what I saw. Kintner spent about a week in hospital after the bombing of the Sistine Chapel in which Pope Thomas and everyone else present died immediately or within a few days—everyone, that is, except Kintner, who had been concelebrating Mass with the pope. He checked himself out of the hospital in Rome and flew to our air base at Har-Megiddo. I was there when Michael ordered the AC-130 configured with a hyperbaric bomb and flew it himself toward some target at which I could only guess. Keep in mind that the bombing of the Sistine Chapel took place after the formal cessation of hostilities."

Bohemund dropped his head for a moment before continuing, "Ask yourself, gentlemen. We are all experienced combat veterans. Would we have acted any differently in Kintner's place? Somehow, I doubt it."

"Then the Vatican did not order it, as *Al Jazeera* reported?" asked Sullivan.

"No. And Kintner never informed Rome about his actions, before or afterward. The Vatican's official response was essentially correct, except for implying that Kintner had died."

"What about the gang that attacked the ranch?" asked General McConnell. "Were they killed or captured? Is there still a threat to Morales?"

"The FBI believe that all the al-Qaeda involved in the attack were killed. But there is no way of knowing if that is true. Even if it is, who's to say that their organization won't try it again? Not only against Morales, but against each of you and everyone else included in their paranoia? No. I'm afraid this is far from over."

"So, all the death and destruction of the Ninth Crusade was not enough to teach them a lesson," said Brigadier Janowiscz. "Does every Muslim in the world have to die before there is any peace?"

Bohemund looked steadily at Janowiscz and then at every other face in the room before speaking.

"I understand your frustration, Brigadier, and I know also that your question is a rhetorical one. But there is an important point to be made here. I know intuitively that there are millions of Muslims of goodwill in the world, people with a sense of an ultimate moral order, which must prevail in every philosophy and every religion if the human race is to survive at all. But if those Muslims who subscribe to this morality fail to root out the evil from their midst, then there is little hope for peace.

"I also know that there are Muslim populations all over the world who live in relative poverty and ignorance—relative, that is, to the standard of living in Europe and America. In my view, there must be a deep-seated frustration and antagonism at being left behind in the dustbin of history, not only in material things, but also in religious dogma, which is, in most cases, literally forced down the throats of people born into their faith. There can be no doubt that in centuries past, Muslims excelled in some areas of science and literature and other fields. But in recent history, they have lost the essential arguments in the 'marketplace of ideas' for their violent and repressive way of life, in much the same way Communism has lost against the ideas of economic freedom."

"All very good observations, Monsignor," said General McConnell. "But neither theology nor philosophy is going to solve the problems at hand. I am sure that Pope Thomas must have believed this also, when he established our holy order."

"Yes, General. I am sadly aware of this as well. Now, tell me how the holy order is going to protect its members and restore the general peace."

"I have told you the disposition of our members across the country and what we know of the local organizations in foreign countries," said Brigadier Janowiscz. "Each of the local organizations is known as a 'parish,' named after a man or woman admired for certain . . . *spiritual* gifts. Each of these parishes has a certain number of attributes in common with all the others, such as combat experience from the Crusade, intelligence-gathering capabilities, and communications. But there are some with unique contacts with sources of power and influence in financial circles, politics, and ecclesiastical members of the visible church. If you can give us an idea of where we can be most helpful, then—"

"Just a moment, Brigadier," interrupted Bohemund. "Did you just say 'visible' church? Did you mean to imply what I think you did?"

Janowiscz looked at the other members present, waiting for help, it seemed, but no one spoke.

"An unintended reference, Monsignor. I meant, of course, to refer to the visible ecclesial structure of the Catholic Church, such as priests, bishops, deacons, and so forth." Janowiscz waited for a moment and then continued, "We have a certain level of encryption capability in our communications with each other, but not nearly as sophisticated as that which exists in national intelligence communities. The FBI would not have much trouble cracking our codes, I'm sure. But it serves our purposes."

Bohemund sat at the head of the table, silently drumming his fingers on the table, trying to decide something.

"It seems to me that it would be best to keep communications at a streamlined function, in which I could talk directly to the local 'parish' where we think the focus of action at the moment might be. To do that, I need you to provide me with a laptop computer with the pertinent communication software and codes that you use in the order. I will also need names or call signs, or whatever you use, to avoid any confusion. I will also need an open channel to your national leader, if you have one, to coordinate the movement of resources and personnel around as needed. Is this a practicable approach in your opinion?" He looked over at Shamus, but it was General McConnell who answered.

"I will act as national coordinator, Monsignor. The communications net to move resources is already in place for some other purposes, so it is a simple matter to put you in the loop. An equipped computer will be delivered to you at your quarters tonight. You are still at the Washington Archdiocese?"

"Yes." Bohemund hesitated for a moment. "But I have decided to move to the San Francisco Archdiocese tomorrow, to be closer to the action. What is the name of the order parish in that area?"

"That would be the Gilead Parish, Monsignor. I will notify them of your plans, and they will be waiting on your call."

"Good." Bohemund stood up. "I feel very good about this. It is comforting to have the Keys troops around me again. And if Father Kintner—that is to say, Knight Commander Kintner—is alive, we will find and protect him." He crossed himself, and the others did, also.

"Fiat voluntas tua, Domini."

Chapter 10

Agent Elise Marquette was not sure she could get by without speaking a great deal of Spanish. But she was afraid her accent would give her away, so she decided that the best tactic would be to speak slowly and act as if she had trouble understanding things. So far, it seemed to be working. The Hispanic housekeeper at Rancho Santiago apparently accepted her slowness as a fact, since she was slowing her explanations down to very simple sentences and that also helped. It had an additional advantage, also, in that the other members of the household staff spoke more freely in her presence than might otherwise have been the case. Now, she would just be patient and alert, without seeming to be. She knew that gossip was endemic to any domestic staff, so she shouldn't have long to wait.

She had been fortunate that the clerk in the sheriff's office had been so willing, even eager, to send her out to the ranch. Elise had heard her phone conversation with the housekeeper at Rancho Santiago and gathered that the place was overwhelmed by the influx of so many outsiders, including state troopers and government agents. But upon her arrival at the ranch, it was still a surprise to see the military-style helicopters and squad and staff cars, even moving vans, parked all over the property around the ranch house. With her work clothes, purchased at the Goodwill store in town, and her diffident demeanor, not one of the outsiders paid the slightest attention to her.

She didn't have to wait long. When she finished the breakfast dishes in the kitchen, the housekeeper sent her out to the patio to clean up after the guests having their coffee and pastries.

When she arrived at the patio, two of the Americans were still chatting with Colonel Morales. None of them noticed her.

"Colonel, I am prepared to be as lenient as possible to your religious considerations. But it is very important to my government to verify Kintner's death. Surely you can understand why."

"*Sin duda.* Of course. But since you are apparently unwilling to take my word on the subject, I at least would like to explore some alternative other than going to court to argue the question in public. If the al-Qaeda are led to suspect that Kintner is still alive, they will not cease their efforts to find him. They are very good at gathering intelligence, even when the American press are not helping them. I also have my brother's daughter to consider. The al-Qaeda are not above going after her and the rest of my household."

He remembered the note Maggie had left him before going away with Michael. He had tried to cover her absence with stories about her being "distraught" and keeping to her room. People on the ranch would notice her absence eventually. But by then, it would not matter.

Jerry Owens could see where this was going. He didn't blame Morales for trying to protect Kintner. But he must know that a refusal to confirm the death would be a tacit admission that Kintner was still alive.

"You probably know, Colonel, that there is a way to confirm Kintner's presence in the casket without actually opening it. A small light tube could be inserted for a view by camera or digital screen. I'm sure that would satisfy my superiors."

Colonel Morales picked up his coffee cup, stood up, and walked a couple of steps away from the table. He turned his head and looked across the courtyard at the little family cemetery, several meters away. Were all his efforts to help Kintner escape going to be for nothing? These men from the FBI could not care less what the consequences might be for Kintner, for his brother's daughter, and for himself. He noticed for the first time the maid, sweeping away some imaginary debris from the patio. A new face, not unusual at his brother's ranch, since American Hispanics seemed not to stay in one place very long—a far cry from his experience with domestic help in his native *Espana*. Then he turned back to his guests.

"I have a proposal for you, Mr. Owens. Would you agree to release a notice to the newspapers that Caballero Comandante Michael Kintner was confirmed dead after you have a look with that light tube of yours into the coffin?"

George Bronson looked at his boss and then turned back toward Morales.

"Do you mean that we would release the notice regardless of what we find?"

"By no means. I am simply saying that I am confident you would agree that it serves everyone well if the public at large, including our enemies, are convinced that he is in his coffin. Which I still maintain that he is."

Owens stood up, walked over to Morales, and put out his hand. Morales, after some hesitation, took the hand briefly and then let it go.

"I also would suggest that you send your men and equipment away from here before we call a press conference—for obvious reasons."

"All right, yes, I agree," said Owens. "I will take care of everything, just as you ask."

Elise finished clearing away the dishes from the little patio table and took them into the kitchen on her platter. The housekeeper was waiting for her.

"What took you so long? It is not good manners to spend more time than necessary around the patron when he is speaking with guests."

Elise gave her the practiced blank stare she used to convey a certain vagueness of mind.

"They were still finishing their coffee, *Maestra*. I did not mean to intrude upon them."

"Very well. But you must learn never to delay in the presence of the patron. He is from a very old Spanish family, and he will brook no unseemly behavior from servants."

Elise hesitated, seeming to think hard about something.

"*Maestra*—the family, does it not have a niece of the colonel?"

The housekeeper gave her a stern look.

"What is this about a niece? Who told you this?"

"*Perdonar, Maestra.* I could not help but hear the colonel refer to her. Does she not live here? I have not seen her."

"This is none of your business. Anyway, it is a very painful subject for the patron. He pretends that she is staying in her room because of all the sadness. But we all know she ran away and no one knows where she might have gone."

Elise started to unload her tray of cups and saucers into the sink. The housekeeper watched for a while before speaking again.

"My heart is breaking for her. I have looked after her since she was a *niña*. And now . . . none of us knows how she is going to take care of herself. It is a sadness."

Elise turned from her washing at the sink.

"But this place is so big, *Maestra*. How could she just walk away?"

The housekeeper shook her head, the tears beginning to show in her eyes. She had tried to block out her thoughts of her little Magdalena in the last couple of days but could not. When she spoke again, it was if she were talking to herself and not to the servant girl.

"The vaqueros, I know they know something, but they are not saying anything. They talk in whispers of the missing truck, which the patron has not even spoken of, and of the old truck that was left in its place, but I do not know how my little one could have . . ."

She lowered her head and wiped her eyes with her apron. "None of this is any of your business, so just forget it," she said sternly. Then she walked out of the kitchen.

Elise picked up a bucket and went out of the kitchen door into the courtyard in back of the house on which the quarters of the ranch hands was located. She walked across the open space until she came to the water spigot a few meters from the door of the bunkhouse. She turned it on to a small stream and placed the bucket under it. She saw one of the cowboys seated in front of the bunkhouse working with a knife on a latigo. She didn't have to wait long before he spotted her and walked over.

"Morning, miss. Carry that for you?"

Elise gave him what she hoped was a fetching smile and answered, "If it's not too heavy for you."

The cowboy grinned. He was on the youngish side, she noticed, and not too bad looking.

"New here, ain't you? Prettiest of the lot, if you ask me," he said, still grinning.

"*Gracias.* You are very cheerful. Everyone else here seems so sad."

"Yeah. Some bad stuff been happening here. Awful bad. There was a shooting here at the hacienda a few days ago. Some foreigners with a grudge against the colonel killed our foreman, from what they said. Then, some friend of the colonel's was shot by the colonel's sister-in-law. And the deputy sheriff shot her. Damndest thing. Then a bunch of them foreigners came back to the ranch. You probably saw it on the news. The colonel took me and seven more of us down to meet them, and we finished them all off, but not before they killed the sheriff and his deputy. Tommy Gray got hit in the leg, but he's going to be all right. FBI everywhere. Never seen the beat of it."

"*Es muy malo,*" she said, crossing herself as she imagined a servant girl would do. "But what about the niece of the colonel? I am told she ran away. Was she so badly frightened?"

The cowboy shook his head and stared off across the plain, as if looking for something.

"Now, that's the strangest part of it all. Not that she took off—I can't blame her for that. Especially after all that happened, even before all these killings took place. Rumors were flying around about Sutter—he used to be our foreman—and the mother and daughter . . . Well, I better not get into that. But if little Maggie did steal that truck and run away, as everyone seems to think, it's mighty peculiar that the colonel didn't go after her or at least send someone. Something just doesn't add up."

He looked back down at Elise and grinned again.

"But I better help you get this water back, eh? I know how your boss is; she yells at the help all day long."

Elise let the cowboy pick up her bucket, and she followed him to the kitchen door. She took the bucket from him, placed it just inside the door, and turned back to the cowboy.

"*Señor*, may I . . ."

"Not *señor*, my name's Billy."

"Billy. What you have said makes me very . . . *espantar* . . . *scared*. I have changed my mind about working here. Could you take me down to the highway so I can get back to the town? I don't want to see the *maestra* anymore."

"I'll do better than that. I'll take you all the way to Ely. Are you sure you . . ."

"*Si*, very sure. I would be grateful."

Billy went back into the bunkhouse for a minute and came back out with a set of truck keys. He motioned Elise over to one of the trucks and helped her get in. As they drove away, she began to plan in her mind what the next steps should be. There now was no doubt in her mind what had happened. She looked over at Billy and spoke to him.

"This is a very nice *camblo*. Are all the trucks so new? Is this like the one the little señorita ran away in?"

"Yeah. This one's a couple of years older. The colonel always buys Fords. Maggie took the best one—dark-blue Ford 150. Pretty piece of machinery."

Elise had all the information she needed. Henri would be proud of her.

* * *

Michael Kintner awoke and looked around at the interior of the closed truck bed, uncertain for a fleeting moment of his circumstances. Then he remembered the dinner he and Maggie had shared and the brief discussion about his abandoned priesthood. Maggie stirred on the carpeted floor and opened her eyes, which immediately met his. A sly smile intruded itself on her features, and she sat up and put her hand on Michael's.

"You look as if you have just broken an expensive watch or something, Michael. Sleeping in the same truck didn't break any rules, did it? If you think it did, then will you give me a tiny kiss, so I won't feel cheap?" she joked, her smile broadening.

Michael reached out both arms and enfolded her in an embrace, his face softening into a smile of his own. He had never had a daughter, but if he had, he hoped she would have been like Maggie.

Maggie didn't raise her face from where it was buried against Michael's chest. They stayed just like that for a long time, allowing their minds to float in the mists of their momentary refuge.

* * *

Elise thanked Billy for the ride and got out of the truck in front of the sheriff's office, it being the least suspicious place she could think of in case Billy mentioned it to someone. It was a short walk back to the motel. When she got back to her room, Henri opened the door for her, and she walked in.

"You look like the cat that swallowed the canary, Agent Marquette. I take it the impersonation worked."

"It did, indeed." She sat down on her bed and took off her shoes. "I'm afraid I didn't fare so well. I followed Suleiman to the airport, where he had an airplane waiting for him. I went over to the field operations office and inquired about the plane. The duty officer said it was on a filed flight plan from Reno, stopping in Ely and headed for San Francisco. I called the Washington embassy DCRI agent, and he said that their surveillance records indicated a call was made to the Saudi consulate in San Francisco from an untraceable cell phone in this area—just a few hours before. That could mean that they are regrouping and probably waiting for additional personnel. But I don't know why they would do that. There's nothing more they can do here. This place will be crawling with FBI agents for a long time yet. What do you think?"

"I think they have guessed at what I already know. Kintner is still alive."

* * *

Monsignor Bohemund was just getting out of his shower in the St. Francis Hotel in San Francisco when his phone rang. He threw on the hotel robe and went back into his bedroom. He had hoped the Vatican wouldn't bother him for a while, but he knew from experience that their proclivity for micromanagement was too ingrained.

"Your pardon, Monsignor," the voice said. "Cardinal Bocelli will be on the line in a moment."

Bohemund waited for the ridiculously necessary bureaucratic pause, and then the Vatican secretary of state came on the line.

"Robert, I hope your trip was pleasant. I received a call from Archbishop Karl Wolnik of San Francisco awhile ago, and he said that you informed his secretary of your intent to visit; he wanted to know from me if this was an official visit, and I told him frankly that I had no idea why you were there. I don't recall your mentioning such a visit at our meeting in Rome."

"No, Your Eminence. I did not know then that this trip would be necessary. I am still just exploring all the evidence for Michael Kintner's status. Ostensibly, he was killed at the terrorist attack on the ranch in Nevada, which has been in all the news reports. You are familiar with the events?"

"I am. In fact, the reports this morning said that the American authorities had confirmed his death. What more is there for you to do?"

Bohemund thought furiously for a moment, trying to come up with something plausible in place of the real reason.

"Eminence, I did not know that such an announcement had been made. But it is just possible that the Muslim terrorists still in America may not accept the veracity of the announcement. I too believe there may be some room for doubt."

"Now, really, Robert. I think your experiences in military intelligence may have made you too cynical. After all, the FBI report said that they had examined the contents of the casket. That report must have been approved at the highest levels."

"Even so, Eminence, the terrorists may still have some acts of revenge in mind. There are other veterans of the Ninth Crusade in America who may be in danger—including some clerics. However, I only want to consult with the archbishop on this possibility, in case he may require our assistance."

"Whom exactly do you mean by 'our'? You don't have the authority to commit Vatican resources to this."

"I have no intention of doing so without your consent, Eminence. But I still think it prudent to explore all contingencies at this point. With your permission, of course."

The line was silent for a long moment.

"Very well, Robert. But I caution you that I don't want to read about any of this in *L'Osservatore Romano*, if you get my meaning."

Bohemund hung up the phone and stood still for a long time, thinking. Then he sat down at his laptop computer and keyed in the passwords he had been given by the order. After a moment, a question and an answer block appeared. "Authority?" He typed in "Knight General McConnell." Then another: "Supplicant?" He typed in "Knight Deputy Commander Bohemund."

He noticed that the camera light on the top margin of the screen went on, and a face appeared on the screen. The face of the man who appeared seemed ageless. He had a light, closely trimmed beard, blue eyes, and dark thick hair. His voice when he spoke was firm without being aggressive, and his eyes were piercing but gentle—a man not to be trifled with, but distinctly approachable.

"Welcome, Monsignor. I have been expecting your call. My name is Gil Berenger. How may I be of help?"

Bohemund hesitated for just an instant. He wasn't sure what sort of man he had expected to see, but this was a surprise. There was something familiar about the man, but he couldn't place it.

"It is good to meet you, Father . . . Mister . . . Berenger. Which is it?"

"Just 'Gil' will be fine. And I will call you 'Robert' if I may."

"Yes. I hardly know where to start. I came to America to determine if Michael Kintner is still alive, but I was informed that the Americans have pronounced him dead officially. Do you know about this?"

"Yes. The announcement is probably salutary in effect, but it is not literally true. And I am sure the Wahabi have not accepted it."

"Whom did you say? *Wahabi*?"

"Yes. It is a very conservative Muslim group who recognize no innovations in the Islamic religion that have occurred since the third century of its existence. They have effectively replaced the decimated al-Qaeda in all its deplorable activities."

Bohemund thought hard; everyone had been making the same mistake in their assumptions. He knew little about the Wahabi, but what he did know was not pleasant. They had tremendous influence in the richest Arab kingdom of Saudi Arabia and believed firmly in conversion to Islam by force, the penalty for refusing being death, much as in the early decades of its existence, when many thousands of Jews and Christians in the Middle East were slaughtered. This news did not bode well for the church.

"I would like to know more about that, but right now, I think we should concentrate on trying to find Kintner—I hope before anyone else does."

"Yes, I agree. Have you contacted Archbishop Wolnik yet?"

"I talked to his secretary and got an appointment for this morning—mostly for reasons of protocol, but I also thought he might have some ideas about canvassing the parishes in the archdiocese to enlist their aid in picking up evidence about Kintner's location. What do you think?"

"Yes, that couldn't hurt. The order has contacts with others in the archdiocese, people who are able to monitor police and other emergency services. But let me caution you on one issue. None of our efforts must be obvious to the American and French agents and especially not to the local police. That is an open line to the news media, and that kind of exposure would doom our efforts to rescue or assist Michael Kintner in whatever it is he is trying to do. By the way, do you have any idea what he might be trying to do?"

Robert thought about the question for a long time before answering.

"I suppose that if I were in his place, I would just be trying to find a peaceful place to die, not to be too morbid about it. I don't know anyone who believes he can last much longer, after the amount of radiation his body absorbed. But, from my experience with him in the Crusade, I know he is a hard man to kill."

Another long silence. Then Berenger spoke again.

"What if we can find him a peaceful place to live? He was, by the abbot's account, a valuable source of spiritual inspiration and awareness to the other members of the Benedictine monastery where he spent a lot of time, both before and after his role as knight commander of the Ninth Crusade. What he has learned in the last few years, both in the spiritual realm and the secular, would be a valuable resource to draw from."

"I'm not at all certain that is a practical possibility. Wherever he goes, whatever he tries to do, people are going to remember what he did to Mecca and the thousands who were killed there—after the war was officially over."

"Yes, I see your point. But I would propose to you that Michael is not beyond redemption. I know that the visible church has by her attitude implied that it may be so. But the visible church has erred in this direction before. The thousands of excommunications will attest to that."

"That is the second time in as many days that I have heard someone in the order mention the 'visible' church, as if there were still an 'invisible' one. I am referring to the—"

"Yes, I know—the Donatist heresy."

Berenger was quite confident the monsignor would know that Donatus and others in the fourth century were protesting the undeniable fact that the church was filled with clerics who had acceded to the demands of the Diocletian persecution. They had given up their copies of Holy Scripture, thereby tacitly repudiating their faith. Many other wealthy Christians did the same in order to preserve their fortunes. Even St. Augustine was sympathetic to the position taken by Donatus and his followers, though he supported the bishops and priests approved by Constantine and his Council of Nicaea.

"You know the history." He paused for a long moment. "Is it possible this heresy has survived?" Bohemund's ironic tone was unmistakable.

"The 'invisible' church alone survived the invasion of the Vandals and the Byzantine reconquest under Justinian I. And they did this by taking arms and opposing the invaders when the visible church was capitulating to them, as they had to the Roman persecution. They also vigorously opposed the Muslim invasions in the seventh and eighth centuries by fighting for the Christian Church when no one else could or would. I believe the Donatists and their breakaway churches disappeared sometime after the Muslim conquests. So, if they were around today, they would certainly be useful, don't you think?"

"Yes," said Bohemund, after a long hesitation. "I believe they would . . . And I think a priest like Father Michael Kintner would fit right in, don't you?"

"Yes, Monsignor . . . I believe so."

"And, uh, hypothetically speaking, Michael could virtually disappear into such an, uh, organization and never be heard of again."

"Hypothetically, yes. If such an . . . *invisible* church existed."

* * *

Michael started the truck and steered it back out onto the highway. As usual, there was no traffic on this famously lonely highway, and that was just what he wanted. He looked at Maggie, seated in the passenger seat, and she looked back at him. The same wan little smile was on her face that had been there when she'd woken up. And the same strong sense of protectiveness welled up inside his chest.

He thought about what it must have been like for Maggie to have been momentarily obsessed with such a creature as Bob Sutter. She had not the maturity to put such things in perspective and probably wasn't sure how her Catholic faith regarded such things. He remembered that the catechism for adolescents did not routinely address such things, beyond an unequivocal rule against sex outside of marriage. Church doctrine on such matters was clear. But what did doctrine and dogma matter to a young girl in "love"?

In any case, the church doctrine on sexuality had never really seemed practical to him, as a man or as a priest. The cynical view of the doctrine was that sex was okay only if you were married and if you didn't really engage in it just for pleasure. That set human nature on its head, if anything did. What of the ontological human need for authentic intimacy, which surely must include the sexual aspects of both male and female?

But Michael knew the inherent morality and stabilizing influence of marriage on society. The church had been right in making it a sacrament, even though the sacrament of matrimony didn't exist until the twelfth century and was created then only at the urging of the landed gentry for the preservation of inherited wealth.

"You look so serious, Michael. Are you worried about what will happen to us?"

"No, little one. *Worried* is not the word that could describe my feelings right now. But I am concerned that you may be in danger from the same people who may be searching for me. The tragedies of the last several days—I am not at all sure that they are over. I know these terrorists well enough to know that they do not give up on such things until their revenge is complete. I am putting you in a danger you would not face if you were not with me. That is the hard truth. And it has to be dealt with. You know that, don't you?"

"Michael, *I* worry that trying to look after me might be risking *your* life. Does that make sense?"

"That doesn't matter to me, Maggie. Up until now, I have not put much value on my life—during the Crusade and especially in the last few weeks. But you have given me something to live for. And that something is making sure you are cared for until you can find your own future—a future free of danger and free of want."

Michael looked in the rearview mirror and saw, far back on the highway, what looked like a red pickup with a black grill.

Chapter 11

George Bronson and Ken Russell came out of the motel office and got back into their van. Their conversation with Colonel Morales the previous day was still very much on their minds. But they had a very difficult job ahead of them and they had to concentrate on that.

The communications technician was asleep in the back and barely stirred when the doors to the van slammed shut. Russell looked over at Bronson and jerked his thumb toward the prone figure in the back.

"I can tell he's going to be a lot of help."

"Well, helpful or not, he's the only one of the three of us who is familiar with that new gear we're carrying. If we're going to catch up with Breuger and the survivor of that shootout, we are going to have to rely on whatever intercepts he can pick up. By the way, do you suppose Breuger and that group of terrorists knew about each other—I mean that they were staying in the same motel?"

"I doubt if the ragheads did, but Breuger is sharp enough to pick up on it. And if he did, my guess is that he would be following the one that's left even as we speak."

"Maybe, maybe not. If he bought that story we put out confirming Kintner's death, he could be headed out of the country. Maybe the other one, as well."

Bronson looked over at Russell, and Russell looked back at him silently. Then both of them shook their heads.

The soft sound of an electronic bell sounded from the back, and the technician was awake at once, going over to the small seat in front of one of the computers. He put on the earphone and waited, listening for several minutes. Then he reached up and tapped Bronson on the shoulder.

"Mr. Bronson, NSA intercepted a call from Breuger to the French embassy in Washington. He and another agent—no info on who he is yet—are following a lead to San Francisco. Seems the Saudi consulate flew someone out of Ely last night, headed to the international airport in Frisco. They also picked up an earlier call from Ely to the Embarcadero Hotel complex, where the Saudi embassy is located. They haven't decoded that one yet. Any of that helpful?"

"Yeah. It gives us a direction, anyway. Thanks, Charlie." He looked at Russell. "What do you think? A lead or a ruse?"

"I think—"

The soft bell sounded once more, and the tech went back to the computer. After a few minutes, he turned back to the front of the van.

"Got a copy of the decoded call, Mr. Bronson. Want me to print you a copy?"

"No, just summarize it for me."

"Caller was Suleiman. Received by the duty officer and passed on to someone named Saleh. Caller says their resources in Albuquerque, Salt Lake, and Phoenix are depleted and they requested more men from San Francisco, but they want to talk first."

"Anything about Kintner or Morales?" asked Russell.

"Yeah. They say they haven't been able to confirm Kintner's death, they are monitoring communications between the FBI and the state police, and they know the FBI is protecting Morales."

"Thanks, Charlie. And pass the information about our compromised communications with the state police to all our field offices in the western states, okay?" He turned to Russell.

"What do you think, Ken? California or bust?"

"Shouldn't you call the San Francisco field office director? They can set up surveillance right away, if the resources Suleiman requested are sent in before we can get there."

Bronson grunted, pulled the van onto the shoulder of the road, and cut the engine. He moved into the back, sat down at one of the computers, and connected a secure voice link.

"This is Bronson. Special assignment from Washington. Please connect me with Field Director Ames."

Thirty seconds later, the director came online.

"John Ames, George. Been awhile since we talked. What's up in the puzzle palace?"

"They're all stirred up about this business at the Morales ranch in Nevada. Have you seen the reports?"

"Yes. How can I help?"

"One of the terrorists escaped killing and is headed your way; in fact, he is probably already there. His name is Suleiman, and he's coming to the Saudi consulate to meet with someone named Saleh. We think he is there to try to bring in reinforcements."

"What do you think his intent is? Didn't they manage to kill the guy they were after—this man Kintner?"

"We don't think so, in spite of the public announcement. And apparently they don't think so either. And they might have some other people on their hit list as well. If Kintner is alive, he's likely headed toward the West Coast. That's our assumption anyway."

"Based on what?"

"Well, for one thing, a French DCRI agent named Henri Breuger, who was sent here to find Kintner, and one other agent, whose name we don't have yet, are headed in that direction."

"Breuger, eh? I thought he was dead."

"Yeah, well, if you know him, you know he's very hard to kill. Anyway, we also have information that a representative of the Vatican, a Monsignor Robert Bohemund, who was Kintner's deputy in the Crusade, is headed for a meeting with Archbishop Karl Wolnik."

"Pretty good indicators, I'd say. If Washington okays it, I can put surveillance on the archdiocesan offices and the Saudi consulate as well."

"I'd recommend you go ahead with it. If Washington has any complaint, I'll take care of it."

"All right. What about the other people on this 'hit list' you mentioned. Who are they?"

"Check your database for the locations of principal participants in the Crusade. The Keys troops. Remember them?"

"Who can forget? More propaganda than the Marines. No offense, of course."

"None taken. We all have a past. If you find any names in your area of responsibility, I would appreciate it if you would let me know who and where they are."

"Absolutely. We should have the surveillance in place in twenty-four hours, maybe sooner."

"Okay. My associates and I will be staying in the St. Francis Hotel. That's where Bohemund is staying, according to my information. I have a remote monitor with me for the van communication equipment, so I will be able to get on a secure link in a matter of a few minutes probably."

"All right, George. Good talking to you. Good luck."

* * *

Archbishop Karl Wolnik was a tall, austere-looking man, somewhat after the East European stereotype, but there was a quality of kindness in his demeanor not as common among bishops as it typically was among parish priests. He had been a priest in Poland before *glasnost*, the beginning of rapprochement with the West. The experience of practicing a faith not in favor with the political and, in some cases, ecclesiastical authorities was burned into his subconscious. His personal spirituality was not as closely aligned with Roman Catholic dogma as that which was presupposed to exist in a bishop—which position was given to him only after the personal intervention of Pope John Paul II.

He had known Karol Wojtyla long before he became pope and had had many private conversations with him on the subject of personal spirituality. Their views had been remarkably similar and bordered on what most conservative Catholics might consider heretical. One of the most mystical subjects they had discussed was the true nature of the Eucharist, the sacrifice of the Mass. They had both regarded it as the "secret sorrow" of the church that the Mass offered to the ordinary communicants had not had the miraculous impact upon the majority of them that it should have had. They each had their own opinions as to why this was, but they agreed upon one thing: The miracle had once existed in the church and now no longer did. They agreed that "once in time and somewhere in the world" a Mass had existed that was of an extraordinary consecration and celebrated by an especially blessed apostolic succession of priests. But Karl Wolnik and Karol Wojtyla had taken very different paths to try to reconcile this sorrow, this hidden wound of the church.

"I am glad to welcome you to the archdiocese, Monsignor Bohemund. I confess that I was surprised not to have received an advance notice of the visit of a representative of the Vatican. Not the usual procedure, I am sure you will agree."

"My abject apologies, Your Grace. In any case, I am pleased to convey the respects and affection of Cardinal Bocelli. My visit was not officially announced because it concerns the safety of some people who were associated with the Ninth Crusade—an enterprise no longer held in much regard by the majority of people, both inside and outside Holy Mother Church."

"I am not among those who have recently suffered an attack of conscience on the subject of the Crusade, Monsignor. I firmly believe it was a necessary thing, and I admire Pope Thomas for his courage in launching it. But perhaps my 'radical' point of view stems from my experience with the suppression of the church in Eastern Europe. That also almost destroyed us, just as the Muslim terrorists are trying to do."

The archbishop walked over to his small conference table and offered the monsignor a seat. A young cleric entered the room, set coffee and tea on the table, and left.

"I am pleasantly surprised at your opinion, Your Grace, because it makes what I have to say easier. I am sure you must be aware of the recent events in Nevada—from the news media, at least. It was announced by an American government spokesman that Father Michael Kintner, the commander of the—"

"I am familiar with the particulars of what happened in Nevada, and I certainly know of the Keys troops and their commander, whose deputy you were. I am on the list, if you are not aware of it, of those church officials who receive intelligence reports from the Vatican. Since you are the one responsible for the existence of this network, I have you to thank for the valuable information this network produces. It reflects admirably the expertise you acquired from French intelligence before you became a priest, if I may say so."

"Thank you, Your Grace. But most of the technology was provided to us by the Americans during the war. It is very advanced—and expensive, as you may imagine."

"And, if I may further speculate, you think Kintner is a fugitive somewhere in my archdiocese."

Bohemund silently stared at the archbishop for a long moment.

"I believe you are doing more than speculating, Your Grace. I think you may also be on the Keys communications network—as I am."

Archbishop Wolnik got up from his chair and walked over to the large window that looked down on Geary Boulevard, stretching toward where it joined Market Street a few blocks from the bay.

"I have done my best to keep this confidential, for obvious reasons, but I am already committed to doing whatever is necessary to help the men who fought in the Crusade as well as their families. It is a disgrace the way the Vatican has neglected them since the war." He turned back toward Bohemund.

"I am pleased to see that the Holy See has changed its attitude, if I am not presuming too much from your appearance here."

"It has for now, but you may conclude that they are still not eager to have any publicity about their involvement."

"All right. Let's get down to cases. What do you propose that we do?"

"First and foremost, we must find Kintner. We have reason to believe that he may also have a young woman with him, the niece of Coronel Lorenzo Morales. She disappeared about the same time Kintner did."

"Have you considered contacting the FBI? We could use whatever information they might have about the Wahabi and the French agents who have been following Kintner."

Bohemund's eyes widened.

"Your information is better than mine. I only recently learned about the Wahabi from a man named Gil Berenger. You know him, of course?"

"Yes. Father Berenger and I have worked together for some time. Gil also has some contacts in Washington, at a very high level, apparently. But we need real-time intelligence, as you professionals call it. The FBI might be willing to help."

"I don't think that would be wise. The American government would kill Kintner in an instant, I believe. They feel themselves exposed on the issue of the destruction of the Grand Mosque in Mecca. Or there might be other reasons. Anyway, I feel we must find Kintner before any of the three—the Wahabi, the FBI, or the DCRI."

Wolnik sat back down at the table. He sat staring at Bohemund for a long time as if trying to decide something. Then he spoke.

"Our motivations in this matter are not identical, as you no doubt have already perceived. But they are similar enough to impel me to trust you in this undertaking. I am not going to ask you to keep everything I say a secret, because you have other loyalties—that is to say, accountabilities."

Bohemund remained silent, his curiosity growing.

"Gil Berenger is the nominal head of an organization that is thoroughly Catholic but unrecognized by Holy Mother Church. If they were, they would almost certainly have already tried to destroy it. I am not referring to the Keys, of course. You have already spoken to Father Berenger, so I think you may have an inkling of what I am talking about."

"Yes, Your Grace. But I am not here to ferret out or otherwise unearth any kind of dissident organization, whether heretical or not. Michael Kintner is a dear friend, whatever he has done or not done, and at this point, I only want to see him safe from the depredations of our enemies. If such a thing is possible."

"It is. I seem to remember a passage of scripture that says that anything is possible to one who has faith."

Bohemund smiled. "Thank you, Your Grace. I need reminding on occasion of the fundamentals."

"All right, then. In addition to alerting the parish priests under my jurisdiction to assist, I am also asking you to follow Father Berenger's every request in this matter. If Kintner is to be saved, only he can do it.

"Now, step one is to check out of your hotel and leave no forwarding address. Do not attempt any unsecure communication with anyone, including face-to-face conversations, with anyone other than Gil Berenger. When Kintner is safe, and with Gil's concurrence, only then should you resurface and continue your duties to the Vatican. Can you do this?"

"I will do my best. But it has been a long time since I had to behave as an operative—I may make some mistakes."

"I am sure you will do fine. Go directly from here to your hotel and change clothes into normal street wear for nonclerics. Two men will come to your room who will identify themselves in some fashion by which you can be certain of who they are. One will be wearing the coveralls of a local electrical repair service, and the other will be in clerical garb. The priest will take your bags down to the desk and check you out of the hotel. The other will provide you with service coveralls, and you will accompany him to the service entrance and then to a van parked in back marked also with the local repair service logo. It will take you to Father Berenger. Any questions?"

Monsignor Bohemund shook his head and stood up. The archbishop made the sign of the cross in blessing, and they parted company.

* * *

Suleiman followed the embassy clerk down the long hall lined with office suites; the clerk turned into one of the largest, bowed, and left. Some meters away stood a tall man in classic Arab gown and turban, staring out the floor-to-ceiling windows, which overlooked the bay. He turned around as Suleiman drew closer and nodded to him. Suleiman made a proper obeisance and wished him peace.

"My pardon for the inconvenience, my Lord Saleh. I had no choice but to—"

"Do not apologize, Suleiman. Sit down and tell me your account of what happened at the Morales ranch in Nevada."

Suleiman went through the story again, putting the best possible face on the ignominious defeat Ahwadi and his contingent of fighters had suffered.

"Well, that is either very unfortunate or very stupid. One never attacks an enemy without knowing his strength."

"We had so little time to prepare, Lord Saleh. The FBI and French agents were closing in very fast."

"Yes, well, we will let it rest; it cannot be undone. What exactly are you proposing to do now?"

"As I explained to the duty officer the night I called, we have exhausted our resources here in America. The field offices in—"

"I know all about that. Get on with it."

"We need the best that the Wahabi can provide us. The al-Qaeda leadership and infrastructure are all but destroyed. The organization Osama bin Laden set up no longer works. The French have committed only an agent or two to America as far as we know, but the FBI committed a small army of troops and gunships after the tragedy at the ranch. But even that is not enough to protect all the devils of the Crusade. I think we need at least two dozen top fighters, armed with the latest technology in weapons and information-gathering equipment."

"To do what exactly?"

"First—and most importantly—we must find the devil Kintner wherever he is hiding and kill him. Then we will go after the remaining leaders of the Crusade in America. One by one, they will be—"

"Wait. What makes you think Kintner is still alive? The Americans have already pronounced him dead."

"Well, I never saw his body. And I have to think the Americans were a little too eager with their announcements of his death. When I returned to the motel where we had been staying in Ely, Nevada, I saw a man I think might have been a French agent. If the French are still here, then they must not believe Kintner is dead either."

Saleh studied the man opposite for a long moment.

"What you say makes some sense. This man Kintner appears to have as many lives as a cat. What about the communications intercepts you collected before the attack on the ranch. Did any of them indicate that Kintner was alive?"

"No. But from the conversations between the FBI and state troopers, they believed Kintner was alive when they decided to send reinforcements. Also, it may not mean very much, but Lord Ahwadi said something just before we attacked—"

"Well, what?"

"He said Allah would not have willed that Kintner be killed by anyone but us—his faithful."

Saleh drew his hand across his face, whether in frustration or in agreement, Suleiman could not say.

"I am going to do two things right away, Suleiman. I am going to direct our intelligence apparatus here on the West Coast to collect, within the limits of their capabilities, whatever it can on the pertinent movements of the state police, the sheriff's departments, and the FBI. Do you remember any of the wavelengths your team was monitoring to pick up the state police and FBI communications?"

"Yes. The FBI has an enormous capability, but the state police are limited and it was these frequencies we monitored. American law requires that anything the government law enforcement in Washington does is coordinated with local authorities."

"Good. That is where we shall start. And I will call the foreign secretary in Riyadh to pass on my request for Wahabi troops and other operatives. There may be some already in America, which we can summon here. Also, I will insist that they send the latest technology, information-gathering equipment, and weapons. Anyway, diplomatic courier aircraft fly in frequently from Saudi Arabia with no interference or inspections. And every Wahabi agent will possess diplomatic immunity."

Saleh permitted himself a smile. Suleiman did not smile. He was thinking about just exactly how secure any call from here to Riyadh might be.

* * *

The flashing light on the dashboard-mounted communications device was very insistent. Henri Breuger pulled the car over to the side of the road and touched the receive button.

"This is the San Francisco consulate. Please provide identification."

Breuger sighed and touched the transmit button.

"This is Breuger. I am not keeping up with your passwords of the day, for all the good they do. What do you want?"

"I am Mondet, DCRI attaché. The DGSE have decoded a transmission from the Saudi consulate asking Riyadh for additional personnel specialized in covert activities, along with their hardware. Are you near San Francisco?"

"We are about two hours away. Was there any mention of Michael Kintner in the Saudi transmission?"

"There seemed to be a veiled reference to 'one who escaped.' We are not sure whether that refers to one of the al-Qaeda or to Kintner."

"I have a request. Have someone who knows what he is doing report a stolen vehicle to the California state police. It would be a late-model Ford F-150, dark blue in color. That is the last known vehicle Kintner and a young girl were traveling in. Contact me immediately with any information you receive. Can you do this?"

"Yes. Anything else?"

"You may want to increase whatever normal surveillance you have on the Saudi consulate and the district FBI office. I believe we may find ourselves up to our collarbone in Wahabi terrorists within a few days, if not hours."

"Thank you for your advice. That is already underway."

"Have there been any interesting activities from this increased surveillance?" Breuger hated having to pull information from someone.

"We know that the local FBI field office director has been contacted on a secure link by newly arrived personnel. We haven't decoded it yet."

Breuger sighed. "Well, let me know when you do." He jabbed at the transmission and turned to Elise.

"Where do we get these people? No wonder France no longer has an empire."

"How is it known that an unusual transmission has occurred in the FBI offices? There must be hundreds of those a day."

"Not every employee in such offices, even the most secure, is a thoroughly known quantity. Uncleared personnel can watch for small events and report back on them. As far as encrypted communications are concerned, one doesn't have to be able to decode them to be able to establish patterns and routines over several months of observations. Any deviation is noticed by the computers and made known to us. I would think you would know this. You are not an amateur."

"No. But I continue to be fascinated by how even the most complex security procedures and equipment can be overcome."

"Well, it ultimately comes down to how well human intelligence can digest information—just like in the days before computers took over." Breuger grinned at his own joke.

"So, what now? Back to some rat trap reeking with disinfectant?"

"We wait. But not in a motel. San Francisco is the most European city in America. I have a friend with a friend, so to speak."

"I'm intrigued."

"Just minutes north of the city is North Bay—completely separated from the city by water but close enough to get there in a short time. Very affluent and very close to a protected beach area and to wine-growing country. There is a well-appointed empty *maison* just waiting for us. Sound good so far?"

"I always said you were a gentleman, Henri."

Breuger grinned again. "Don't insult me. I am a Frenchman. That is sufficient."

* * *

"General Kane, Dr. Weiss is on the line. Are you able to take the call?"

The national security advisor to the president dropped the paper he was reading and reached for the phone, selecting the lighted line.

"Judy. Glad you called. I never got a chance to talk to you about that little meeting in the Oval Office. What was your reaction?"

"Come on, David. There is no such thing as a 'little' meeting in the Oval Office. But I was just glad to get out of there before I started to bleed from Senator—I mean President Hilton's dirty looks. She didn't seem very comfortable with her chair, just yet, if you know what I mean."

"Yes, well . . . Sorry you had to put up with that. Anyway, what did you think about her decision to pursue Michael Kintner?"

"It worried me then, and it worries me even more now. I need you to level with me, David. After all that business at the ranch in Nevada, is Michael alive or not?"

"Well, he was at the time of the attack. How he could have been, I don't know, but . . . This phone isn't secure, Judy, as you know. Would you like to meet for lunch at the Hawk and Dove? Say in about twenty minutes?"

Judy hesitated; the Hawk and Dove was a favorite watering hole up on Capitol Hill, but it had, in the old days of the war, been a code between Kane and Judy for a meeting in the Old Executive Office Building. There were plenty of secure rooms there.

"Twenty minutes. Right."

Exactly twenty minutes later, Judy and Kane sat down in the conference room reserved for them in a hurry.

"A good deal has happened that wasn't in the news, Judy. First, we allowed Colonel Morales to preserve his fiction that Kintner was buried on his property. The reason is obvious, but we knew that it was a temporary measure. We are pretty sure, and we think the French are sure, that Riyadh is sending Wahabi terrorists to the West Coast. We can't stop it without a major diplomatic dustup, but we know pretty much how they will get here and we can keep an eye on them afterward. They are not on their home field anymore, as they were in Afghanistan. I don't think the president will hesitate to wipe them out if they try anything."

"I don't think the Wahabi will care about their own losses, if they can take Michael Kintner out in the process, do you?"

"No, of course not. But we cannot give them such an obvious victory. That's why we have to find Kintner first."

"But you have already declared him dead. So you must be planning to kill him if you find him."

"Give me some credit, Judy. I wouldn't countenance that, and I can assure you that I would oppose any idea the president might have that we should take such an action."

Judy stared for a long moment at the painting on the wall of the victory at Saratoga. Then she turned her face back to Kane.

"How did we get to this kind of world, David? Did all this get started just because we and Britain wanted to give the Jews a homeland? Is all this a Muslim reaction to that?"

"This has been simmering on the back burner since the fall of the Ottoman Empire, Judy. Well, since the start of the Muslim conquests in the seventh century, actually. However it started, we have to deal with it realistically and avoid pretending that we are all just one big, happy human family at heart."

"That's what I think, as well. We could toss Israel to the wolves tomorrow, and it would solve nothing. We have to try to make this sort of thing unthinkable—and the only way I know of is to make the consequences of terrorist activity too high for anyone to consider."

Kane gave Judy one of his wry smiles.

"Yes. I remember that was what we all thought in September 2001."

"What exactly is happening now, David? Are all the agents collecting in California waiting for someone else to draw first?"

"No. Well, it's true that the FBI and the DCRI are out there in some force, but we have an ace in the hole, which I hope we can play. Monsignor Robert Bohemund is in San Francisco, conferring with Archbishop Wolnik on the best way to locate and bring Kintner to safety. Holy Mother Church can be extremely resourceful when she has to."

Judy's eyes widened at the thought.

"David, I think I might be able to help . . . No, please hear me out. If either Wolnik or Bohemund is able to get word to Kintner that I am there, it could be the impetus for his coming in from the cold, to use a hackneyed phrase. I would stay out of the way of your agents or theirs or anyone. Would you consider that?"

Kane put his hand on his jaw and rubbed it. He was thinking that she might be of some help, at that. After all, she had been in his position for the whole of the recent war with the Muslims. She wasn't the type to try anything crackbrained. He hoped.

"All right, Judy, you convinced me. I think you may want to contact Bohemund, whom you have met, first. He is staying at the St. Francis Hotel in San Francisco."

Chapter 12

Michael kept driving, silently, the phantom truck no longer visible in the mirror, if it had ever been there at all. The road sign said Reno was ten miles ahead. Already, the desert emptiness was filling up with signs and billboards advertising all the heavenly joys and adventure of laying down your small fortune, certain to come away richer and happier—the fools' paradise, doubled and redoubled.

Maggie stirred from her nap, rubbed her eyes, and looked around. The advertisements were starting to include those that made garish and not very subtle references to "chicken ranches" or to "bunny havens," the adolescent appellations used to identify legal whorehouses in Nevada. The appalling glitz and chintz long since had overwhelmed the once charming little guilty-pleasure township, which it had been in the beginning, little more than half a century ago.

"Michael, I just remembered a place not far from here that not many people know about that Daddy used to take us to when I was a little girl. That might be a good place to rest and catch our breath. Want to hear about it?"

"You're not referring to some sort of resort, are you? That could be pretty risky."

"No. It's just a cabin, and, as I remember, the nearest store of any kind was about a half-hour drive away. It was by a little creek, deep in the forest, up around the Truckee River. A person would have to be very lucky to discover it by accident."

"Okay. It sounds like the kind of place we need right now. How do we get there?"

"Just go straight through town. The turnoff is hard to spot, but I'm sure I will recognize it."

Michael eased the truck into the right lane as he encountered heavier traffic in the city. He didn't like being this exposed, but sometimes a crowded venue was the best place to hide. What should he be looking for as a permanent home for Maggie? A monastery? A girls' school? Maggie had to be his first priority; how could she not be? But he couldn't let her out of his sight until a haven had been found for her. Then he could start thinking about himself.

He didn't know what to make of the improvement in his physical condition. Getting shot didn't exactly help matters, but it was minor compared to the radiation poisoning. No one ever recovered from that kind of dosage, did he? Yet here he was, feeling more pain-free and alert than he had since the explosion. He had even been having thoughts of sex, the last thing one would feel in the throes of radiation sickness. If he were on the way to recovery—no, how could he be? It reminded him of the Groucho Marx joke: "Who are you going to believe, me or your own eyes?" But it certainly seemed possible. What could he possibly do with a new life? Everyone—and that really did mean everyone—wanted him dead. There was no place for him in the world.

"Why so glum, Michael? You seemed in so much better spirits earlier."

Michael managed a smile.

"Just thinking about what a terrible reflection on human nature this awful little city is. Can there be any redeeming virtue to such a place? Very depressing."

"Well, the ones who own the casinos and hotels, the theaters and strip joints and whorehouses are making a pile of money. I'll bet they never stop to think about what the redeeming virtues might be."

"I'm sure they don't. They are too happy with being rich to feel guilty. I wonder if very many of them obtain genuine happiness from their lives though."

"My daddy was rich. And he was the unhappiest man I knew. His wife was unfaithful, his foreman was a thief and a cuckold, his little innocent daughter was—well, not innocent anymore. And then he was murdered. His wealth couldn't save him from all that."

"No. But in my belief system, in my faith, there is a cosmic justice present in the universe. There are pandemic forces and influences that restore the natural balance to things. Whether one believes in it or not, it is an immutable fact. There is no such thing as coincidence—as a causal force, anyway. The Greek philosophers knew and believed this, as well as the ancient mystics and holy men of every part of the world. It was well established long before Christ appeared on the scene to draw everything together."

Several minutes later, the traffic thinned and a sign indicated that they were on Interstate 80 headed toward San Francisco.

"We're going to have to get off this route now, Maggie. Everyone is going to have some surveillance on the interstate highways. There's a turnoff to Highway 395. I'm going to take it and try to find a county road of some sort. Let me know if you spot anything familiar."

"The sign says we're headed toward Lassen Volcanic Park. I guess we might as well sightsee while we're running, right?"

"Not very funny. This whole thing could . . ." Suddenly, he thought of an acquaintance from Georgetown University, a Jesuit priest and professor of mathematics named Dennis Parker, who had been on the faculty with him.

"Maggie, you wouldn't happen to have a cell phone with you, would you? I know cell phones are easily traced, but I think it might be worth the risk. I just remembered a colleague from some years ago who hailed from a parish not far from that park you just mentioned. It's just possible that . . ."

Maggie grinned.

"A teenage girl never leaves home without her cell phone, Michael. You should know that."

"I confess to knowing almost nothing about teenage girls, dear. But, well, it would be taking a risk, but we might try to contact my old friend's parish church if I can just— Oh, yeah, now I remember. I used to kid him about his growing up in a church dedicated to St. Francis of Assisi and then joining the Jesuit Order out of seminary instead of the Franciscans. Kind of an inside joke."

"What exactly would that do to help us? Your friend wouldn't be there, would he?"

"No. It's the location I'm thinking of. He told me the church was near the Shasta National Forest. In a pinch, we could lose ourselves in such a wilderness without half trying."

"You mean just camp out until everything calmed down?"

"Why not? We've certainly got all the gear we need in the back. Your uncle saw to that."

Maggie grinned again. It seemed to Michael that she was recovering nicely from the recent tragedies.

"It sounds like fun. Sure, why not? Let me look up the number on my search app. What was the name again? Oh, yeah, St. Francis of Assisi. Do you remember the town?"

"I'm trying. Something like Gurney, Burnout, or . . . Oh, yes. Burney, California."

Michael spotted a truck turnaround area and pulled over. He cut the engine and waited for Maggie to finish whatever ritual she was performing on her cell phone. He hoped that whoever traced the call would not be able to react quickly enough to apprehend them before they moved on.

* * *

203

Bronson and Russell and their technician, Charlie Simmons, were just finishing up their lunch at Scoma's Fisherman's Wharf. Ken was watching a small contingent of young girls passing around their cell phones, showing off pictures of some kind and giggling wickedly. *Signs of the times,* he thought. Not like when he was—

"George, I just thought of something. Morales's niece—Maggie, wasn't it? She's presumably with Kintner, right? She is about the same age as those youngsters over at that table."

Bronson looked over at the activities of the girls with their iPods and phones or whatever they were. He looked back at Ken, his eyes widening.

"Great thinking, partner." He looked at the technician. "Charlie, have we—sorry, I meant have *you* got access to phone account search software from our mobile station in the van?"

Charlie gave him a deprecating smile.

"No, not exactly, but I can get any information we need to bug someone's calls—especially from cell phones. As long as you know the name and address her account is listed for. That's what you want, isn't it?"

"Yes. Let's get back to our comm equipment and ask whomever it is we need to ask to start listening for calls from Miss Maggie Morales's phone."

* * *

Maggie read off the phone number of St. Francis of Assisi parish in Burney, California, from her small screen and then dialed it with a touch. She handed it to Michael when it started to ring the number.

"St. Francis Parish, Father Parker speaking."

Michael was dumbfounded. "Not Dennis Parker, the Georgetown professor?"

"Well, yes. Who is calling, please?"

"Dennis, it's Michael Kintner, department of physics and astronomy. Remember me?"

"My God, Michael! What in the name of . . . Where are you? What has happened to you? I heard on the news that you had been killed!"

"I was, officially, so let's leave it that way for now. But what are you doing back at St. Francis? Wasn't that the parish you grew up in?"

"I'm back visiting my family. My mother was ill, so I . . . But where are you? Do you need help of any kind?"

"That's putting it mildly, old buddy. Listen, I don't really feel safe talking from this phone, so I was wondering if we could meet. I can find you anywhere you—"

"Okay, let me think. There's a quiet little campground named Lakeshore East near here. Have you got GPS?"

"Yes. But so has everyone else."

"Okay, I get it. Let's try this: Head for the campground, and somewhere along the way, you will see a disgracefully dirty red Toyota sedan, vintage 1993, parked on the shoulder. From there, I will lead you to it. Okay?"

"Okay, buddy. Sometime in the next few hours. And many thanks. God bless."

"You, too, Michael. May Our Lady Mother be with you."

Michael handed Maggie her phone, started the truck, and pulled back on the highway.

* * *

Father Dennis Parker got up from his desk and walked over to the library where he knew the pastor, Father Dooley, spent most of his time. His mind was still reeling from the conversation with Michael. Imagine, after all that had happened—the war, the business at that ranch in Nevada—and now Michael Kintner, former university colleague and knight commander of the Sacred Order of the Keys of St. Peter, had washed up on his doorstep, well, almost.

He tapped softly on the library doorjamb and walked in.

"Pardon me, Father, but something has happened, which you may need to be aware of and which may require me to be gone for a while."

Parker recounted the conversation with Michael, how they knew each other, and what they had planned to do. Father Dooley listened carefully to everything Parker had to say.

"Well, I'd say offhand that the phrase 'God works in mysterious ways' is particularly apt here."

"I'm sorry, what?"

"I received a phone call from Archbishop Wolnik just last night. He has contacted practically every priest in the archdiocese. He told me that Michael Kintner was being pursued in this part of the country, and he was determined to do everything in his power to help him. Apparently, there are still a lot of terrorists after Kintner, and they mean to attack some of the other leaders of the crusade as well. He wanted to be notified immediately if Kintner contacted any of us. He has some resources at his behest, even someone from the Vatican."

"But . . . what can I do? I have to keep my promise to meet him. I can't leave him high and dry. He is my friend, among other obvious reasons."

"I don't want you to break any promises you made to him, Dennis. But Michael would benefit from the archbishop's help, I think. What if we do this: you take your Toyota where you intended and park it and wait. In the meantime, I will call the archbishop back and tell him what we are doing. I am sure he will do nothing to put you or Michael in danger and just may be able to bring Michael to—well, wherever he would be safe."

Dennis grimaced slightly and looked out the window of the library into the garden beyond.

"Okay, Father. Tell the archbishop that I intend to park and wait for Michael about three miles short of the boat dock at the Lakeshore East campground. No, wait. Michael alluded to the fact that a lot of electronic surveillance is being directed at him. Leave my exact location out of your conversation with the bishop."

"All right, Dennis. But it might save some time if—"

"Please, Father Dooley. I can't sandbag Michael on this."

Parker left the room and headed toward his quarters to get a few things Michael might need. He thought about what Dooley had told him and wondered if he might have left something out—like what these other resources the bishop had might be. He hoped desperately that he wasn't leading Michael into a trap of some sort.

* * *

Michael's GPS had gotten him to Highway 299 West, and he was straining to catch sight of any sign of the Lakeshore East campground. He saw a sign that indicated he was headed for Interstate 5 in a few miles, but he wanted to avoid that. It was a good bet that the FBI had put the state troopers on watch for the vehicle. They would certainly know by now which vehicle they were traveling in, just by asking a few questions at the Morales ranch. Then he spotted it, just as Maggie did.

"Look, Michael! There it is! The turnoff is only a mile ahead."

"I see it. Let's get a plan here. When and if we spot Dennis's Toyota, I will drive toward him, and when we are fairly close, I will flash my lights. If he notices it and pulls out, then we can follow him to a good place to pull off. I know it sounds hokey, but we don't have a lot of options."

"It sounds like it might work. But if anyone else is watching, they are going to catch on anyway, don't you think?"

"Yes. But they might not have had time to react to my phone call yet. That's what I'm counting on."

A few miles farther on, they both spotted the beat-up old Toyota. While they were still at some distance, Michael flashed his lights on and off. The brake lights on the Toyota briefly flashed, and Michael slowed down to see if Dennis would pull out, which he did. They drove on toward the lake, Michael following just close enough not to lose him on the winding road.

* * *

"My name is Judy Weiss. I have a reservation."

"Yes, Dr. Weiss, we have your room ready. I hope you enjoy your stay with us at the St. Francis." He rang for the bellman.

"By the way, can you tell me which room Monsignor Bohemund is in? I am an acquaintance of his, so I don't think he would mind if . . ."

The clerk looked down at his computer screen and punched up another screen.

"I am sorry, Dr. Weiss, but it appears that the monsignor checked out yesterday. He did not leave a forwarding address."

Judy stood speechless, feeling very foolish. *Now what?* she thought. The archbishop—that was who he came to see, according to Kane. That was the person she would contact.

"Dr. Weiss?"

Judy turned to see a dark, broad-shouldered man who looked familiar. *Breuger.*

"Well, the DCRI is still on duty, I see."

"Yes. Sorry about the little charade back in Georgetown. I think we can help each other. If you are willing."

"I doubt it. From what I understand, your mission is pretty clear. You intend to see Kintner dead, no matter what."

"No. Are you willing to discuss it?"

Judy hesitated. This was the last thing she had expected. Breuger must know he was taking a risk to come there. He must be running out of options.

The agent from the San Francisco district FBI office was seated across the lobby from the admittance desk. He took out his secure cell and punched up a number.

"Mr. Ames, this is Agent Colman. Dr. Weiss just showed up here at the St. Francis, I suppose to find Bohemund. But someone else has showed up. Breuger. He is talking to her now. What are your instructions?"

"Follow them, if they leave. Pass them off to your link as soon as you see him. I'll contact the Washington contingent and let them know what's happening."

Colman put his cell away and saw, over the top of the magazine he was pretending to read, Breuger and Weiss leaving the hotel. He also saw the bellman pick up Dr. Weiss's luggage and take it toward the elevator. As he was instructed, he got up and followed them out of the hotel. Outside, he saw the pair get into a dark SUV. He also spotted his hand-off man behind the wheel of his car, who made a gesture to him that he was on the move.

Judy sat back in the passenger seat of the SUV and buckled her seat belt. She felt something cold and metallic against the back of her neck.

"You are in no danger, Dr. Weiss. Just a precaution. Would you give me your handbag, please?"

Judy dutifully handed her handbag over her shoulder to the feminine voice behind her. She heard the bag being searched and then saw it handed back to her. She took it, looked briefly inside, and could see nothing missing or added.

"Dr. Weiss, this is Elise Marquette, my colleague. We will not take much of your time. As soon as I lose the tail the locals now have on me, we will go someplace to talk."

Breuger took the turn onto Highway 101 to cross the Bay Bridge to the north.

"Am I your prisoner, or do I have a choice?"

"I will take you back anytime you say. If you like, we can talk in the vehicle."

"All right then, what is it you want?"

"When last we talked, you said that you were sure that Kintner's injuries were terminal and that he would have no interest in any further actions against the terrorists. Since that time, you have attended a meeting with the president in the Oval Office and have met several times with members of the intelligence community. Are you still certain that Kintner plans nothing more in the way of retribution against the Muslims, either on his own or at the behest of the Vatican?"

"It seems that your own intelligence apparatus has been pretty busy also, Monsieur Breuger."

"Yes. Please understand that the government of France is at least as eager to avoid further conflict as your own government no doubt is. I see no reason why we cannot cooperate to see that this does not happen. I am not referring to the two governments. I know you are in no position to speak for yours anymore than I am for mine. I am merely suggesting that—"

For a moment, Breuger's attention was not on the traffic or on the agent following him. At that moment, a huge semitrailer truck in the passing lane swerved violently into his van, crushing the driver's side and pushing the vehicle through the guardrails and following it 220 feet into the water below.

* * *

Director John Ames hung up the phone, his face livid with frustration. They had dumped this whole business into his lap with no chance to prepare a plan, and now they were blaming him for the mess. "They" being practically the whole security apparatus in Washington, including his own chain of command.

"I am sorry, John," said George Bronson. "I am the one to blame, not you. I tried to explain this to Mr. Owens, but he was too busy trying to cover himself to listen to me."

"It's okay, George. This new administration still has to learn the limits of its control over people and events. I don't know what spin they are going to put on this for the news media, but I am prepared to be amazed. I'll bet that the first words out of the White House are what a bad situation they inherited from the last bunch that was in power."

Ames looked over at Ken Russell, the CIA liaison George had brought with him, much to Ames's discomfort. If the past was prologue, the CIA would find a way to make this a jurisdiction fight.

"What about your people, Ken? How deeply are they involved in this?"

"Not very, I shouldn't think. When I got this assignment, I was given strict orders not to interfere with FBI operations—except to provide whatever help you might need from us."

"Well, was this little episode the work of the Wahabi or not? Or doesn't the CIA keep track?"

"Come on, John," said Bronson. "Let's not follow Washington's lead and smear everybody with this. The only relevant question is what are we going to do about it?"

"Yeah, you're right, George. Sorry, Ken." John thought for a moment. "You know, it seems strange to me, assuming that it was the Wahabi, that they would go after the French agents and a retired bureaucrat. What exactly does that get them?"

"It's consistent with the distorted mind-set of these characters," said Russell. "The fight with the French has been going on since the colonization days in North Africa. But maybe more to the point, they think that if anyone wastes this guy Kintner or the other leaders of the Crusade, it has to be those faithful to *Allah*."

"Well, why wouldn't they wait to see if Weiss and the French found him and step in then?"

"They're taking no chances—not after what happened at the ranch in Nevada. They took a beating there, and they must be anxious to get themselves in front of this situation."

"Well, that makes sense to me. What do you think, George?"

"I think we had better start worrying about Monsignor Bohemund—and maybe the archbishop, as well. They are the other people involved in trying to find Kintner. Plus, don't forget that Bohemund was Kintner's deputy in the crusade. I'm sure the terrorists haven't forgotten that."

"No, I'm sure not. But where is he? He seems to have disappeared right from under your nose and mine. Do you think the *Wahabi* might already have him?"

"It's possible, I suppose. But if they did, wouldn't Archbishop Wolnik have notified you by now?"

John Ames looked at Bronson and Russell steadily for a long moment. Then he got up hurriedly and put on his jacket.

"Come on. We're wasting time."

The three men got out of their chairs just as Bronson's cell went off. He took it out of his pocket and held it to his ear as the others waited for him.

"All right, Charlie. Is he on foot or in the Ford pickup? . . . Okay. I am in Mr. Ames's office right now. Keep me posted." He put the phone away.

"I think we may want to postpone the visit with Wolnik, John. Our surveillance has just located Michael Kintner at a campground on the lake up in the Shasta National Forest."

Ames walked back to his desk and punched up his intercom.

"Alice, contact every agent we have in the district who is not on stakeout duty. Get as many resources as you can muster up to the Shasta Lake area. Then contact the California State Troopers and have them block off every possible route in and out of that area. Hold on a minute."

He turned back to Bronson.

"Is he still traveling in the Ford?"

"Yes. He's meeting someone in a 1993 red Toyota sedan."

He passed the information to Alice and punched off the intercom.

"I am going to head up there myself, George. Do you want to come with me or go meet with Wolnik?"

"Wolnik can wait. Kintner's the key to everything in this affair."

* * *

Dennis Parker pulled into the boat dock, away from the marina office building, and got out of his Toyota, just as Michael and Maggie pulled up next to him. Michael got out and went over to Dennis, took him by his shoulders, and looked hard into his face. He was still the fresh-faced youngster he remembered, almost, but time had treated him with kindness.

"Who'd have thought it, Dennis? Two beat-up professors from a Jesuit university mixed up in something like this?"

They grabbed each other in a bear hug and pounded each other on the back, like two old fraternity brothers. Then they backed off from each other a pace.

"I hate to say this, Michael, but you look like . . ."

"Yeah, I know, buddy. The strange thing is, I feel better than I have in weeks. Let me introduce you to someone who looks a great deal better than either of us."

"Before you do that, Michael, I must tell you something. The pastor at St. Francis told me that Archbishop Wolnik had called almost every one of his parish pastors and told them to watch for you. He said that the archdiocese had resources to help you find safety."

"Dennis, are you telling me that you ratted us out?"

"No, no, Michael, nothing like that. I told Father Dooley that we were going to meet but not where. But he might have passed that on to the archbishop."

"Did he say what kind of resources? Should we look for angels or cops?"

"Michael, please. I didn't know what to do. I . . ."

Maggie came up to them with a timid little smile, uncertain how to act in the situation. Michael turned to her and smiled.

"Maggie, this is one of a handful of mathematicians who believe, as I do, that complexity theory may be the next best thing to gospel. But he is otherwise pretty smart."

"I have no idea what any of that means, but I am pleased to meet you, Father."

"No, just Dennis, please. I am a little out of my element as a priest at the moment."

"I am sure the both of you have a great deal to talk about, but don't you think we had better get on with whatever we can to disappear?"

"Quite right, Maggie. Michael, I lived in this area growing up, as you know, and there are lots of places you could hide—but for how long, and on what resources, I am not sure. There are a couple of old logging roads that lead from the other side of the lake up to the area around the volcano. And there are still some old stone cabins from the time of the influx of Italian stone masons to this area, more than a century ago."

"Stone masons?" asked Maggie. "What made them come here?"

"Lots of mill work, economic developments of various sorts in the postwar boom. The Italian immigrants also account for the strong Catholic presence in this area."

Michael was looking at the lake and the surroundings. He noted the aluminum racks with various kinds of small boats stacked in them and looked up the shore where he could make out the marina and the docks for the larger boats. He gestured toward the racks of boats and spoke to Dennis.

"Is one of these our transport to the other side? Where the logging roads are?"

"Yes. The large green one on the bottom rack belongs to the parish. It should hold whatever gear you have. And it has an outboard motor, as you can see. For us sedentary priests."

Dennis grinned at his own joke. Neither he nor Michael had ever led sedentary lives as priests, preferring sailing on the Chesapeake and hiking in the Shenandoah Valley to hiding in the bookshelves of Georgetown University. Michael smiled and turned toward his truck.

"Might as well get started. There are some backpacks and carrying belts in the truck. And some luxuries, but we'll pack only the food, medicine, and weapons. Help Maggie with hers, Dennis— the light stuff—and I'll pack the heavier stuff in mine."

The three of them turned to their task, with Michael deliberately taking some of the heavier items, such as cooking ware, weapons, and ammunition. When they had finished, Michael and Dennis moved their vehicles into a space as far under the trees as possible, and then they put the boat in the water and loaded the packs and belts.

"Maggie, if anything should happen on the water, and we have to abandon the boat, grab whatever you think you can swim with and forget about the rest."

"I've been camping with Daddy for years, Michael. I'm not a child," she said, feigning a pout.

Michael grinned at her. No, indeed, she was not. Then his smile disappeared as he thought of a long-ago time.

He looked around and saw that the road watch team were all assembled and waiting for the order to move down the mountain. The team leader came up to Kintner.

"*Sir, I'm Sergeant Bill Tunney. Your radio operator is going to stick close to you for communications with Starlight, your command post. And I would be obliged if you would stick close to me, sir.*"

The burly man spoke in an authoritative tone. This was his team, and he ran it. He knew that the Keys troops' commander knew it. He had spent ten years in the US Army Special Forces and the last six months in training with troops of the IDF. He knew his business.

"*Whatever you say, Sergeant. But you look to your team. I don't need babysitting.*"

Chapter 13

Dennis made sure his passengers were sitting and then shoved the prow of the boat to free it of the shore and jumped in after. He took a position by the outboard motor in the stern and started the engine. They slowly moved out toward the center of the lake. The scenery around the lake was a panoply of old-growth forest and rising bluffs covered with mosses and ferns. The tall sequoia trees had ferns and mosses growing out of the trunks up as high as one could see from the lake. In the far distance, the four cones of ancient volcanoes rose upward as if in supplication to heaven. The plights and ploys of men were as trivial to the forest as if they existed not at all. It had been here for millennia and would be here for millennia more if man didn't manage to destroy it.

They had reached the center of the lake before they spotted the helicopter. It was moving slowly down the east-west axis of the lake and crossed over them as it continued on to the east. Michael looked at Dennis and puffed out his cheeks as if breathing a sigh of relief. The noise from the helicopter engine had almost faded when it started to build again. They looked in the direction it had gone and saw it returning, several hundred feet lower than before. It moved in close to shore and slowed to a hover close to the rack for small boats. Even from the distance they were, they could see two men alight from the helicopter and disappear into the trees, where the truck was parked. Then they returned and reboarded. The helicopter moved to an altitude of about fifty feet and headed toward the boat.

"Who do you think they are, Michael? Are they going to be shooting at us, or are they the good guys?"

"I don't know, Dennis. But right now, I don't know who the good guys are." He watched the helicopter as it continued slowly toward them. He wasn't sure diving overboard would make any difference. They were too far from shore to make a quick escape. He hoped he had been right about moving fast enough to escape whoever might be following the traced phone call. He had been a little desperate, especially with Maggie to think about.

The helicopter kept slowly moving at the same rate toward them. When it was overhead, someone called to them from over an amplified speaker.

"We are not your enemy, and we are not from any government agency. Please follow us to the shoreline."

The aircraft moved away slowly and then slowed again to a hover on the far shore, away from where they had embarked. The three looked at each other, waiting for someone to speak.

"No markings," said Michael. "That kind of narrows it down."

"To what? Does every legitimate flight have to be in a marked aircraft?" asked Dennis.

"Yes, but markings can be concealed quite easily just before takeoff from a private airport or after a brief stop at a concealed location. The FBI wouldn't want their identity concealed, and any foreign entity would be taking quite a risk to do it. These days, Air Force fighter jets are on call from any civil airport. Observing an unmarked aircraft would set off alarm bells in any controller's head. Besides, why would anyone care whether we identified them or not? We're about as helpless as we can get."

Michael kept staring at the shore where the aircraft had stopped. He wondered if it might be from the archbishop's "resources," whatever they were. He thought again about what he had just said to Dennis. Why *would* anyone care whether they were identified?

Dennis headed for the shoreline, just as the disembodied voice had ordered him. Like Michael, he realized they were totally vulnerable to whatever weapons might be aboard the aircraft. He had no idea what to expect, but he had to stick with Michael and the young girl. He could not leave them no matter who or what was in the aircraft. He prayed that it might be someone sent by the archbishop, but he was trying to prepare himself for the worst.

When they were a few meters from the shoreline, two men descended down the line from the helicopter to the ground. Neither of them appeared to be armed, but the way they were dressed made Michael's eyes widen in astonishment. They were wearing black uniforms with gold piping down the trouser legs; their collars were stiff and bore a gold insignia of crossed keys on one side and a gold military emblem of rank on the other. Their black berets also bore a shield containing crossed keys—the keys of St. Peter. *My God,* thought Michael. *They are Ordo Sacer Clavium Sancti Petri.* They were the first he had seen since that day—

"What is it, Michael? You look as if you have just seen a ghost."

Knight Commander Michael Kintner, Societas Jesu, did not answer. He rose, stepped into the shallow water, and walked ashore. The two men stopped a few meters from him, came to attention, and gave him the ancient Roman military salute—the closed fist was placed against the heart and then raised forward with an open hand, palm down. It was similar to the salute used by the Fascists in the twentieth century but no less sacred for that unfortunate coincidence. Michael returned the salute, striking his breast harder than necessary, trying to stop the tears from coming to his eyes. But they came anyway.

The Keys trooper with the chevrons on his collar walked over to the boat and helped Maggie to shore and then started to unload the gear. The other trooper with a star on his collar extended his hand to Kintner, and Michael took it and clasped it firmly.

"Commander, I am Knight Brigadier Peter Janowiscz. Please board the chopper as quickly as you can. We are expecting lots of company very shortly."

"What about—"

"They will come with us also, Commander. We can get them to wherever they need to go later, but right now—"

In the background, the sound of a large motorboat engine at a high rpm came to them clearly. Michael looked up the lake in the direction of the sound and saw the prow of a speedboat heading in their direction.

"That will be the park rangers, I believe, sir. And they will have state troopers aboard."

Another trooper had come out of the aircraft and was helping to load the gear and the passengers into the chopper. Kintner and Janowiscz followed them aboard, and the Blackhawk helicopter flew up out of the forest, heading west. Just as they cleared the trees, thirty-millimeter tracer rounds shot across the nose of the aircraft. The pilot banked hard to the left, toward the tracers, and then back to the right. It was an old aerial combat maneuver Michael recognized. Janowiscz, seated in the left, copilot seat, turned back to the passenger compartment and shouted, "Tighten your seat belts, sir! This is going to get rough!"

The pilot banked back steeply to the left, again, and an Apache Longbow helicopter shot past them. Then the pilot turned sharply in behind the Apache and fired his two M60D 7.62-millimeter Gatlings toward the other helicopter. The Apache went almost inverted, pulled toward the trees, and then lifted up again and came back toward the Blackhawk. Michael had never heard of air-to-air combat between helicopters before, and if the situation were not so desperate, he would have been fascinated. His own military background had been in F-15 fighter jets before he resigned and headed back to graduate school in physics and astronomy.

The Apache was positioning itself for another clear shot at the Blackhawk when it exploded in a large fireball. The Blackhawk turned back toward the west, and an F-15 Eagle shot past, waggling its wings in salute to them before turning back in the direction it came from.

After a few minutes, Janowiscz got out of his seat, came back to the passenger compartment, and sat down next to Kintner.

"What the hell was all that?" said Kintner. "Am I crazy or did an Air Force fighter jet just shoot down an Army Apache helicopter that was trying to shoot us down?"

"You are almost right." Janowiscz grinned. Then the smile vanished from his face.

"There are a great many things to explain to you, sir, and there will be time to do it when we get to where we are headed. But the first thing I will say is that hardly anything you may see is exactly what it appears to be. That is true at the visceral level as well as with your five senses."

"Sorry, Brigadier, but just what the hell are you talking about?"

"Indulge me, sir. But I can tell you that the Apache helicopter you saw did not belong to the US Army. Neither does this Blackhawk. But the Eagle you just saw is indeed an Air National Guard aircraft. The pilot was on a scheduled live-fire mission from the 144th Fighter Squadron at Klamath Falls, Oregon. Some of the pilots know us and are eager to lend a helping hand when necessary. None of this interferes with their NORAD Air Defense mission, however. In fact, it's good practice for them."

"Well, now I am totally confused. Is the order still on active combat status by some miracle or anomaly?"

"We are. Your deputy commander, Monsignor Bohemund, was made aware of our existence just a couple of days ago, when we found out about the situation with you and the terrorists. We offered to help, and he accepted."

"Does the Vatican know about this? I thought the pope disbanded our order."

"Actually, no, he hasn't. I think he preferred to ignore us, perhaps hoping we would just go away."

"Well, I am thankful that you did not. My friends and I wouldn't be alive right now otherwise."

Janowiscz excused himself and went back to the cockpit, leaving Michael to think about what he had just been told. It was a solid comfort to know that the order still existed and was still performing the mission for which it had been formed. The Crusade was still being fought, and it looked as if the fight was going to get a lot hotter.

* * *

John Ames, George Bronson, and Ken Russell climbed out of the park ranger patrol boat at the site where, just a few minutes before, the Blackhawk had picked up its human cargo. Ames was on his wireless secure link, talking to another Blackhawk, one that belonged to the FBI.

"We couldn't see very much of what happened from here. Fill me in."

"I am still a few miles out from the lake, sir. What we saw—whatever that dustup was—you are not going to believe. I don't even believe it."

"Spare me the verbal histrionics, Jordan. What happened?"

"An Apache Longbow was firing at another helicopter, I think a Blackhawk, but no markings that I could make out. Then a fighter, looked like an F-15, smoked in at low level and took the Apache out with one burst of its guns. I never saw where the Blackhawk went, and the F-15 was gone before I could turn my aircraft around for a better view."

Ames was taken aback, considerably. At what point, he wondered, did this pursuit of Kintner turn into a shooting war—and with aerial combat! There had to be a great deal more to this than he had thought.

"Is there anything else? Can you see anything?"

"Just the column of smoke where the Apache went down. Want me to take a closer look?"

"No. Come over here, and pick us up. You already have the GPS coordinates, I assume."

"Roger that, sir. Be there in about two minutes."

Ames put his cell away and turned around to speak to the park ranger captain.

"We will be picked up in a couple of minutes, Captain Craig. I recommend you alert some firefighting personnel about a downed aircraft, just a few miles away. The pilot coming to get us will give you the coordinates."

"What about a rescue team for the downed aircraft crew?"

"Won't be needed. But I know there is a fire there."

And there is going to be a fire in Washington about two minutes after I report this, he thought. *I wonder who they will blame this time?*

* * *

Archbishop Wolnik could not believe his ears. What could it mean? He looked back at his secretary, who stood waiting for his answer.

"Did the imam say what this was about? I do not trust these self-appointed prophets of the new Shiite Messiah."

"He would only say that he thought you had some mutual interests and that he thought you might be able to help each other." The young priest was unsure of his ground, because he had not routed this request through the monsignor who served the archbishop as his executive secretary. "The imam specifically asked that I go directly to you on this but would not say why."

"There can only be one reason. He knew Monsignor Walsh would insist on security for such a meeting. And he would have been right. It would be stupid of me to take the bait. That's why I . . ." He sat very still, thinking about the obvious dichotomy between a possible avenue of accommodation and a poorly conceived trap. The risk was so blatant he was tempted to take it, even though there was absolutely no logic behind such a decision.

"Tell him I will meet him. And get Father Berenger on the phone." *There was another way*, he thought. "Where did he say again?"

"The Kokkari Estiatorio. It's a Middle-Eastern restaurant close to the Embarcadero."

"Yes, I know it. Not very far from the Saudi embassy, is it?"

"No, Your Grace. About four blocks north." He waited a moment and then left to place the call the archbishop had asked for.

Two hours later, Archbishop Wolnik walked into the Kokkari and looked around. He saw no sign of the imam, nor of anyone in Islamic robes. A waiter walked up to him.

"If Your Grace pleases to follow me?" He turned and walked away, toward the back of the restaurant, where the private dining rooms were located. The archbishop followed, still looking about for anyone he might recognize. He was reminded of nothing so much as the clandestine meetings he became used to in Cold War Poland. It was not a comfortable feeling.

The waiter opened the door to the dining room and stepped aside deferentially for the archbishop. As Wolnik walked inside, a turbaned and robed man arose with a sickly smile. *Much like that of Osama*, thought Wolnik. The man walked forward, made a gesture with his hand upward about his face, and spoke.

"*Asalaami aleikum*," he said. "Peace be upon you."

"*Suhl*," replied the archbishop. "May we be reconciled."

"Indeed so, Your Grace. That is why I am here—why *we* are here. Please to sit down."

They both sat, and as if by signal, coffee was brought in. They waited in silence until the waiter had left.

"We have met before, Archbishop, but perhaps you do not remember. It was at an embassy reception some years ago, before the recent unpleasantries. I am Saleh Rahman. I am the spiritual leader for the people of the embassy—"

"I remember, Imam. I don't mean to be abrupt, but I would remind you that several recent homicides have taken place, with a good deal of reason to believe that terrorists under your protection have committed them. I hope you do not expect me to ignore these depredations in our efforts to achieve some kind of truce."

The imam's face became dark, and his posture subtly changed.

"I am not here to answer to you about these unfounded and offensive allegations. I come here to offer peace."

"The founder of my faith once observed that only the dead are truly at peace. But, if your intentions are sincere, I will listen to whatever you are about to propose."

The imam continued to stare in silence for a long moment, and then he softened his expression again.

"I assure you that I am sincere in what I am about to propose," he said ambiguously. "I think that you have the appropriate influence in the American government to stop these attempts by the FBI and others to intimidate us with this overwhelming surveillance they have put upon our embassy and its officers. In addition, we received a naked threat from your state department only this morning to invade our sovereign territory at the embassy to arrest certain of our diplomats and to confiscate the property we have stationed at American military bases, property which the Saudi government legally purchased from the American military. These actions threaten to put our two countries in a state of war, a situation which I would think the Americans and the Catholic Church would wish to avoid."

So that is what this is about, thought Wolnik. The administration in Washington had finally found some intestinal fortitude. But he knew from long experience that what the US State Department threatened and what it was willing to do were usually very different things.

"I do not have that kind of influence, Imam. And if I did, I would certainly not discourage them from carrying out their warning to you. You have mistaken me for someone who subscribes to the delusional notion that every aggression can be dealt with by forbearance and good intentions. The insane aggression that Islam has consistently practiced against Christians and Jews since the seventh century speaks for itself. This could have been overcome long ago, if not for fanatics such as yourself."

"It is plain to me, Archbishop, that you do not love the peace that Yeshua himself taught. It comes as no surprise. But it does make easier what I have to do to prove to your government that we will not be deterred from our holy mission."

The imam raised his head slightly and nodded. The archbishop heard the door behind him open. He turned without rising and saw a small group of large men standing at the door. Beyond the men at the door, there was neither sight nor sound of any customers or activity. The restaurant was empty.

He had been arrested twice by the KGB in Cold War Poland, and he knew what to expect. His only chance for escape was now, just at the beginning. In a few minutes, it would already be too late.

He slowly slid to one side out of his chair and then rose quickly, grabbing the chair by its back and swinging it hard in the direction of the nearest man. The man had not expected such a reaction from this older man, and a priest at that. It was the edge that Wolnik needed. The man caught a chair leg across the side of his head and staggered backward but did not fall. The other man stepped in quickly, grabbed the chair Wolnik was holding, and flung it out of the way. He produced a knife and went after the archbishop.

"No, you fool, not here! Bind and gag the infidel. I have other plans for him before we gut him like a rabbit."

The large man stepped to the door and gestured for the two other men waiting outside to enter. His groggy partner was still standing, doing nothing. Then he fell heavily to the floor. The other two men came in; one held a gun, and the other took Wolnik by the arms, pinning them behind his back, slid a plastic restraint around his wrists, and pulled it tight. Then he produced a roll of duct tape, cut off a strip, and put it across Wolnik's mouth.

"Take him out back to the van, Ali. I will remain here awhile for the benefit of the FBI surveillance and to give you time to get back to the compound."

"What if we are stopped? If the FBI agents—"

"Do not stop. But don't be stupid and start blasting away at the first sign of trouble. The FBI is great at intimidation, but they are bound by laws and regulations. They cannot act without restraint, and I don't want you to either."

"Your pardon, Lord Saleh. If they should do so, anyway—"

"Then you will immolate yourselves and the infidel with the explosives you have in the van."

Ali nodded and took the archbishop by the arm while the other two hefted the dead weight of the man whom the archbishop had laid low. When they reached the back alley, Ali looked around and saw no one. The van was parked only a few meters away. When he saw that the driver was still in place, he headed for it with the others following.

Ali went to the back of the van and opened the rear doors; four men in black combat utilities and black berets came out quickly, carrying M27 automatic rifles, which they leveled at the group of Wahabi. One of them took the archbishop from them and removed his restraints and gag.

"I am Sergeant Kelly, Your Grace. Are you all right?"

Wolnik nodded, visibly shaken. He looked around as if seeing everything for the first time. At some point during the fray, he had retreated into an inner state, which he had mastered years ago while a prisoner of the KGB. Now that he was back to awareness, he looked at the four Wahabi and noted the driver of the van, seated unmoving in the left front seat.

One of the Keys troopers looked up at Sergeant Kelly from where he was kneeling by the driver's comatose body.

"This one's dead, Sergeant."

"They are all dead. Take care of these three and put them all into the van."

The trooper rose, took out a garrote, snapped it quickly into place over the head and around the throat of Ali, and whipped the head back with an audible snap. The other two terrorists tried to run, but both received the butt ends of rifles to their heads and collapsed on the pavement. The trooper with the garrote finished the job on both, and the other troopers moved the bodies into the back of the van. Sergeant Kelly spoke briefly into his secure cell and then turned once more to his troopers.

"Our ride is on its way. Billings, are those explosives we found in the van equipped with time fuses?"

"No, Sergeant. But I have a timer fuse in my kit. I will tape it to the bombs, if you want."

"Good. Set it for one minute."

Billings did as he was told and closed the van doors just as another van, marked with the logo of a local utilities company, came up the alley. Everyone piled in the back of it, and it drove away, turned up the side street to Battery, and headed south toward Geary Avenue and the archdiocese office building.

"Pardon me, Archbishop, but you still look a little spooked to me," said Kelly. "Shall I call your office and get medical attention ready?"

"No, that won't be necessary. It's been a long time since . . . Well, I had quite forgotten what it is like to be a part of violence of this kind. Was it necessary to kill those men?"

Kelly gave the archbishop a wry look.

"No, Your Grace. I considered letting them off with a stern warning. But I thought we might have to fight these bastards again, if you will forgive my language."

The irony in Kelly's response was not lost on Wolnik. But it still sickened him that it had come to this. *No,* he thought, *it came to this the day they bombed the Sistine Chapel.*

Chapter 14

Michael looked down at the ground from the aircraft window and saw what looked like a busy interstate highway. *Probably Interstate 5,* he thought. If it were, then they must be headed west. He turned around and looked at Maggie to see how she was taking all this. She seemed a lot calmer than he felt—and a lot calmer than Dennis looked.

"What's the matter, Dennis? You look as if you swallowed a frog."

"That's exactly what I feel like. Where do you think we might be headed? Didn't I hear the officer say they were part of the old Crusaders' order?"

"Yeah. Lucky for us. I never dreamed that they were still around. I guess they must be the 'other resources' the archbishop has. If so, I can tell you that we have some very powerful guardians." He looked at Maggie. "Maggie, I don't know what we are in for, but if it's what I think, then I'm sure they will find a safe place for you to go."

Maggie's face went very somber.

"I am not leaving you, Michael. I am not going to end up in a convent somewhere. You said you wouldn't abandon me, right?"

Michael didn't remember saying that exactly, but he had never intended that he would leave her alone without anyone to protect her. He knew he was a danger to her because he would more or less always be a hunted man, if he did survive the radiation—something he was beginning to think might be possible.

"I never thought of leaving you in a convent." Michael grinned. "But I am sure it would be an interesting adventure for you and the sisters too."

Maggie turned away and looked out her window as well. She was not frightened in a way that felt familiar. The recent weeks had turned her whole world upside down, and the contradictions that had been there before were gone—along with the people responsible for them. Now she felt oddly liberated. Sure, there was still a lot of danger and violence in this world of Father Michael's, a world she could not even have guessed existed before that night she met him in the arroyo where Selena had been hurt. But it was both fascinating and horrifying, threatening and comforting, all at the same time. Michael was the key to her future now. And she didn't intend to be parted from him if she had anything to say about it.

The terrain below was getting even rougher from the looks of it, and Michael wondered that, even in this impossible forest, the order had managed to stay undetected. *There must be others in authority besides the archbishop, helping them surreptitiously,* he thought. That fighter jet for one thing. It had an international mission, defending the continent against air and missile attack for NORAD. What kind of influence could command a response from that resource? That would have to reach almost to the level of the White House.

The pilot changed his power settings and banked to his left. So far, Michael could not see anything below that resembled an air station. Then, as if by sleight of hand, an opening appeared in the thick tree canopy below. He could see a helipad and hangar and several vehicles built to service aircraft. The pilot let down onto the pad and started shutting down his engines. Janowiscz came back to the passenger compartment, swept his arm around once, and pointed to the door. Everyone disembarked cautiously, as if the place might disappear. An officer and two enlisted men in Keys uniforms walked toward the group of passengers.

The officer saluted Brigadier Janowiscz and then Knight Commander Kintner.

"Sir, welcome to Rogue River country. Please follow me, and I will take you and your companions to your quarters. When you are rested, Father Berenger will join us in the dining room, if that's all right?"

"Of course. We are very grateful to you."

Kintner and his little entourage followed the man to their quarters. Just a few meters from the service buildings, a small group of cottages appeared in front of them, nestled among the ancient trees, ferns, and moss. It looked like something out of a fairy tale.

* * *

General David Kane hung up his secure phone and sat silently for a long time. It was not unusual for him to receive a direct call from the director of the National Security Agency, the department responsible for the gathering and analysis of data from every corner of the world that could impact the security of America and her allies. The NSA converted this data into hard information, with a minimum of assumption and bias. When the director, Vice Admiral (Retired) Richard K. Dowling received this information from his subordinates, the priorities for action were usually quite clear—as they were in the present case. And, as was his habit, he passed these findings directly to David Kane, his longtime friend and colleague from their service in the Department of Defense.

Kane pushed a button on his terminal and asked his assistant to come in.

The executive assistant to General David Kane walked briskly into his office with her pad and recorder in hand. She recognized that tone in his voice and knew something significant must have occurred to get her boss on edge. She sat down and turned on her recorder.

"Turn off your machine, Betsy. What we are about to get into will have to remain sub rosa for now."

She did as she was asked and sat very still.

"Get on the secure phone and set up a meeting with Dick Dowling and Jerry Owens. I think Tom Valence is out of town, but if he isn't, then include him as well."

"Sir, I'm pretty sure that the directors of the CIA and the FBI are available, if you would rather have them instead of Owens and Valence."

"No. The directors are political appointees, not professionals. I would like the meeting to take place away from the White House, preferably in Area Three, where we can have an electronic conference call. For the conference hookup, call General Margaret Simmons at Area Three and see if she can get General Telford from Special Ops, Admiral Collins from Pacific Combatant Command, the NORAD commander, General Jameson, and General Barrow from Space Command online. Also, find out if the Coast Guard commandant, Admiral McBride, would place himself on call from me. Insist on talking directly to the people you invite and not to their assistants. I don't want this meeting to appear anywhere on anyone's schedule."

Betsy Turner felt her stomach sink. She knew from experience why these back-channel meetings were necessary, and she didn't want to think about what might happen if she screwed up the proceedings. Whole governments had been brought down by disclosure of such goings-on.

"Don't worry, sir. I know what to do."

Two hours later, the national security advisor to the president, the director of operations for the CIA, the deputy director of the FBI, and the director of the NSA met on the lower deck of the metro station for the Pentagon. They walked together under the escalator to a locked steel door flush with the concrete wall and let themselves through. After locking the door behind them, they walked another few meters to another underground metro station, one that was part of the metro no one ever saw or knew about except key members of the government. It had been constructed in parallel with the public metro and stretched far beyond Washington to the foothills of the Allegheny Mountains in Bath County, Virginia. It was known as Area Three. Key congressional leaders knew about part of the secret system but by no means all. Security among congresspeople was a joke.

When the metro car stopped, the group of men disembarked and took an elevator up to a small but comprehensive communications center. The uniformed US Air Force officer who met them ushered them into a room with a conference table with communications terminals by each of the seats. They seated themselves, and General Kane turned to the Air Force brigadier escort.

"Thanks, Margaret. It's nice to see you again. Were you able to get hold of the commanders I asked for?"

"Sir, I have the CINC Special Ops Command, the CINC Pacific Combatant Command, the CINC Space Command, and the commander of NORAD online. The commandant of the coast guard is on standby."

"Very well." Kane turned to his terminal and saw the faces of the men he had asked for on one screen. "Gentlemen, thank you for your attendance. None of what we say here today has the knowledge of anyone other than us, and no official command decisions are asked or expected. While entirely legitimate, nothing of what we say or decide here today has the official participation of the National Command Authority, *per se*. Is anyone here not okay with that?"

No one spoke.

"All right then, let's proceed. Dick, summarize for us what you told to me earlier today about the recent events in Saudi Arabia."

"This morning at 0100 GMT, three cargo ships fitted out as troop carriers embarked from the port of Jeddah on the west coast of the Arabian Peninsula. Two hours later, they received encoded orders from Riyadh to rendezvous with an Iranian navy escort at a point twelve hundred kilometers south of Karachi in the Arabian Sea. We were unable to determine exactly what the escort comprised, but there will be at least two missile frigates of the Mowj class, two— and possibly three—Qa'em class submarines, and an undetermined number of logistics support ships. Whatever their destination might be, it is clearly a considerable distance from home waters."

Dowling stopped talking and looked at Kane to see if he wanted him to say anything further. Kane nodded toward Owens.

"Before we go any further with the international situation, Jerry, maybe you ought to bring us up to speed on what's happening on the West Coast."

"Very well, sir. A few hours ago, I received a report from the San Francisco office of the FBI that four confirmed members of the Wahabi, a Shiite terrorist group, were found dead in a van a few blocks from the Saudi Arabian embassy. Indications are that they had been involved in an attempt on the life of Karl Wolnik, the archbishop of the San Francisco Archdiocese. This occurred subsequent to a meeting between the archbishop and a man named Saleh, a senior official of the Saudi Arabian embassy, who is also *Aya tu Allah* to the Wahabi, principally based in Saudi Arabia. Subsequent to that, a Saudi military Apache helicopter was shot down in the Lassen Volcanic Park while attempting to shoot down a . . . uh . . . civilian helicopter."

"Shot down by what? The civilian helicopter?" asked General Jameson.

"No, General," said Kane. "By one of yours, an F-15 out of Fresno, the 144th Fighter Wing."

"This was not on any official report that I have seen," said Jameson. "Are you sure?"

"If you recall, John, we talked some time ago about the possibility of support we might need from your organization, and you okayed a working agreement between some of your tactical commanders with the Keys tactical outfits. We also agreed that they would have to be compatible with your mission training requirements and that no special reports would be prepared on the use of that support. For obvious reasons. Remember?"

"Yes, certainly. I guess I didn't realize—well, it just came as a surprise to me; that's all."

"You mean the Keys are involved in this?" asked General Telford. "Level with us, David. What's this all about?"

"I am sorry, gentlemen. Let me start at the beginning, as I should have."

Kane looked around the room and then back at the screen. "This little group assembled here has come together by the circumstances of the recent war and by other compelling interests. By whatever path, each of us has arrived at a point in our lives—both spiritual and secular—in which we are committed to a higher cause, higher even than our love of country. That cause is the preservation and advancement of Holy Mother Church, and more than that, to the very spiritual heart of the church, which, unlike the visible church, has continued unchanged for seventeen centuries. In the seventh century, this ancient hidden church was the only part of the Catholic Church to oppose the Muslim takeover and obliteration of half of Christendom, until the creation of the First Crusade by Pope Urban II in the eleventh century. We are the modern remnants of that invisible church, along with the members of the Sacred Order of the Keys of Saint Peter and certain members of the *ecclesiam mystici corporis Cristi*, such as Archbishop Wolnik and others."

Kane paused for a moment in case someone wanted to challenge his characterization of the hidden church.

"In recent months, the intelligence organizations of France and the United States have discovered the resurgence of Muslim terrorist groups intent upon revenge against the former members of the Order of the Keys. Their first priority was clearly the knight commander of the Order of the Keys, Father Michael Kintner. The Muslims somehow learned that Father Kintner had survived the destruction of the Sistine Chapel, which was bombed by these same terrorists. You are all no doubt familiar by now with the attack by the terrorists on the home of Knight Colonel Lorenzo Morales at his ranch in Nevada. Kintner was also there but managed to escape again. He is now in the protection of the Keys after they rescued him in the Shasta National Forest. That was what the dustup with the Saudi Apache helicopter and the air force fighter jet was about. Kintner was in the Keys Blackhawk, which the Apache was trying to shoot down."

"Is all that related to the attempt on the life of Archbishop Wolnik?" asked General Telford. "And who wasted the thugs who were trying to kill him. The FBI?"

"No, General," said Owens. "The FBI had them under surveillance, but we didn't have any orders to move in on them. The Keys troops took care of that on their own."

"And the man you called Saleh, do you have him under arrest?" asked General Jameson.

"No, sir, I'm afraid not," answered Owens. "He has diplomatic immunity, and we can't prove it except for the possible testimony of Archbishop Wolnik."

"Let me guess," said Telford. "He can't testify because he doesn't want to implicate the Keys troops who rescued him."

"That's it. At this point, the FBI can only sit and watch. But there are bound to be lots of questions about who really killed the four Wahabi, if that information gets out. We haven't gone public with the attempt on Wolnik's life either."

"Have you briefed the president on any of this, General Kane?" asked Admiral Collins.

"No, Admiral. But I will have to pretty soon. I tell you in all confidence that President Hilton would just as soon see Kintner dead than risk another worldwide *jihad*. And she probably isn't the only one who would think so, if this information gets into the news media."

"No doubt," put in Dowling. "But when we take these reports of Saudi and Iranian tactical movements to her, she's bound to connect them to the activities in San Francisco, just as we did."

"Wait a minute," said Admiral Collins. "Just how, exactly, do you connect the two together? I can think of a half dozen reasons why the Saudis and Iranians might be exercising their forces jointly. Maybe it's directed toward Israel—or maybe it's just one of the military masturbations these Muslims like to engage in."

"I agree," said General Telford. "I don't see any chance in hell that Iran and the Saudis would challenge US naval and military power because of losing a few terrorists. They have always been expendable."

"Yes," said Kane. "And they no doubt still are. But just suppose that Saleh and his Wahabi have come to believe, just as the Ayatollahs in Iran have been preaching, that the arrival of the prophesied Islamic messiah is imminent. The recent defeats in the Ninth Crusade, as some have called it, have thrown the Islamic world into chaos. Those are the very conditions the Ayatollahs have said will foretell the coming of the *Mahdi*. Perhaps they even believe the Mahdi is already here. That kind of obsession might motivate an actual assault—whether against Israel or the Great Satan, as they like to call the United States, would make no difference."

"Well, even if you're right, that's not the kind of thing we can decide. That's got to be in the White House, David; surely you can see that," said Admiral Collins.

"Bear with me on this, Mark," said Kane. "I am not asking this group for a decision, one way or another, just as I said in the beginning. This is purely a precaution on my part, in case we get a decision from the president that compels us to go against the Order of the Keys of Saint Peter or against the church in general. Let me get even more specific—if the Saudis do manage to put troops ashore in the United States specifically to go after the remnants of the Keys, whether under diplomatic guise or not, then we need to give the

Keys all the military assistance they need to survive. I think we can do that so long as it is disguised as training exercises or preplanned military and naval forces maneuvers of some other sort. Now, if President Hilton decides it's in the country's interests to assist the Keys against the Wahabi, then we are all right. But if she doesn't, then we must do it ourselves."

"Well, I don't know about the rest of you, but I would have to see exactly what that so-called 'assistance' would consist of," said Telford. "If it stays well within the realm of training exercises, then I don't see a problem. But if it goes any further, then it has to be a National Command Authority decision."

The others all indicated their agreement.

"I am grateful to all of you," said Kane. "I know we are all risking a great deal, but the Keys fought, bled, and died alongside US, French, and Israeli troops in the last war. I believe we owe them this much."

Kane crossed himself, and the others followed his lead. Then they all intoned the same prayer.

"In nomini Patris, et Filii, et Spiritui Sancti. Amen."

$$* * *$$

Maggie stepped out of the shower and picked up the towel from the rack on the wall. It was large, soft, and fresh. The last time she had felt like this was back at the ranch, before all the trouble, before the deaths, which really began with the murder of her father. She pushed the memory out of her mind and slowly dried herself off, including a thorough toweling of her luxurious dark hair. She regarded her naked body in the mirror with a critical eye. At her young age, there were still noticeable changes occurring but much more slowly than they had in the last few years. She started to remember the rough hands of Bob Sutter, and she shuddered, deliberately blocking it out of her mind. She thought of Michael and the way he had helped to rescue Selena, her young filly, in the desert and then the way he had protected her since they had left the ranch.

He had changed so much in the days she had known him. His hair had begun growing back in dark, replacing the total whiteness it had earlier. The tired look was gone, and he was more vibrant and alive. He was the only stable point in her life now, and she wanted nothing so much as keeping him close.

There was a knock on the door to her little cottage, and she instantly hoped it was Michael. But it was not. The woman standing on the porch was dressed in a plain black dress with a high black collar like the priests wore, but instead of the one square inch of white in the front, it had a white ruffle extending all the way around. She was not wearing a headdress. Maggie remembered that she was still wrapped in her towel and was embarrassed in front of the nun, if that was what she was.

"Maggie? My name is Sophie. Please forgive me for intruding, but I thought you might like to join us for breakfast. Did you have a good sleep?"

Maggie was struck by the reminder that it must be morning. She had completely lost her sense of the passage of time in the last few hours.

"Oh. Yes, I . . . I'm sorry, but I kind of lost track of time."

"Yes, I was told what you have been through the last few days. You are free to just rest, if you like. I will come back later."

"Oh, no. I'm sorry. I was just surprised; that's all. Would you like to come in? I started the coffeepot before I got in the shower. You're welcome to—"

"Good. I will pour us both a cup and wait while you get dressed. There should be some comfortable clothes your size in the closet. We have been expecting you for a while."

Maggie busied herself and quickly finished combing out her hair and pinning it up. When she came back into the bedroom, some underclothes had been laid out on her bed, along with a simple black skirt and white shirt with a Peter Pan collar. Also on the bed beside the dress were the washed and pressed dungarees and shirt in which she had been traveling. On an impulse, she picked up the black skirt and white shirt and put them on. She regarded herself in the mirror and saw that the little skirt had a very flattering, feminine cut and length. She walked back into the sitting room and sat down by the little table where her coffee cup had been placed. The coffee was hot and delicious.

"After breakfast, I will be glad to show you around, if you like. There is no pressure to do anything right now."

"What about Michael? And his friend Dennis?"

"They should already be in the dining room with Father Berenger. I think they are going to get some briefings and an orientation to this place and its functions. You are welcome to join them if you like. Or I can give you a tour of your own."

Maggie didn't quite understand what kind of choice she was being offered, but she would wait and see what Michael had to say.

When they walked into the large dining room, it looked to Maggie as if they were just cleaning up most of the tables and only a few stragglers were still having coffee. At one of the tables still occupied, she saw Michael and Dennis talking rather intently with four men, three of them in the by-now-familiar black-and-gold uniforms of the Keys troops. One of them was a striking-looking man whose high military collar had a patch of white in the front— the Roman collar of a priest. Another priest had scarlet piping around the edges of his cassock; she remembered from Catholic school that this meant a monsignor or something. Michael looked up, saw her, and beckoned to her.

As they came to the table, the men all rose, introduced themselves, and helped Maggie and Sophie into their chairs. The names of the men were Father Gil Berenger, Brigadier Peter Janowiscz, Colonel Timothy O'Reilly, and Monsignor Robert Bohemund. Berenger caught Maggie's eye again and continued speaking to her.

"Miss Morales, I am very glad you could join us. It's important for you to understand what is going on here and what you can expect, because there is at present no way to predict how long you and your companions will have to stay here. Until the outside world is safe again for you and Michael, you will be in our protection here. Is that all right with you?"

"Yes, Father. Is this a good time to ask some questions, or do you wish me to wait?"

"I think it best to introduce you into our community gradually, so that you can fully appreciate the logic and scope of our activities and functions here. Sophie will be your guide for now. She is a graduate student at Saint Miriam of Magdala Seminary for Women and has graciously consented to take you under her wing."

"I didn't know you had to go to a seminary to be a nun."

"You don't. The Magdalenes are studying for the priesthood."

"What?" Maggie was staggered. There weren't supposed to be any female priests. "I thought the Crusade soldiers were a Roman Catholic order."

"They are." Berenger looked at Michael and Dennis. "Perhaps I had better explain about the invisible church at this point—at least give you an introduction to it." He turned and looked at Monsignor Bohemund.

"Monsignor, I do not wish to make you uncomfortable as I explain our order and . . . well, our piece of the church."

"It's perfectly all right, Gil. Archbishop Wolnik and I had a long talk about it. I am an official representative of the Holy See at the Vatican, but I see nothing about your 'invisible' church that would warrant my opposition to it. And I do not intend to make it a part of my report to Cardinal Bocelli."

"Thank you, Robert." He looked back at Maggie.

"First, the Sacred Order of the Keys of Saint Peter is a traditional military order, consecrated by Pope Thomas I, may God give him peace. Not all the members of the order are part of the invisible church. And by no means are all the members of the invisible church part of the Order of the Keys. They coexist here by mutual respect and tolerance, but most of all because—in a sense—the invisible church is 'more Catholic than the Pope' to borrow a phrase."

Berenger looked slowly around at the little group before continuing. He knew the necessity for going slow in his explanation.

"Father Berenger," said Michael, "I think we might well postpone anything beyond what you have already said. For reasons too complex to go into now, I would like Miss Morales—Maggie—to just be assured that she is safe and is not going to be shuttled about without her assent and comfort. Can we do that?"

"Certainly. Let me just add that, while the probability of the terrorists attacking here is small, it is not zero. But there is no place on the planet that is guarded as well as this place, in every sense of the word."

Maggie had been looking intently for some minutes at Sophie. Finally, she turned her head and spoke to Father Berenger.

"Please answer one more question before you leave the subject of the nature of this place, Father."

Everyone looked at Maggie because of the tone she had in her voice. It was not that of a teenage girl.

"You want to know about the seminary."

"Yes, Father."

"The question of women priests and the division of opinion it always evokes goes back to the beginning of the church—to a time before the miracle of the raising of Lazarus from the dead. The miracle which, of them all, really set the known laws of nature on their head."

Berenger looked at his little audience. Every face turned toward him was infused with curiosity.

"Much recent scholarship has shed light on the reasons St. Augustine and many others have called Miriam of Magdala the founder of the faith. She was present at the crucifixion and first at the tomb, but, before that, she was the one who anointed Christ when her sister Martha was complaining about her absence from the kitchen. The other disciples also complained, especially Judas, who complained about the waste of expensive unguent, the oil used for the chrism. But Jesus explained that what she did 'helps prepare me for my burial.' This implies that Miriam is aware of what is happening at a much deeper level than the other disciples. It puts her in the same category and tradition of other ancient priests and priestesses, whose anointments were intended to ease the transcendence of death by retaining consciousness for the person at that threshold. The question was asked: 'By what authority does she anoint him?' Remember that the very word *Christ* means 'anointed one.' By another account in the Gospel of Mark, Jesus said, 'Verily, I say unto you, wheresoever this gospel shall be preached, what she has done here will be told in remembrance of her.'

"One may well ask: how is it that most remember her as a reformed prostitute, an egregious error made by Pope Gregory in a homily, an error not officially corrected until 1968."

"But what are we to conclude from that, Gil?" asked Michael. "We know her as '*Apostola apostalorum*' from St. Augustine. Does she really stand in precedence and authority over that of St. Peter and St. Paul?"

"I will put it this way: her presence at the tomb and virtually every other significant event and circumstance in the life of Christ certainly makes her unique among the apostles. The one exception—her absence at the Pentecost, when the others were sent out into the world to proselytize—implies that her sort of wisdom was not one that can be preached about to the masses, at least not at that period of history. Instead, Miriam focuses on the inner world of spiritual awareness or elevation of consciousness. This might also be called 'inner knowing,' an idea which was officially ruled out at the Nicene convocation in the fourth century. The so-called 'Gnostic' heresy was banned and all its gospels burned and not rediscovered until the twentieth century. Not a coincidence by any stretch, in my opinion."

"So, you're saying that the Gospel of Mary, which was discovered in the late nineteenth century, is not really a Gnostic gospel?" asked Michael.

"In my opinion, no. It does not contain the elaborate cosmology usually associated with Gnostic writings. But neither is it inconsistent in the essential message—that one may achieve an inner knowledge of God with or without the intercession of a priest."

The group was silent. This was, for most of them, an entirely new perspective on the priesthood and on Holy Mother Church as well.

"And this . . . noncoincidence of the recent discoveries of the Gospel of Mary and the Gnostic books, have relevance to the 'hidden church'?" asked Dennis.

"Most particularly. The history of the hidden church closely parallels that of the Gnostic orders. But—we agreed to leave that part until later, right?"

Everyone looked around and tacitly agreed. Only Maggie was looking somewhere else. She had a distant, unfocused mien. As Michael studied her, the look reminded him of one he used to search for in the faces of his troops during the Crusade. The thousand-yard stare, they used to call it.

Chapter 15

The president was not happy. She sat silently looking at the men assembled in the Oval Office as if they were condemned prisoners waiting for sentencing. A few of them felt exactly like that. Secretary of Defense Darryl Cosetta, appointed to his office primarily because of his political reliability to the administration, had to be present for this meeting because it would involve some very high-ranking military officers, who apparently had circumvented the secretary's authority—or so it seemed. One of them, Admiral Mark Collins, was there because he had personally instigated this meeting with the president through Secretary Cosetta.

David Kane, her national security advisor; Dick Dowling, director of the NSA; Tom Valence, director of operations at the CIA; and Jerry Owens, deputy director of the FBI were also present.

"Dr. Kane, I am informed by the secretary of defense that you have exceeded your authority in the handling of some recent national intelligence information. This is a very serious accusation—especially in light of my instructions to most of you here a few days ago that I was to be kept aware of this new terrorist threat, or whatever it is, whenever any new information was acquired." She had deliberately refrained from using Kane's military rank, and the message was not lost on him.

"Madam President, I never had any intention—"

"Intentions? Since when can we consider intentions—good or bad—as anything but irrelevant?"

"The meeting in question—for surely it must be that which you brought us here to discuss—was one in which I stipulated that nothing we said was to be regarded as bearing any kind of National Command authority."

"I have heard from Admiral Collins about the substance of your meeting. What stood out for me was that if my decisions didn't correspond to your idea of what they were supposed to be, then you and your military colleagues would do as you pleased."

"That was not my purpose then, nor is it now. But if you are saying that you have lost confidence in my ability to carry out your decisions, then you will have my resignation within the hour."

The room was silent. No one knew exactly what to expect from this president.

"That is not sufficient. We are looking at a defiance of the federal statutes that define my authority as commander in chief. We may be looking at not just dismissal but prison time, as well."

"Madam President, if I may, I don't believe it would be in our political interest to do that." Darryl Cosetta, whatever else he was or was not, was an astute student of political protocols. He shuddered to think what the press would do with such a calamity. These were all respected men, with considerable political support from both sides of the congressional aisle.

"Yes. You are no doubt right, Darryl. Thank you for the catch. My apologies, gentlemen. I guess I expected too much from you."

She took a long pause, looking first at one of the men and then at another.

"Over the next few months—no, make that the next few weeks—each of you will, one at a time, in whatever sequence you choose, resign your office for personal reasons. Of course, that does not include you, Admiral Collins, nor you, Darryl. Does everyone understand this?"

There were no questions. One by one, the men left the Oval Office.

* * *

It was dark and cold, and the muffled thunder of the Rogue River was audible in the predawn darkness. Michael felt a hand on his shoulder, firm and insistent in its grip. He rolled on his back and saw the faces of Gil Berenger and Robert Bohemund. They were in the combat dress of the Keys troops.

"We have to move out in just a few minutes, Michael. I have your combat utility dress and gear laid out for you. Take a quick shower if you like, but meet us at the heliport in fifteen minutes." Berenger and Bohemund turned and went out the door of the cottage.

Michael sat up in bed, rubbed the sleep out of his eyes, and sat very still for a long moment. He was remembering similar times from the Ninth Crusade:

The crossed keys painted on the side of the helicopter were in subdued green against the black background so as not to be visible from any distance. Michael Kintner had opted not to burden himself down with the standard gear his special ops troops carried into battle. The only items he really needed were his personal survival items, his GPS, his radio, water and rations—and the two items he had always carried on his missions in Bosnia: a Colt .357 Magnum and a Bowie knife.

Kintner shut out the noise and vibration from his consciousness. He remembered the prayer he had always prayed before his missions in Bosnia and in Desert Storm. Back then, it was the procedure for pilots to turn off to an arming ramp before taking the runway, so that the ground crew could pull all the pins from the bombs and rockets. Kintner used those few moments to pray what he came to think of as the "dead man's prayer."

"Lord, now accept the soul of thy servant Michael. For mine eyes have seen my salvation. Now let thy servant depart in peace according to thy Word." He had come to know that it was far easier to accept the

*fact of death before entering into combat. It established in his mind an
ineffable peace and radical acceptance for himself of what he was about
to inflict upon the enemy.*

* * *

When he got to the helipad, he saw five Blackhawk helicopters
with their engines running and the troops lined up ready to board.
Gil and Robert were by the door of the nearest aircraft, and Gil
motioned him over. Michael trotted over and swung up into the
open door of the helicopter. Brigadier Janowiscz and two other field-
grade officers were already seated inside. Berenger and Bohemund
swung into the aircraft, and a crewman closed the door. Gil sat down
next to Michael.

"Sorry I couldn't give you more warning, Michael, but I received
word only an hour ago from Archbishop Wolnik that our tactical
support from American forces was no longer available to us. In fact,
it seems likely that the national leadership views us as only a little
less dangerous than the Wahabi terrorists."

Michael looked at Gil, puzzled as to how such a thing could
happen.

"I know, it sounds incredible, but the archbishop talked directly
to David Kane, the national security advisor to the president. Hilton
is getting rid of every official she knows about, which is quite a few,
who are affiliated with us in any way. She got the information from
one of our own, Admiral Mark Collins, CINC Pacific. Sad, isn't it?"

"Are you sure?"

"Sure of what?"

"Of his name. Shouldn't it be Judas Iscariot?"

Gil shook his head.

"He is an ambitious man, perhaps to the point of zealotry, I
don't know. But there is bound to be a reckoning of some sort at
some time. That is how the cosmos functions. Balances are restored,

wrongs righted, crimes punished. There isn't much more to be said about that. But I have quite a bit to pass on about the emerging crisis. That will come when we get to our tactical base in southern Oregon."

It was past first light when the Blackhawks reached their destination. Once again, as Michael watched from the port, the forest just seemed to open up. Foliage faded away to the facilities of a forward assault base. It still seemed unreal.

Berenger's Blackhawk landed first, and the door was shoved open quickly; the men were out of the chopper and running toward a bunker about twenty yards away, following Brigadier Janowiscz.

When all were assembled inside, Janowiscz stood up and began to speak.

"A couple of weeks ago, a combat force left Jeddah with an Iranian navy escort, headed, as it turns out, for the west coast of the United States. They should have been intercepted by now, but, on orders from the president, they were not. Two troopships are now anchored twelve miles off the coast of Oregon, due west of a little fishing port named, simply enough, 'Harbor.' Their troops have been disembarking in small boats for several hours, headed for the beach just north of Brookings, a small resort town one mile north of Harbor. Except for traveling at night, they have made no attempt to conceal their activities."

"Pardon me, Brigadier," interrupted Knight Colonel Morgan. "But how can this be? I am from this part of the country. I know there is a coast guard station in Harbor, and I believe they have at least two frigates assigned to them."

"Good question. It appears that the government of Saudi Arabia has been granted permission to conduct 'joint' tactical exercises off the coast of the United States in at least three areas: the Siskiyou National Forest, the Siuslaw National Forest, both in western Oregon, and one other—unknown to us and to my contacts in Washington, which are rapidly dwindling in number."

He looked around the room at the astonished faces of his audience of senior officers.

"I will continue with the order of battle. Please reserve your questions at this point until I have got through it once." He smiled at his own joke. "Our estimate is that each of the Saudi transports can carry no more than three thousand troops—that would mean that, at most, two reinforced brigades of heavy infantry can be landed. No one has used troopships since the Falkland War, so we are guessing a bit here."

Janowiscz turned on a projector showing an annotated map of the southern Oregon coast.

"As you can see, there are very few major routes of communication through the mountainous regions of these two national forests. Combat maneuvers in these forests would not be visible from the air, but they can be seen quite clearly by infrared sensors, from which these troop deployments on the map are derived. They are not complete, because we do not have the access to the national intelligence assets we enjoyed before recent events."

A second projector was turned on, and it revealed the West Coast deployments of Keys troops, both tactical bases and forward deployments. There were not many.

"You see here the locations of our three main tactical bases in the northwest, in California, Oregon, and Washington. The little crossed keys identify them. The principal refuge of the Church of the San Graal and its schools and communities are not shown, as there is no reason for doing so."

Janowiscz paused, just long enough to see what effect his briefing was having so far.

"The red Templar crosses mark the present, approximate locations of the forward deployments of Keys infantry. The helipads are not shown. We are dug in at platoon strength just below Pollywog Butte a few miles east of Brookings, another position five miles east of the town of Pistol River below Big Craggies, and the third just east of Gold Beach on Lawson Creek. They are heavily armed with automatic rifles, antitank weapons, and rocket-propelled grenades but no artillery. The Blackhawks will provide close air support. Patrols from these positions will call in airstrikes and reinforcements, which will come from here at Tincup. Any questions?"

"Who is providing real-time aerial surveillance?" asked a voice from the back of the room, which Michael recognized at once: Knight Colonel Lorenzo Morales, Maggie's uncle.

"Very good question, Colonel Morales. That may just be our best weapon, for as long as it lasts. We are using armed drone Predators, compliments of the 114th Air Force Fighter Squadron at Klamath Falls. This support will continue until the American national command authority finds out about it, at which time— well, there is no need to go into that right now."

There was a general shuffling about by the officers present, all waiting for some word of dismissal or orders. Michael looked back behind him, trying to catch the eye of Morales. Finally he saw him. Morales gave him a wry grin and then went back to his notes.

Gil Berenger stood up and made the sign of the cross.

"In nominum Dominum Jesum Christum. Amen. Gentlemen, please leave your mobile com sets on and be prepared for immediate deployment. You are dismissed to your separate commands."

Gil motioned Michael and Robert over toward him.

"Michael, you and Robert and I are going to have a dedicated Blackhawk with an assault detail—just for quick response and coordinating field actions. I am going to rely on your experience and instincts, which are legendary among the Keys troops."

Michael shook his head slightly, thinking, *Yeah, legendary mass murderer, that's me.* He looked again, and Gil was staring hard at him.

"I know you can never forget what these people did to the pope and to the Sistine Chapel, Michael. And you more than anyone believes Thomas Merton's words, that 'A theology of love cannot afford to be sentimental. It must seek to deal realistically with the evil and injustice in the world—not to merely compromise with them.' And you of all people know that Holy Scripture is not a suicide pact."

Berenger started to walk away and then turned back to Michael once more.

"It is a terrible truth that, even in the medieval Grail legends, it is not uncommon for certain people to put themselves beyond the redemptive power of God. In the legends, no fault or sin attached itself to a knight who slew such a person—not to Gawain, the knight who lacked compassion, nor to Galahad, who was the purest knight of all."

"Really, Gil? Are you putting the Grail legends on the same level of certainty as Holy Scripture?"

"Michael, the hand of God is not only in history but in folklore. It was written in the Middle Ages that 'The language of the court is not the language of fields and forests, nor is it the voice of the nooks and byways heard among rushing waters and the open sea. It is the voice crying in the wilderness in an unknown tongue.'"

Bohemund broke in.

"You astound me, Father. You seem to be saying that the ordinary people of the world see from the evidence of their own life experiences, the traditions, the legends, from nature itself, certain truths that the formal dogma of the faith fails to impart. Is that right?"

"Precisely. I am saying even more than that, however. The Grail at its highest is the representation of the divine mystery within the church. To the extent that the visible church has failed so far as an institution to accomplish the transmutation of humanity, it is because in the mystery of her development, she has still not evolved into the fruition of her higher consciousness."

"How can any immutable truth or the institution that guards and perpetuates that truth evolve to a higher state of consciousness?

By definition, it must already be at the highest level. I know you remember the ancient dictum: *Extra nulla salus ecclesiam mystici Christi.* There is no salvation outside the church. Isn't that right?" said Bohemund.

"The evidence is to the contrary, Monsignor. One of the misjudgments in the spiritual life in the Roman Catholic Communion has been the frittering away of the spiritual powers in the popular devotion. If the great mysteries of the church are insufficient to command the dedication of the whole world, then the world is best left under interdict—no art is better than bad art, so to speak."

"So, if I understand you, you are saying that the message of God in folklore—in this case, the Grail legend—is that there is more untapped power in the Eucharist than is indicated by the sufficing graces imparted to the ordinary communicant."

"Yes, Monsignor. This undeclared excess is that which has always been kept secret by the invisible church and by the wisest in the visible church—est in sacramento quicquid quaerunt sapientes."

Bohemund sat still for a moment before answering. "Your words are hard as steel, Father."

"If you wish to understand fully why the hidden church exists, this must be understood: Hereof are the wounds of the church, and for this reason she has been in sorrow through the ages. The mystery of the Christian faith is in the Eucharist, but because of the interdictions of our long exile, we receive only a substituted participation in the Communion with God in the visible church, as compared to the participation in the transcendent mode in the hidden church.

"It is precisely because of this that the invisible church exists at all. When she last appeared on the open landscape of history, the hidden church was fighting off the invading hordes of Muslim fanatics in Europe and Africa, a time when the visible church was cowering behind the walls of its dogmas and doctrines and *ecclesia.* Now we are visible again. And again we are fighting off an implacable enemy, which the visible church and most of the rest of the world refuses to acknowledge—at least in the nature of the threat. Can you understand that?"

Michael stared silently at Berenger for a long time, the impact of his words working more deeply into his consciousness. Finally, he spoke.

"And you have always been there, haven't you, Father Berenger?" The full significance of his name had finally dawned on Michael— Gil . . ." "Gilead," another name for Christ and "Berenger," another name for shepherd.

"Yes, as I will always be."

Father Gilead Berenger walked away toward the command post, leaving two stunned supplicants behind him.

* * *

US Marine General Paul Telford, CINC Special Ops Command, was watching in disbelief at the foreign helicopters coming in to land at the Naval Amphibious Base in Little Creek, Virginia. This was the home base for the Seal teams, the joint expeditionary forces, and several more of the most sensitive black ops units in the US arsenal. Telford had been apprised of the intention of the JCS to entertain Saudi troops and aircraft, but not here, not in the very cradle of the sensitive missions. He turned to his adjutant.

"Major Templin, I want you to get me on the secure phone with the chief of naval operations and the secretary of defense as soon as we arrive back at the war room. I don't care what they are doing or whom they are with. I want them now. Understood?"

"Yes, sir. There might be a problem getting the CNO, today. There is a change of command ceremony for the CNO at the Pentagon. Admiral Mark Collins is replacing Admiral Fleming . . ."

"Collins, eh? Might have known. The fruits of betrayal."

"Pardon me, sir?"

"Never mind. If you can't get Collins or the SecDef, get me the White House. Is General David Kane still there?"

"I believe so, sir. I will get him, if he is."

Twenty minutes later, General Telford was seated at the console in the war room at Little Creek. Secretary Darryl Cosetta and General Kane were on the screens in front of him; neither of them looked very happy. They knew General Telford, and they both dreaded a confrontation with him, especially Cosetta, a mild-mannered politician caught up in a world he didn't feel competent to be in.

"Mr. Secretary, I don't relish intruding upon your no-doubt busy schedule or yours, either, David. But I feel that a grave error in judgment has been made with the permission given to the government of Saudi Arabia to infest the most sensitive military facilities in the country with their own forces. Furthermore, the exact nature of this permission was not given to me in any earlier communication. This situation, in my opinion, must be rectified immediately."

"I know it must appear that way to you, Paul. I think everyone involved in the decision process knew what your opinion would be—that may have influenced our . . . uh . . . poor judgment in not giving you all the details. But I think the president made her decision based upon the best available information and was intended to forestall any further diplomatic difficulties with our ally in the Middle East."

"Our ally? Diplomatic difficulties? Doesn't the president get any intelligence reports? Does she even know who the Wahabi are? David, I can't believe you let this happen."

"You must know I opposed it, Paul. But I am a lame duck here in the White House. My opinion counts for very little."

"I can verify that David stood up for what he thought. I believe he said what needed to be said. But, as David just implied, the president is still smarting over the secret meeting at Area Three.

Incidentally, she is wondering why she still hasn't received your resignation. We don't want any unwarranted publicity, do we?"

"Warranted or not, Mr. Secretary, I am ready to go public with this whole affair—whether with threats of court-martial or not. There are many in Congress who would not sit still for this, as you no doubt are aware."

"Yes, I can understand how you feel, Paul. But the decision has been made at the highest level. What more is there to be said?"

"Just this, Secretary Cosetta. There is always a higher court of appeals, call it cosmic justice, for want of a better phrase. I intend to use it."

Telford clicked off his receiver and stood up. This outcome was not unexpected, but it still made his skin crawl to be reminded of what stuff politicians were made. He turned to his adjutant.

"Order my aircraft prepared for a cross-country trip, Major Templin. Destination Klamath Falls, Oregon. And have the commander of the 173rd Fighter Wing prepare a helicopter to be ready when we arrive."

Telford turned to leave the room and then looked back at Templin.

"Make sure you have my secure laptop with you—the one without the sanction of the Department of Defense. Understand?"

Templin snapped to attention. He knew something of General Telford's contacts with the Keys troopers. This could not bode well for the general. But he knew it must be necessary if Telford was prepared to go that far for what he believed.

* * *

The long column of visitors to the White House was a mixture of civilian tourists and a sizable contingent of men in the uniform of Royal Saudi Armed Forces. They were queued up at the metal detection machines. When the first of the Saudi soldiers came to the machine, he held up his hand and halted the men behind him. Then he turned to the White House security guard nearest him and said something in a low tone. The guard looked at him for a long moment and then picked up his phone.

"Ms. Caldwell, this is Sergeant Morris at the gate. We have a situation here with the Saudi visitors. They say that subjecting themselves to the detection machine violates their religion. What do you want me to do?"

"What do you usually do when someone refuses to go through the search?"

"I always turn them away. But the shift commander said he didn't want the Saudis to be offended in any way. You're the protocol officer. I can't take the responsibility of creating an international incident. Is there any way you could check with . . . well, the president?"

"You must be joking. I can't bother her with anything like this. She has important things to deal with. We have to do our jobs."

"Well, my job is to provide security. And I can't do that without scanning every mother's son who comes through here. So what's your call?"

Sally Caldwell remembered well what the president had warned her about. No insults to Muslim visitors on pain of being fired.

"Let them through, Sergeant. There should be nothing to worry about. I'll take the responsibility."

Thirty minutes later, the group of visitors were gathered outside the door to the Oval Office. The tour guide was speaking.

"And this is the world-famous Oval Office, where many of the most important decisions affecting the United States and, indeed, the world, are made. I am certain that—"

The door opened, and President Catherine Hilton stepped out.

"Well. What a nice group has come to visit. I am pleased to welcome you."

A man in a Saudi uniform stepped from the crowd and walked up to the president, smiling. He raised his hand and slipped it inside his tunic. He found the cord and pulled it.

* * *

The Blackhawk command ship was hovering over the town of Brookings, watching the *Wahabi* landing craft hitting the beach just below a low cliff, at a calm body of water protected from the full force of the ocean waves by a circle of stone, a few meters below the surface.

"Pollywog Platoon, this is Warlock. Move out and deploy on both sides of the Chelco River. The enemy is moving off the beach through the north end of Brookings up the Chelco in column. Appears to be about a battalion in strength. I have already called in airstrikes. Be in position to block their escape from the river road on the north and south sides. You copy?" Michael Kintner had just given his first combat order since the Ninth Crusade. All the time and events since the war faded into dim obscurity in his mind.

Michael remembered that someone had once said that nothing concentrates the mind so wonderfully as the knowledge that one was being hanged in the morning. So did going into combat. He knew once more exactly what he was trying to do and the consequences of failure. His self-pity and confusion about his place in the Church and in the world were over.

"Roger, Warlock. We are monitoring the air support frequency and will move in immediately they pull off the target."

Michael looked at Gil and Robert, who were listening to the exchange.

"I am going to move up the coast and check out the beaches at Pistol River and Gold Beach."

"I agree," said Robert. "Are you getting any images from the drones on your screen?"

"Yes. Looks as if the three enemy contingents committed so far are about battalion in strength. That would be about twenty-five hundred troops in total. Our lads should be able to handle them if we catch them cold. Keep them bottled up before they can get to cover in the forests."

As they flew north, the landing craft committed to Pistol River could be seen clearly on the beach disgorging troops. Kintner keyed his microphone again.

"Craggies Platoon, this is Warlock. Do you read?"

"Roger, Warlock, Craggies here. We have the enemy in sight, forming up on the beach south of Pistol River. I am ready to commit the Predators to attack while they are still on the beach. You approve?"

"At your discretion, Craggies. Make sure no one gets across the coast highway."

Kintner looked up at the pilot and motioned for him to fly north, where Gold Beach lay just twenty-three miles away.

Five minutes later, he saw the beach to the north lit up in a fire fight, tracers streaming in thick trajectories down upon the beach. As he looked, he also saw the deadly sparkles of antipersonnel bombs from the drones cover the beach in waves of fire. *Nothing is going to survive that,* he thought. And he was right.

The pilot turned from the right seat of the aircraft and held up his hand to Michael, motioning him forward. Michael came up to the cockpit and knelt down.

"Sir, we just got a call from General Paul Telford on company frequency. He's headed this way from Klamath Falls. He wants to meet us back at the monastery. Something extremely urgent. Can we break free from the action?"

"Yes. Everything looks pretty well in hand," said Michael. He turned toward Gil. "General Telford is in the area? Isn't he CINC Special Ops? What's he doing out here?"

"He's an old friend. Same as David Kane, if you get my drift."

Kintner didn't reply. This had to be something very big. He didn't like the sinking feeling he was getting about this.

* * *

The flames from the West Wing of the White House were soaring into the night sky. The fire departments attending the blaze had been trying for hours to control the conflagration as best they could, but the heat and intensity of the fire was unlike anything the firefighters had ever seen.

Chief Thompson was still staring in disbelief at the apparent futility of their efforts. Nothing had prepared him for this kind of fire. As he stood, feeling almost helpless, his deputy ran up to his side.

"Chief, I just talked to the EPA technicians. They're getting some horrendous radiation readings. He said it isn't safe for anyone to be near the fire."

"Well, what the hell do they expect us to do? Go home and wait it out? See if you can get anyone from the Defense Nuclear Agency or Homeland Security over here—someone who knows something about nuclear weapons."

His deputy looked at the chief in horror. Until this moment, he hadn't imagined this thing could get any worse. But it just had.

* * *

Every form of news media outlet was broadcasting the events at the White House, and every one of them had a different take on the situation. But it didn't deter them from making their guesses sound authoritative.

Fox News: "It's clear that Hilton's permissive, even obsequious attitude toward the Muslim terrorists has come home to roost. It is far too high a price for this nation to pay for the president's lack of judgment."

MSNBC: "There are unconfirmed but reliable sources who assert that the bombing was the work of a group of dissident Catholics who resent the fact that their Crusade against the Muslims ended in failure."

BBC: "There are reports coming out of Riyadh, Saudi Arabia, that a self-declared Mahdi, or Muslim messiah, has taken power by force from the king and his government. The feeling in Europe is that the tragedy in Washington is related to the revolt and that the Saudi-based group of activists known as the Wahabi may have been involved in the bombing of the White House."

CBS: "Reports coming from our offices in San Francisco say that active fighting between military units of uncertain origin has broken out in the coastal region of southern Oregon. We believe that this may be related to recent events in Washington. Reporters have so far been unable to get access to the region because of blockaded highways and closed airports. Local police and the FBI have refused to comment."

* * *

General Telford was standing waiting on the tarmac as the Keys helicopter landed. He was wearing his trademark desert combat utilities and carried a baton, a long-forbidden accessory for Marine Corps officers. He watched while the Keys officers disembarked from their Blackhawk and came over to where he stood. Telford snapped to attention and saluted—to the surprise and dismay of Father Berenger and Knight Commander Michael Kintner.

"I regret having to call you away from your duty stations, but desperate times are once more upon us. The president, most of her staff, and General Kane have been killed by a terrorist bomb. The White House, from the intelligence reports I have been getting, was hit by a low-yield 'dirty' nuclear bomb carried in by Saudi soldiers. Soldiers who were given access to our bases by the president and her SecDef. Now, what can you tell me about your situation here? Archbishop Wolnik told me that you were repelling Saudi invaders. Is that true?"

"It is, General," said Kintner. "As bizarre as it sounds, three battalions of Saudi troops came ashore at three locations, presumably bound for the Keys headquarters and probably the monastery as well. How they got the information about our locations, I can't guess."

"Well, I can. Indirectly from the new CNO, Admiral Collins. He is the only possible source, and he no doubt shared this information with Cosetta and Hilton before his appointment."

Major Templin came up to the general and spoke to him in a low voice. Telford's face grew dark.

"It seems the scenario we have all been expecting has happened. My adjutant tells me the news services are reporting a *coup d'état* in Riyadh. Seems the Mahdi has arrived at last. A man named Takhte Suleiman Saleh. That sound familiar?"

"Yes," said Berenger. "Until a few days ago, when he disappeared from our surveillance, he was the Saudi charge d'affaires at the consulate in San Francisco. He was responsible for the abduction and attempted murder of Archbishop Wolnik."

"You seem to have things well in hand here. I had feared the worst, but you won't need my assistance with this dustup. I have to hightail it back to the Pentagon and try to bring some order out of chaos. We can't afford to have a man like Cosetta calling the shots. I have some powerful friends in Congress, and I intend to use them to the fullest. We can't worry about the niceties of formal chains of command now. What are your intentions, Gil?"

"I also will try to bring some order here. But I am sure our two friends will need Archbishop Wolnik to arrange transportation back to Rome. Am I right, Monsignor?"

Bohemund looked at Kintner and saw the determination in his face.

"Yes. His Holiness is going to need the best advice he can get. But he is not surrounded, as Pope Thomas was, with courageous men. I am bringing his most courageous to him. Knight Commander Michael Kintner."

"I agree. Michael, her uncle and I will see that Miss Morales is cared for and given the finest education available. You must have no concerns on that." Berenger put his hand on Michael's shoulder.

"Now, you go to your greatest sacrifice, my son—greater even than that which you have already given. My prayers go with you. In nominum Dominum Jesum Christum."

* * *

Pope John XXIV put his face in his hands and wept. He had prayed that all the violence and depravities of war were behind them. What had the Crusade accomplished? And now, he was hearing from his people the same cries Urban II and other popes, right down to Thomas I, heard. Take arms, they cry, the future of the faith is threatened. Now he was besieged by the same entreaties. When would it end?

The president of the Pontifical Council for Justice and Peace watched his pontiff in his distress and struggled with all his might to say something that would comfort him. But he could think of nothing hopeful to say. Pope John looked up and saw the look on Cardinal Abrusco's face. He wiped the tears from his face and smiled.

"You know, Abrusco, you look even more mournful than I feel. But we are wrong to mourn. Grief is forbidden to such as we, the keepers of the faith. Don't you agree?"

"I do, Your Holiness. But the memories of the Ninth Crusade are still fresh in my mind. It is impossible not to feel sorrow at the prospect of more violence."

The young priest in attendance at the pontiff's chambers walked softly in and stood waiting for acknowledgment of his presence, which the pope gave him with a look.

"Your Holiness, Secretary of State Cardinal Bocelli is here with Knight Commander Michael Kintner and Monsignor Robert Bohemund. They beg an audience—immediately, if possible."

The pope glanced at the face of Cardinal Abrusco to see if there was any reluctance there and saw nothing but surprise.

"Please have them come in."

The three were ushered in, and the pope motioned for them to sit down, which they did.

"Monsignor Bohemund, it is good to see you have returned safely from your mission. Cardinal Bocelli has kept us informed of your efforts to rescue Father Kintner, and we are all very grateful to you.

"And you, Knight Commander. We are overjoyed to see that you have recovered from the terrible wounds you suffered in the Sistine Chapel with our brother Thomas, may God give him rest."

"Thank you, Your Holiness."

"Your Holiness, we are here to offer what may be a way to avoid another disastrous war between Islam and Christianity," said Bocelli. "You are well aware of the events at the end of the war, when the Sistine Chapel was almost destroyed by a radioactive 'dirty' bomb and our beloved Pope Thomas was killed. Father Kintner was the only one to survive the blast. When he recovered sufficiently, he flew one of the aircraft under his command to Mecca and destroyed the Grand Mosque with a hyperbaric bomb. He did this without the authorization or knowledge of the Holy See. Since that time, he has been hunted like an animal by the remnants of the al-Qaeda terrorists and then by the emergent Wahabi fanatics, who are even now in control of the government in Riyadh."

"I am aware of these things, Cardinal Bocelli. But we have prayed many times for the forgiveness and reconciliation of Father Kintner's soul. We do not judge or condemn him. Even Christ forbore judgment of sinners, preferring compassion in its stead. Can we do less?"

No one spoke for a long time.

"Your Holiness, I readily confess and heartily regret my offense. But I am here to offer atonement. I was healed from my wounds by God, I believe, so that I could come here and offer an even greater sacrifice. The enemy have used my atrocious act to justify renewing the war against Christianity. I propose to take that justification away from them."

"But, Michael, our dear son, we cannot countenance another—"

"Your pardon, Holiness, but I am not offering to take up arms again. I am offering myself, everything I have or ever will have. I am offering my life to the enemy. I will deliver myself to the Mahdi at Mecca, where the Grand Mosque was destroyed, to do with as he pleases."

The room was deathly silent. An unknown, compelling force seemed to cover everything and everyone there. Such must have been the feeling that night in the Garden of Gethsemane.

* * *

"This is the bombardier, Commander. Target dead ahead."

Ahead, in the gathering twilight of the Hijaz, was the brilliantly lighted Grand Mosque of al Harram, in the very center of the ancient and holy city of Mecca, the place toward which hundreds of millions of people bowed to pray five times each day. It was Ramadan, the ninth lunar month of the Islamic calendar, and a million people were performing their hajj, their sacred, once-in-a-lifetime pilgrimage to the birthplace of the prophet. The nine tall minarets, the slim towers from which the faithful were called to prayer, showed white in the dusk. The three domes, surmounted by four-ton gold crescents, were illuminated by great spotlights.

The pilot began to read off the bombing checklist. Kintner threw the necessary switches on his side of the cockpit and again raised his eyes to the city. He could now just make out the brick temple of Abraham's well, the Ka'aba, draped with black silk embroidered with gold, ironically the colors of the uniforms of the Keys. A huge crush of people swirled around and around about the temple, in their ritual of devotion, oblivious to the catastrophe about to befall them. Kintner could now make out the five hundred great marble columns surrounding the courtyard.

* * *

"Wake up, Commander. Mecca is dead ahead."

Kintner looked out the porthole and saw the lights of the city. On the east side, he could make out the twin beams at the airport, where they had been granted permission to land. Except for the aircraft crew, he was the only one onboard. Bohemund had begged go with him, but he had refused. This was a solitary journey.

He had been a captive of Muslim soldiers before, in Pakistan, months before the advent of the Ninth Crusade. He had been held in prison and tortured relentlessly, until he had got what he came for—an audience with the leader of the *intifada*. But it had come to nothing. The war could not be avoided.

He knew that he would not be interrogated this time.

As the aircraft landed, Michael Kintner allowed himself one final meditative moment, remembering once more the words of his old mentor, Father Toriano, at Christ in the Desert Monastery.

"Michael, I have been your counselor for a long time now. You remember that I once told you that the most profound values of a society, of a culture, can be transformed and reconstituted by spiritual renewal, but only at great cost. The blood of martyrs has not always nourished

a transformation and regrowth, of course. But such profound changes never occur without it, my son.

"I don't think anyone can know how far one ought to go in the preservation of their culture or their religion. I doubt that few have gone as far as you have. The sacrifice of one person for another is considered holy, yet the sacrifice of thousands for the sake of many other thousands is considered monstrous. An appalling contradiction.

"The truth, Michael, is always more than the sum of its parts. All the faithful of the world since time began do not, in their individual essence, add up to the sum of what faith means, or of what the truth is. Yet, each of us can glimpse his piece of it.

"But how fleeting are the most closely held values and principles when driven out by the human thirst for revenge, for justice, for retribution. What are those compulsions, really, but an indulgence of one's most primitive and destructive instincts, no matter how we justify or excuse them? Yet they have formed the basis for human sociology for tens of thousands of years. They will never disappear. And some questions will forever remain unanswered.

"Remember also the words of the anonymous fourteenth-century mystic: 'The Fiend must be taken into account.'"

Down by the river bed, now flooded with bright moonlight, another whippoorwill had added its voice to the first. Soon, the mournful soprano of the coyotes would fill out the chorus. And the whole of Chama Canyon would echo with the sounds of life—and of eternity.

* * *

Michael walked down the stairs leading down from the aircraft. Waiting there on the tarmac was a red Dodge pickup truck with a custom black grill.